BY C. J. TUDOR

The Chalk Man
The Hiding Place
The Other People
The Burning Girls
A Sliver of Darkness

A SLIVER
OF DARKNESS

A
SLIVER
OF
DARKNESS

STORIES

———

C. J. TUDOR

BALLANTINE BOOKS

NEW YORK

Published in the United States by Ballantine Books, an imprint of Random House, a division of Penguin Random House LLC, New York.

BALLANTINE is a registered trademark and the colophon is a trademark of Penguin Random House LLC.

Originally published in the United Kingdom by Michael Joseph, Penguin Group UK, a Penguin Random House company.

"The Lion at the Gate" was first published in the Tesco special edition of *The Other People* by C. J. Tudor (January 2020).
"Final Course" was first published in *Tales of Dark Fantasy 3* by Subterranean Press (July 2020).
"Butterfly Island" was first published in *After Sundown* by Flame Tree Press (October 2020).

Library of Congress Cataloging-in-Publication Data
Names: Tudor, C. J., author.
Title: A sliver of darkness / C. J. Tudor.
Description: First edition. | New York : Ballantine Books, [2022]
Identifiers: LCCN 2022020848 (print) | LCCN 2022020849 (ebook) |
ISBN 9780593500163 (hardback ; acid-free paper) |
ISBN 9780593500170 (ebook)
Subjects: LCGFT: Short stories.
Classification: LCC PR6120.U36 S55 2022 (print) | LCC PR6120.U36 (ebook) |
DDC 823/.92—dc23/eng/20220428
LC record available at https://lccn.loc.gov/2022020848
LC ebook record available at https://lccn.loc.gov/2022020849

Printed in the United States of America on acid-free paper

randomhousebooks.com

2 4 6 8 9 7 5 3 1

First U.S. Edition

Book design by Victoria Wong

For Dad

Contents

Introduction

In January 2021, my dad passed away.

He had been in a nursing home for two years, but his death was still a shock. Due to the pandemic, we'd only been able to visit him for thirty minutes every two weeks and had to talk to him through Perspex.

The first time I hugged my dad in over a year was on the day he died.

2020 had already been a tough one (like it was for everyone): the pandemic, lockdown and home schooling all took their toll. Plus, I had spent October through December attempting to relocate my parents from Wiltshire to Sussex so I could help out more.

Mum was still living in the family home so the logistics of finding Dad another nursing home, selling the house and buying Mum a separate retirement apartment were complicated, to say the least.

Throughout all of this, I was trying to write a book.

I'm not someone who likes to admit they can't cope, so even though I was finding the writing process much harder than usual—to the point where I would wake with a hard knot of anxiety in my stomach every morning—I told myself that I just had to plow on. Every book was difficult at times. I would fix it all in the edits.

After Dad's death, things got even harder. I hated sitting at my laptop. Every word felt like an effort. The characters' voices, usually so real to me, felt forced and unnatural. Still, I persevered, telling myself it was just my frame of mind. It would get better.

But in my gut, I knew.

This book wasn't working.

Somehow, I managed to finish the manuscript, and I sent it off to my editors, hoping that I might be wrong.

When I got my notes back, I knew it wasn't just me. Normally, I take a big edit in my stride. This time I knew, whatever I did, I couldn't fix this book. I *hated* this book. It had come to represent everything horrible and painful that had happened in the last year, and I couldn't go back to it. If I tried, I thought I might break.

So, after a good cry and a very long chat with my lovely agent, Maddy, I approached my editors and confessed. I asked if I could scrap the book, skip a publication year and use the time to work on another idea—a passion project that I had put on the back burner, waiting for the right moment to write. This felt like the right moment.

However, I still felt bad about letting my readers (and my publishers) down and not putting a new book out in 2022, so to fill the gap, I suggested a short-story collection. I love writing short stories and it seemed the perfect opportunity.

Thankfully, because I have wonderful, supportive editors, they agreed.

A weight was instantly lifted.

The passion project—*The Drift*—will be published in January 2023, and you're reading the other fruit of my labors right now!

The book that I scrapped will probably never see the light of day, and that's okay. Sometimes, you need to take a couple of steps back to go forward. But I always believe that nothing in life, or writing, is ever wasted: I ended up taking a section of that failed book and reworking it as a short story in this collection. (I'll let you work out which one.)

My dad was a man of few words, not prone to praise or big displays of emotion. But I know he was proud of my writing. I'm glad he saw me achieve my dream and become an author. I'm sad he won't be able to read any more of my stories.

I guess we all have to mark the page and close the book one day. This one is for you, Dad. They all are, really.

A SLIVER
OF DARKNESS

End of the Liner

Introduction

In 2021 my family and I went on a cruise for the very first time.

This was during the pandemic, so it was a "staycation cruise." It only lasted four days, and the ship never left British waters. But it was fun and very family friendly. It was bound to be. It was organized by *the* major operator in the family entertainment market. (Think mouse).

One day, while Betty was in the pool and Neil and I were on deck, sipping iced cocktails, conversation turned to the pandemic, space programs and the apocalypse (as it does). We stared out over the expanse of water, and I remember Neil saying: "If a virus really obliterated the world, you wouldn't need to send people into space. Just stick them all on giant cruise ships."

The comment and the idea stuck.

One of the reasons I love theme parks is because they tread a fine line between magical and creepy. Especially if they are abandoned or run-down. Anyone who has seen *Donnie Darko* will know that there's something quite sinister about someone dressed up in a big furry animal costume. And while everything being shiny and magical is nice for a week or two, would you really want to live like that for the rest of your life? Wouldn't it perhaps feel a tad authoritarian? Especially if you were in the middle of the ocean with no way to escape.

It was with those ideas in mind that I sat down to write "End of the Liner."

I hope you enjoy the magic. All aboard now.

S he often dreamed of drowning.

In the empty hours between midnight and dawn, she lay in her narrow bunk and imagined the waves taking her. It would be cold. And if she was lucky, the freezing temperatures would claim her before the dark water invaded her mouth and lungs. Or, if she was even luckier, perhaps a Sea God would be merciful.

She wondered if she could request a winter ceremony.

She wondered how it had been for the others.

And when it would be her turn.

Not today. Today she had a packed schedule of breakfast, followed by aqua aerobics on the main deck. Then, an hour or so in the shade, reading. Perhaps she might stroll around the ship before lunch. In the afternoon, the crew often tried to provide entertainment, although the theaters were looking a little tired these days; no amount of clever lighting could disguise the fact that the paint on the elaborate sets was peeling and the velvet upholstery on the seats was faded and patched. People tried not to notice, and for many, it had been that way for all their lives.

But she remembered. And occasionally she felt a yearning for the old days. For a time when this existence was a privileged luxury rather than a slow torture. She glanced at the photographs she kept on her tiny dresser. One of her and Nick when they boarded with her parents. She looked so young, with her new husband—and they *were* young, she supposed. She was twenty-five and Nick was only two years older. They had hardly lived, really. Barely built up a bank of experiences before they boarded the ship and their lives shrank to these decks and corridors.

The other picture she looked at less often, because even a short glance drew fresh pain. Sometimes, she wondered why she kept it at all. Certainly, it did her no favors with the Creators. Those who were "lost" were never spoken of, nor commemorated. Keeping mementos was frowned upon. But it was the one thing Leila couldn't let go of.

Her daughter, Addison.

This was the last photo ever taken of her little girl. On the verge of becoming a young woman. Celebrating her eighteenth birthday. Dark hair falling over her face, a wide grin, blue eyes glinting with mischief—and rebellion. Too much rebellion, perhaps.

Maybe Leila should have been sterner. Maybe she should have encouraged her willfulness less. When Nick had tried to cajole Addison into partaking in traditional female pursuits such as sewing and cookery, perhaps she should have backed him up rather than supporting Addison's decision to enroll in maintenance and engineering.

Regrets. Mistakes. No life lived long is short of them.

Leila turned away from the photograph. She couldn't be late for breakfast. The Creators liked routine, and any small aberration meant that questions might be asked. She faced herself in the mirror. Unlike many of the older passengers, whose skin had weathered like leather from the abrasive winds and unforgiving eye of the sun, Leila had always protected herself from the elements. Her skin remained pale and soft, criss-crossed with a myriad of fine lines. Her blue eyes were clear—no cataracts yet, although she needed glasses for reading—and her long, thick hair was pure white, secured into a sensible bun.

Leila smiled at herself in the mirror. Past her heyday, but still holding up. Much like the ship itself.

In two days, she would mark her seventy-fifth birthday, and fifty years on board.

BREAKFAST WAS IN the Grand Suite today.

There were three main dining areas and passengers were rotated around them for breakfast, lunch and dinner, grouped by room number. Leila joined the queue to be seated. The queue was the usual mixture of older people like herself and younger families. Children scampered around the atrium playing tag, faces happy and eyes bright. They had never known anything but the ship. The fourteen decks and one thousand two hundred feet their whole universe. Of course, they had the pretense of space and freedom all around them. The skies above, the endless expanse of ocean. But sometimes, Leila thought, that only served to emphasize how small their world had become.

The queue shuffled forward. Leila nodded and smiled at familiar faces. Eventually, she reached the maître d's desk.

"And how are you this morning, Mrs. Simmonds?"

The maître d' was a small, coiffed man with tanned skin and sharp black eyes. His name was Julian. He had been the maître d' here for ten years, ever since his father was retired. Leila didn't like Julian so much; he had a reputation for *snitching*. Passengers had learned to be wary around him.

Leila smiled back. "Very well, thank you, Julian. And yourself?"

"Oh, I am always good, Mrs. Simmonds—and all the better for seeing you." He smiled, slick and unfelt. "Your companion is already at your table. Let me take you through."

Leila frowned. "Am I late?"

"No, no. Your companion is a little early this morning." His smile widened, but it looked strained at the edges. Something was wrong. "Please, come this way."

Leila followed him between the rows of perfectly laid out tables. The Grand Suite was decorated in the style of a Victorian tearoom. Fake candelabras, walls patterned with floral paper and hung with pictures of the Creators' famous animated characters in their Victorian finery. The servers were also dressed for the period—high-necked blouses and long, full skirts for the women, a suit and waistcoat for the men. Such pretenses, under the circumstances, might seem silly, but it was part of the Creators' policy. The fourth wall must never be dropped. The passenger experience never compromised. At any cost.

The smell of cooking—bacon and waffles—filled the room. Synthetic, of course. They pumped it in via the air vents. No one had eaten real meat in a long time and the breakfast choice was mostly limited to cereals, toast and whatever fruit was in season on the huge floating farms, the Harvesters.

Voices rose and fell. The dining area was large and there had to be a hundred people seated already. But it wasn't normally this noisy. Often, people ate their breakfast in complete silence, the only sound the scraping of cutlery on bone china. After all, what was there to discuss? No news or politics. No celebrity gossip or scandal. Just the same "blissful" routine, day after day, year after year. This morning, however, Leila could feel a heightened energy in the room.

"And here we are, Madam."

Leila's companion was seated at their usual table by one of the round porthole windows. Julian pulled out the chair opposite and Leila sat down.

"Thank you," she said.

Julian bobbed like a bird. "I will fetch you some coffee, Madam."

Leila turned to face the woman opposite. In contrast to Leila, who was tall and angular (and had always felt self-conscious about her height), Mirabelle was a tiny wisp of a woman, barely five foot tall, with wiry limbs, tanned a deep brown, and a massive mop of brittle, bleached hair. In all the time she had known her, Leila had never seen Mirabelle without a massive pair of sunglasses hiding her face, even indoors.

Before Leila even had a chance to pick up the menu—out of habit rather than curiosity, as she had eaten the same breakfast every day for the last five decades—Mirabelle leaned forward and lowered her voice.

"Have you heard?"

Mirabelle was posh. Very posh. Leila had always thought of herself as cultured, and her parents had certainly been comfortable; comfortable enough to pass the Creators' assessment for boarding. But Mirabelle was "old money," as they used to call it. One of her ex-husbands (now deceased) had been the ship's original First Officer and her eldest son was a Deck Officer. Not to mention her daughter, who headed up Entertainment. Even here, where everyone should be equal, some were more equal than others.

While Leila had been obliged to give up her double cabin and move to a smaller single when Nick died (as per Creators' policy), Mirabelle had kept her expansive suite after being widowed, although her predilection for marrying frequently and briefly might have also had something to do with it. In the time it would take to assign Mirabelle a new cabin, she would probably have assigned herself a new husband.

Leila slipped on her glasses and picked up the menu.

"Heard what?" she asked, as casually as she could, conscious that the Creators discouraged gossip.

One perfect eyebrow arched above the rim of Mirabelle's designer sunglasses.

"One of the crew—" Mirabelle pulled a scarlet-tipped finger across her throat in a dramatic gesture.

Leila regarded her over the menu. "OB?"

Mirabelle smiled with a little too much relish. "Fished out of the children's splash pool this morning."

Leila continued to stare at her. "Mikey's Mini Fun Pool?"

This was new. People, both crew and passengers, had jumped ship before. But to drown yourself in a swimming pool when all around lay vast miles of sea seemed odd.

"Suicide?" she queried.

"Well, that's it," Mirabelle whispered. "Rumor is, no. Murder."

Leila's eyes widened. "Murder?"

Mirabelle nodded enthusiastically. "Stabbed."

Stabbed. No wonder the dining room was buzzing. A murder on board. In fifty years, there had only been one other murder, when a passenger had strangled his wife after an argument. Of course, that was the only one officially documented. There were rumors that there had been more. It wasn't exactly difficult to dispose of a body on a ship. So, to leave one to be discovered in a swimming pool was strange.

For the first time in a long time, Leila felt the stirrings of curiosity.

"Do they have any idea who's responsible?"

Mirabelle shook her head. "No. They're trying to keep it hush hush."

Obviously. Nothing must be allowed to spoil the facade. And they all played along, because to do otherwise would result in *consequences*. Although, from the buzz in the dining room, the crew didn't seem to be doing a very good job of containing this particular piece of gossip.

"Of course," Mirabelle said now, sipping her tea, "I expect it will turn out to be another crew member. Some grubby little dispute over a girl or drugs."

She sniffed disdainfully. Even though Mirabelle had been her closest friend for most of her life, Leila still occasionally found her snobbery distasteful.

"What if it's a passenger?" she couldn't help saying.

Mirabelle snorted. "Why would a passenger kill a crew member? Honestly, darling, don't be so silly."

Leila felt herself bristle. But they were saved from an argument by the arrival of their waitress, a wide-eyed Latino girl called Luciana.

"Good morning, ladies. Are you ready to order?"

"Yes," Leila said quickly. "I'll have the oat yogurt, granola, toast and jam."

"Very good. And for you, Madam?" She turned to Mirabelle.

Mirabelle smiled mischievously. "You know, I could *murder* some eggs Benedict."

THE SHIP HAD two outdoor decks, three pools, two water slides and half a dozen al fresco eateries and bars. Inside, there were three huge restaurants, two smaller cafés, another half a dozen bars and two theaters, plus a gym, a wellness center and several shops containing a selection of souvenirs and fancy goods which no one ever bought, because who wanted a souvenir from a ship you never left?

But it all worked to maintain the pretense. Otherwise, passengers might have to face up to the reality of their existence here—and no one was willing to do that.

They knew what happened to those who did.

Leila walked twice around the top deck. Some people were already out on the sun loungers. It was a balmy seventy-two degrees with only a light wind. The sky was a sapphire blue, strung with a few wispy clouds. A beautiful day. Another one. The captain tried his best to keep them in good weather. And yet sometimes Leila longed for storms and rain. For winds and lightning. For the crisp crunch of autumn leaves beneath her feet, the soft spring of grass or even the squelch of boots through mud. All forgotten pleasures. Here, there was only the familiar creaking wood of the decks or the soft tread of the now worn but once luxurious carpets in the lounges and restaurants. Leila hadn't stepped foot on land for five decades. Now she was about to turn seventy-five, she never would again.

She upped her pace and tried to tell herself not to be morose. Introspection did no good. She greeted a few of the couples on the loungers. Lithe, tanned youngsters. She hoped they enjoyed these lazy days. Once they turned twenty-one, most of the younger passengers would be conscripted to work as crew for at least two years. It was part of the arrangement of being on board. Surprisingly, some even stayed on as crew. Or perhaps it wasn't so surprising. Leisure was a wonderful thing when it was a treat. But days and weeks and years of leisure were different. Many of the crew here had started out as passengers. Work gave them a purpose. Funny how we yearn for the things we once hated and hate the things we once yearned for. Life on board the ship was, in so many ways, topsy turvy. But at least it *was* life. The fate of those left behind was much worse.

She made her way back to the lower deck. Children and adults splashed in the main pool and whooshed down the water slides, but the smaller pool remained closed off and covered. "Mikey is working hard to re-open the fun," a sign read. Or was Mikey working hard to clear up the blood? Leila wondered. Dead. Stabbed. In a children's swimming pool. Why hadn't they dumped the body overboard? Perhaps they had been interrupted or hadn't had time?

She found herself macabrely intrigued, her brain actually working for once. She glanced around the deck. There were more sun loungers arranged around the pools, and tables and chairs where people could sit and enjoy a snack or relax. She tried to assess whether people were chatting to each other more than usual or whether they were holding back. There were plenty of crew up here and it wouldn't do to be caught publicly speculating that things were less than perfect on board. Not until anything official was announced.

"Spreading malcontent" was a serious infringement of the rules. There were measures to deal with people who spread malcontent. Persistent offenders were taken to the Re-education Center, a large room below the main theaters that used to be the liner's nightclub— Mikey's Fun Lab. What exactly went on during re-education was never spoken about, but Leila had seen a few of the re-educated afterward. They had a look about them. Glassy-eyed and somehow . . . hollow.

She recalled one—a vibrant young waiter with a brilliant smile who had enjoyed making off-color jokes about "the regime." Bobby, his name was. One day, he had disappeared for re-education. When Leila saw him again, his brilliance had faded. He walked with a tentative shuffle. His smile was hesitant and his eyes were vacant. When the Creators' famous characters emerged for their twice-daily song and dance routines, he stood rigid, clapping so hard it felt as if his very life depended on it.

One day, Leila had found herself walking toward Bobby on deck.

As she raised a hand in greeting, he'd tripped and stumbled, crashing to the floor. Something had flown from his mouth. Leila had bent to pick the item up, but he'd grabbed it first. Dentures.

As Leila stared in horror, he'd shoved them quickly back into his mouth.

"What did they do to you?" she'd asked.

His eyes filled with tears. "My smile," he'd whispered. "They took my smile."

That had been the last time Leila saw Bobby. The next day she heard that he had had a tragic accident and fallen overboard. For such a safety-conscious and well-regulated ship, it was surprising how many people had tragic accidents.

She jumped as a hand touched her arm.

"Are you all right, Madam?"

She turned. A young crew member. Blonde, blandly pretty— "Chrystelle," her name badge read—was looking at her with concern. Leila tried to gather herself. It wouldn't do to let them think anything was wrong.

She forced a smile. "I was just thinking what a beautiful day it is."

Chrystelle's smile widened.

They took my smile.

"Yes, it is, isn't it?"

"And so nice to see the children playing in the pool."

"We love to see happy children."

"A shame Mikey's Fun Pool is closed."

The smile didn't falter. "Well, Mikey's pool just needs a little TLC. We can't have the little ones playing in a pool that isn't properly maintained now, can we?"

"Of course not." Leila widened her own smile, so much her cheeks hurt. "You all work so hard here to look after us."

"Oh, we're just doing our jobs."

"Well, we're all very grateful."

Chrystelle nodded and skipped off again, obviously satisfied.

Leila let her smile fade. She had become adept at the simple-old-lady act. Sometimes, she even believed that was who she was. It was easier to fall into your allotted role here. Just like it was easier to keep up the facade. Why—forgive the pun—rock the boat?

She sat down at her usual table and opened her book, a well-thumbed mystery novel, but she was distracted. She stared at the words, but they refused to sink in. Her mind wandered. A murder. The Creators would be unhappy about that. Everything here was planned. Even death. And much as they might try to cover it up, rumors still seeped out. It would be bad for morale, especially so close to the next Retirement Ceremony.

The Retirement Ceremonies were big events on the ship, almost more so than Christmas. Posters and decorations had already started to go up. By the end of the week, the ship would be fully kitted out with streamers and balloons, the cast would be rehearsing their special Retirement Show in the theater, menus would be prepared for the Grand Banquet and the Creators would decide which child would pick the Retirees.

Normally, this would be one of the youngest passengers, and it was regarded as a huge honor. Parents were fiercely competitive about the selection. Leila had already seen pushy mums with little girls in bright Princess dresses queuing outside the theaters. She had smiled at them as she passed. The children had smiled back, but several of the mothers had dropped their eyes, perhaps embarrassed. After all, Leila was old. Soon, it might be her name that their child picked.

And one day, it will be yours, she had felt like saying. *Retirement comes to us all. Unless we have a tragic accident first.*

She closed her book and stared out over the deck. There was a burst of static through the speakers positioned around the pool and squeals from the younger children as a loud, cheerful voice announced:

"And now it's time to say a big howdy-hi to Captain Mikey and his crew!"

Captain Mikey's theme tune blasted tinnily through the speakers. Character parade time. The younger children cheered and waved. The older children carried on playing. They'd seen this a million times before. As had she.

Still, Leila watched as the characters ran through their usual song and dance routines. From afar, they retained some of the magic. Up close, the fake fur was threadbare and matted, the costumes faded and restitched multiple times. Even the songs sounded tired. But they would never change. Nothing here ever did. Except . . . she frowned, staring harder at the characters over her glasses. Captain Mikey, Rachel Rabbit, Susie Squirrel, Chrissy Cat. Something *had* changed. One character was missing. Donnie Dog. Addison's favorite. With his jaunty red collar and curled tail, he was the cheeky one. Mischievous. Prone to playing tricks on Mikey and the rest of the gang.

Nothing here ever changed, so where was Donnie?

"Your water, Madam," a muffled voice said.

She looked up, about to tell the server that she hadn't ordered any water . . . and her heart leaped into her throat.

Donnie Dog stood by her table. One furry paw placed a glass of water in front of her. His large, shaggy face bobbed at hers, mouth open in a wide grin, pink rubber tongue lolling from side to side.

But that couldn't be right. Characters didn't serve food, and Donnie should be dancing up there with the others. Before her brain could make sense of it, Donnie had shuffled off again, bobbing and weaving across the deck. Leila stared after him. *What was going on?*

Momentarily, she felt a terrible swell of nausea, just like she used to get when the ship occasionally hit a rougher patch of sea. But the sea today was calm, the sun shining brightly; the only instability was within her.

Was this it? she thought. Was her mind finally starting to fray? The ship's doctor had said she was fine at her last checkup, but was he just being kind, not wanting to scare her? Everyone knew, when your mind went, a quiet early retirement was deemed the kindest option.

Leila could have told the doctor she wasn't afraid of death. How could she be? The only two people she had ever truly loved were dead—her daughter and her husband. Even if she didn't believe in an afterlife, at least death meant she wouldn't have to endure the hollow pain of missing them every day, an ache so ingrained that she barely noticed it most of the time, except for that first moment of waking. Then, the agony of their loss was as fierce and raw as when it first happened.

She reached for her water and paused. A small slip of paper had been tucked beneath the glass. She glanced around. No one was watching her. All eyes were on the characters doing their dance. Leila carefully slipped the paper out and tucked it within the pages of her book. She glanced down.

12 a.m. Life Station 1.

Her fingers trembled, a renewed dizziness sweeping over her. The characters on the upper deck sashayed their way through the last song in their set.

"Because we're loving life—and loving you and you and you . . ."

The last chorus.

Life Station 1.

The last place her daughter had been seen alive.

ADDISON HAD ALWAYS been a willful child. She had walked and talked early. Eager, even then, to run away from her mother's arms or keep her at bay with a fierce "No!"

Leila's own mother, Addison's grandmother, had found her only grandchild joyful and infuriating in equal measure.

"You need to be stricter with her," she would often tell Leila and Nick. "She walks all over the pair of you. Discipline is what she needs."

But Addison didn't respond well to discipline. Or rather, she questioned discipline. Even from a young age, she was a child who felt the injustice of an unfair reprisal. "Because I said so" was not a good enough answer for their little girl. "Why?" she would ask, eyebrows drawn into a frown. "That's not a reason."

Perhaps Leila should have realized that Addison's demands for answers would always be her undoing. By the time Addison was ten, Leila had lost count of the times she had been called to the Tutor's office to discuss Addison's over-inquiring nature. On the final occasion, the Tutor had fixed her with a meaningful stare and said softly: "While it's wonderful that Addison is such a bright little girl—and one day she will be an asset to the ship—if she continually questions the Creators, it might be necessary for her to have a *more intensive education.*"

That day, Leila had sat Addison down in the cabin and patiently explained that, although she might have questions, she must learn to keep them to herself. At least in class. Otherwise, the Creators would get cross, and they might punish all of them.

Addison had considered this, eyes wide.

"Why don't the Creators like questions?"

Another good question. Leila had sighed. "I think they're afraid that people won't like the answers." She took her daughter's hand. "It's hard to understand, Addison, but please, promise me. No more questions. Just accept what the Tutor tells you. Please?"

Addison had nodded. "Okay. I promise."

Leila had smiled sadly. "One day you'll understand how lucky we are to be here, on the ship. We're safe, the Creators look after us. We mustn't spoil that."

Addison had nodded again and then—because there was always one final question—she had asked: "But if the ship is so wonderful, and we're so lucky, why is everyone so scared?"

LUNCH TOOK PLACE in the Artist's Suite, a sophisticated black-and-white space, the walls adorned with original concept drawings of Mikey and his gang, plus the many other beloved characters originated by the Creators. They beamed down benevolently at the diners, a reminder of more innocent times.

Children—and adults—could still watch reruns of the old cartoons and movies, although not all of them. Ones which depicted the world as it had been, showing people living in real cities—an unfamiliar concept to many on board—had been banned years ago. They offered false hope and an unrealistic vision of life, it had been decided, as if tales of princesses and dragons, aliens and spaceships, didn't.

What an odd world they lived in, Leila often thought. Where children knew more about imaginary kingdoms than the land that Leila had been born on.

She allowed herself to be led to her usual table. Mirabelle was, again, already seated. For such a tiny woman, she made damn sure she never missed a meal. But she was never usually this early. There must be more news.

As Leila suspected, her bottom had barely touched the seat when Mirabelle leaned over the table toward her:

"Have you heard the latest?"

Leila made a concerted effort to pretend to be looking at her menu.

"About what?" she asked.

Mirabelle trilled like a canary. "The murder, of course."

Leila caught her breath and glanced around. No one appeared to be looking at them, but you couldn't be too careful. The servers here moved like ninjas.

"Should we really be discussing this?" she whispered.

"Well, if you'd rather talk about the weather . . ." Mirabelle faked a yawn.

Leila sighed. "Go on, then."

"They've identified the victim."

Leila stared at her friend. Mirabelle had more ears to the ground than a herd of sleeping elephants. Her sources were impeccable. As were her family connections. It was why she always got away with her gossip. She held a privileged position. And, by association, so did Leila, she supposed.

But Leila also had a mark against her name. Because of Addison. She couldn't be as reckless as Mirabelle. The Creators would not be so lenient. Mirabelle was a friend. But she didn't always understand that her protected status did not apply to everyone.

"So, who is it?" she asked in a low voice.

Mirabelle smiled smugly. "Well, it's very interesting, actually."

Then she paused, her smile widening. She turned her head toward an approaching waitress. "Lucy, darling. I was wondering when you were going to come and take our order. I'm famished."

They ordered quickly. Salad and soup, as always. Once Lucy had departed, Mirabelle picked up her white wine and took a sip. Leila tried to fight back her curiosity and failed.

"You were saying?" she prompted.

"Ah, yes." Mirabelle grinned. "Well, turns out it's someone you know. One of the kitchen staff—Sam Weatherall."

Leila dropped her butter knife with a clatter. The sound seemed to echo around the dining room. A few heads turned in their direction. Damn.

She bent to pick the knife up from the floor, but a server had already swooped in, brandishing a clean one.

"Here, Madam. Let me get that for you. Is everything okay?"

"Yes, yes," Leila said. "Just a little clumsy."

"I think there was a small swell just then," Mirabelle said smoothly. "Didn't you feel it, young man?"

"Err . . . yes. Sorry about that."

He slid silently away again. Leila took a breath and tried to compose herself. She reached for her wine and took a swig.

"I'm sorry," Mirabelle said, in a rare moment of contrition. "I thought you'd be happy."

Leila regained her composure. "Why would I care?"

Mirabelle eyed her steadily. "Well, if it was me, darling, and I'd just found out that the man who betrayed my daughter had finally got his just deserts, I'd be fucking delighted."

Leila felt a tightness in her chest, a lump in her throat. "Well, I'm not you." She pushed her chair back. "Excuse me. I'm going to the bathroom."

She managed to walk steadily, face controlled, from the dining room to the Ladies. But by the time she reached the bathrooms her legs were shaking and her facial muscles taut from the strain of trying to keep a neutral expression.

Fortunately, when she walked in, the Ladies was empty and all the cubicles were vacant.

Leila leaned over the sink and dabbed at her face with cold water. She took several deep breaths. Then she went and shut herself in a cubicle. One of the few places you could get some privacy on board, other than your cabin, and even then it was mandated that you should spend no more than ten hours a day in that.

She perched on the toilet lid, head resting in her hands, trying to calm her racing mind.

They've identified the body. One of the kitchen staff.
Sam.

He had been one of Addison's friends. Since they were young children. Part of the group that Addison had grown up with, played with, gone through the awkward teenage years with, served time working on board with.

And finally, planned to escape with.

There had been rumors over the years. Of those who had tried to "go aft," as the phrase had become known. To jump ship. They were never substantiated. Of course. The crew would never let it be known that anyone might want to escape this cruise of a lifetime.

But people had disappeared. Never spoken about. Written off as another "tragic accident." Even if that was a lie, Leila had wondered how many survived their escape attempt. Adrift upon the endless ocean, at the mercy of the Sea Gods and other creatures that lurked beneath.

Mostly, the liner sailed far from shore, for fear of contamination through treacherous winds. Food was procured from the floating Harvesters. And because the captain tended to sail in circles, following the fair weather, it was almost impossible to keep track of where on earth—or ocean—you were. Even the stars and moon seemed to lie after a while.

Very occasionally, usually at night, the ship drew closer to land, especially if the weather looked bad further out at sea. Close enough for a tantalizing glimpse of a more solid mass far in the distance. Terra firma. A world left behind. But in all the years that they had sailed, Leila hadn't known of anyone who had made it there.

And only one lifeboat had ever got away from the ship.

The one containing her daughter.

THERE HAD BEEN five of them. Friends since childhood. Buoyed up by youthful rebellion and frustration. You saw it in the teenagers, and, like acne and hormones, it usually passed. But Addison had fire in her belly. Leila should have known that the curious little girl would grow into an adventurous young adult. While most eventually settled into their life on the ship, Addison was a caged animal. She wanted more.

She hid it well, achieving outstanding grades and performing her roles diligently, all the time smiling widely and reciting the Creators' lines to perfection.

But Leila could tell—her eyes were always on the horizon.

Nevertheless, Leila hadn't known what Addison and her friends were planning. That pained her at times. Other times, she told herself that Addison had been trying to keep her safe. If questions were asked afterward, then Leila's ignorance would protect her—and it did. Still, there were often days she wished she had known her daughter better, had talked to her more, been a closer confidante. Selfish, she knew. Just as it was selfish that there were days when she wished Sam's betrayal, his attempt to thwart the lifeboat leaving, had actually worked.

After he raised the alarm, the crew tried to stop the boat. There had been a scuffle. An escapee had gone overboard along with two crew members (all rescued). But the lifeboat had deployed and three of the youngsters had got away, including Addison.

Of course, the chances of them making it safely to land were minuscule. And land itself was a poisoned chalice. Everyone knew that it was contaminated and would be for hundreds of years to come. Those left behind, unlucky enough to survive, were probably barely human by now. Mankind had been laid to waste and only the ships, the great floating arks full of survivors, were safe.

So why is everyone so scared?

Leila sighed. She couldn't blame Sam.

But neither did she feel sorry that someone had killed him.

She had seen him only fleetingly in the years since Addison had disappeared. For his part in the plot to escape (even if he had had second thoughts), he was sent for re-education and then deployed "below deck." Their paths had never crossed. What would she say to him, anyway? *Why did you betray my daughter? Where did you think you were going?* Twenty years. It probably didn't matter now.

They never found the lifeboat. But that wasn't surprising. It could have capsized. Been smashed to smithereens against rocks at the shore. Grounded. The sea was harsh and merciless. Leila wanted to believe Addison was alive out there somewhere, but clinging to hope was sometimes worse than allowing yourself to drown in grief.

She tensed as she heard the door to the Ladies open. It wouldn't do to be caught in here crying, or malingering. She stood and quickly flushed the toilet. Then she adjusted her clothes and composed herself before unlocking the door and letting herself out of the cubicle.

The room was empty. Leila looked around. No one was standing at the sinks. No other cubicles were engaged. She frowned. Odd. She had definitely heard someone enter, although the flushing of the cistern might have disguised their exit.

She walked over to the sinks to wash her hands and glanced in the mirror. She mustn't return to lunch looking out of sorts. Mirabelle would notice, as would the servers.

In the harsh light, she looked older. Hard to see the person she once was beneath the fine wrinkles and softly sagging skin. But then, time is a vandal, wreaking its havoc upon all of us. Perhaps better that she had never been a great beauty when she was young. There was so much less to lose. And perhaps she wouldn't have minded losing her youth at all if those lines had been earned. With experiences, excitement. With work and travel and *living*.

But no. Leila had remained static, rotting quietly, like a plant in a pot. Her growth restricted by the confines of her situation. Of course, she was watered and tended to, but now she was withering without ever really having grown.

She turned on the taps and looked down. There was something in the sink. She reached in and picked it up. A small rock. She turned the rough stone over in her hand. On one side, small grooves ran in circles. An imprint of a long-dead beast. *A fossil.* Leila hadn't seen one of these since she was a child. There were no rocks on a ship. No stones or sand or grass or earth.

A rock like this came from land.

Leila felt her world waver. *No. Impossible.* She shoved the fossil into her skirt pocket and hurried out of the Ladies. She looked left and right along the corridor. A flash of brown fur disappeared past the portholes at the end of the corridor. She scurried after it as fast as her aged legs would take her, rounding the corner just as the unmistakable shaggy shape of Donnie Dog disappeared through the double doors that led to the atrium.

Leila tried to hurry after him, but her chest felt tight; she couldn't seem to get her breath. She paused, reaching for the wall for balance. But the ship swayed, or maybe she did. Her hand flailed, she felt herself lose balance and fall, hitting her head on the porthole frame as she went down. She groaned and the corridor shrank to darkness.

IT WASN'T SO bad. The darkness. She floated in the twilight waters. Her breath had gone, but she didn't mind. There was a strange feeling of euphoria. Distantly, she could see twinkling lights. Fluorescence. Tiny fish like sparkling jewels. And larger masses. Bulbous eyes and beautiful orange and turquoise tentacles. The Sea Gods. Only seen since the Event. She let herself drift into their embrace . . . and then a soft voice whispered . . .

"Are you all right, darling? You had a bit of a turn."

Leila blinked her eyes open. Momentarily disorientated. She turned her head. She was lying on her bed in her cabin and Mirabelle was leaning over her, looking worried.

"I . . ."

"You fainted. In the hallway." Mirabelle clutched her hand. "I told them you hadn't eaten your lunch. I told them it was nothing to worry about. It isn't anything to worry about, is it?"

Leila struggled to push herself into a sitting position. Her head and her bones ached where she'd fallen.

"No. Of course not." She hesitated, thinking about Donnie Dog and the fossil in her pocket. Mirabelle was her oldest friend. "Belle . . . can I tell you something?"

Mirabelle's face twitched. "You can tell me anything."

"Okay."

"But why don't we get you some fresh air first?"

"But I . . ."

Mirabelle grabbed her arm and stood, pulling Leila up from the bed. "Agree . . . I know. Sea air is the cure for all ills."

"But I'm a little cold."

"Nonsense. Here." Mirabelle grabbed a blanket and threw it over her friend's shoulders. "Remember how blessed we are to have the invigorating ocean all around us."

Leila stared at her friend, wondering if she was feeling all right herself. Mirabelle wasn't usually one to parrot the Creators' lines. However, she allowed herself to be guided over to the door. Mirabelle pushed it open and bundled Leila outside, on to the small balcony, shutting the door behind them.

The wind was surprisingly brisk this afternoon. It whipped their faces and snatched at their hair. The sea frothed and churned around the ship. Stormy waters. Something they didn't encounter very often.

Leila turned to Mirabelle, eyes watering. "Why have you brought me out here? Are you planning to push me in?"

Mirabelle chuckled. "No, my dear. But out here it's safer to talk."

She slipped off her sunglasses. Behind them, her gray eyes were milky with cataracts. Leila couldn't hide her surprise.

Mirabelle nodded. "The glasses aren't just an affectation. They disguise my infirmity."

"Cataracts aren't necessarily—"

Mirabelle cut her off sharply: "Yes, they are, Leila. If anyone knew, I would face an early retirement. And I don't intend for that to happen." She gazed at Leila fondly. "How long have we known each other?"

"Well, as long as we've both been on board—fifty years."

"How many birthdays have I had?"

Leila frowned. "Fifty?"

"No."

"No?"

"Because if I'd had fifty birthdays," Mirabelle said, "I'd be older than you. And I'm only seventy-two."

Leila stared at her. "Really?"

Mirabelle smiled thinly. "I've been seventy-two for the last five years, Leila."

It took a moment to sink in. "You've been lying."

Mirabelle shrugged. "A little. I pulled a few strings. Bought my-self a little extra time. No one takes much notice if you miss an odd birthday or five over fifty years. I might miss a couple more before they finally call my name."

"But . . . that's . . ."

"Against the rules. Punishable by re-education. True. But there's not a lot they can do to an old woman like me. Of course, I'd still rather they didn't find out, which is why we're talking out here, where no one can hear us."

Another jolt. And now Leila understood. Nothing to do with sea air. But everything to do with listening ears. She glanced back into the cabin. Again, she had heard rumors that the crew had monitor-ing devices in random cabins. But she had always dismissed this as fanciful gossip.

To hear Mirabelle confirm it sent a chill through her that had nothing to do with the brisk afternoon breeze. All this time. All these years. Had they listened in the old cabin too? Had they heard the intimate moments she had shared with Nick? Their arguments, their occasional doubts? She felt sick.

"Why are you telling me all of this now?" she asked.

Mirabelle slid her glasses back on. "Because your name will be called at the Retirement Ceremony."

Leila nodded. She wasn't surprised to know that it was predeter-mined. "I suppose it's time."

Mirabelle clasped her arm. "You are my oldest and closest friend, and I don't want to lose you, but even I can't stop it."

Leila nodded again, feeling tears well. She wasn't sure why. She had been prepared for this moment ever since she boarded. Every passenger was. Being a passenger gave you immense privileges. But your journey couldn't last forever. It had to come to an end. In your seventy-fifth year, you were retired. It was as it had always been. The population of the ship had to be maintained at a level that was reasonable for everyone. Older people became a drain on resources. Similarly, anyone with a life-limiting illness or disability would be retired early. That was just how it was. It was necessary, for the greater good. That was what they had always been told.

So why did Leila feel that she wasn't ready? Despite everything. Despite her frustration with life on the ship, the loss of her husband and daughter, she still wished to see another dawn, to watch a pod of dolphins gracefully arc over the waves or the majestic Sea Gods wave their long tentacles in the dying light of a sunset. There was still life out there, even if she was only a spectator. There were still things she would miss, like the children's happy smiles, and Mirabelle. Dear caustic, gossipy, indomitable Mirabelle.

As if reading her mind, Mirabelle smiled sadly. "Once you have gone, dear friend, I have no one. So I want to give you one more thing."

She reached into her pocket and took out a small vial of liquid.

"What's that?" Leila asked.

"Morphine."

"*Morphine?* Why would I need morphine?"

Mirabelle pressed the vial into her hand. "Slip it into your champagne at the ceremony. You'll be asleep before you hit the water."

Leila frowned, confused. "But why would I need that? In the water, the Sea Gods will take me down to sleep. It will be quick, peaceful."

Mirabelle shook her head. "Leila. Do you *still* believe what they tell you? Do you remember when I fell in, when I was young? They fished me out, but I only just made it."

Leila did remember vaguely, but time made memories cloudy, obscuring them with minutiae and false perception. And sometimes it seemed like the waves stole away her thoughts on the changing tides.

"*Leila,*" Mirabelle continued. "Trust me—it is not calm or peaceful. Fighting to hold your breath until your lungs burst and icy water floods in. It's agony. Torture. Terrifying."

Mirabelle clasped Leila's hands together tightly. "Take the morphine. At least, allow yourself a more peaceful death. It's your best option."

Or was it? Leila thought again about the fossil in her pocket. Donnie Dog. *12 a.m. Life Station 1.* What was going on? Should she share it with Mirabelle? And then the decision was taken out of her hands as someone rapped loudly on the balcony door.

They both jumped and turned. A young man with slicked-back hair, dressed in the standard crew hospitality uniform, stood on the other side of the glass. He had let himself into Leila's room.

"Cabin Service, Madam," he called through the door.

Leila glanced nervously at Mirabelle. A random cabin check. She hadn't had one of those in over a decade. Mirabelle raised an eyebrow.

"We're just coming in, darling," she called back.

She threw Leila a warning look and pulled open the balcony door. Leila slipped the morphine into her other pocket and followed her friend back into the cabin.

The young man smiled widely, betraying yellowed, chipped teeth, a far more common sight than Bobby's brilliant smile. Dentists were scarce on the ships and toothpaste was not widely available. Most young people hadn't heard of braces or whitening.

"I just came to check on you, Madam," he said. "To see if you needed any further medical assistance?"

"No, I'm feeling much better," Leila stuttered.

"We were just outside taking some reviving sea air," Mirabelle added smoothly.

The young man—"James," his name tag read—nodded. "An excellent idea. Fresh air and rest. You must be tired?"

His eyes found Leila's and she felt a tremor run through her. Tired. Ready to be retired. That was what they wanted, these youngsters. When they looked at her, they saw someone whose days were numbered. Whose time had almost run out. Taking up space from others. Had someone already put their name down for her cabin, her clothes, her belongings?

She forced out a smile. "You're right. I am tired."

Mirabelle threw her another sharp look.

"That's why I'm so looking forward to the Retirement Ceremony on Friday," Leila continued. "I hope my name is called. I've had my time and I'm so grateful."

James's face softened. "That is wonderful to hear, Madam. I'll leave you in peace. Please, rejoin the ship when you're ready."

"Thank you, James."

"You're welcome, Madam."

"I should be going too," Mirabelle said quickly. "I just wanted to make sure you were okay, Leila."

"You're a good friend," Leila said, weighting her words with just enough meaning. Mirabelle nodded and followed James out of the cabin. Once the door had closed behind them, Leila collapsed onto the small bed.

She had always thought she would be ready for retirement. What did she really have left here to live for? But now, things had changed. Something was happening. The murder, the fossil, the message. She was feeling emotions she hadn't experienced in a long time. Curiosity, excitement, fear, anticipation.

Was she really going to go to the illicit rendezvous? She could be meeting a murderer. What if whoever was in the Donnie costume had killed Sam? On the other hand, what difference did it make to her? She was due for retirement in just a couple of days anyway. *Dead if you do, dead if you don't.* A hysterical giggle rose inside her. She coughed it down, remembering that "they" could be listening. She mustn't arouse suspicion now.

Everything must look normal. She had to keep to her routine. An early dinner with Mirabelle, then a couple of drinks in the Piano Bar. Normally, she was back in her cabin by ten thirty at the latest. Of course, these days, she usually found herself getting up at least once in the night to use the bathroom. Did they listen to that too? she suddenly wondered, feeling a hot flush of indignation. Well, the joke would be on them, because that would be her cover for getting out of the room. The cistern was noisy, so it should adequately disguise the sound of her leaving.

And then? What next?

For the first time in fifty years, Leila didn't know the answer.

DINNER WAS SERVED in the Royal Princess Suite. Ornate gold pillars stretched up to the ceiling, from which massive chandeliers dangled, sparkling with light. A few had bulbs missing and most were draped in wispy cobwebs. The faded wallpaper was patterned with tiny crowns and fake flaming torches hung from the walls.

The servers here glided around in velvet and tulle finery—the girls in fancy dresses with laced bodices and the men in jodhpurs and long jackets. Costumes that had been patched, darned and re-sized dozens, if not hundreds, of times.

Like everything on board, it was all a facade. Scratch beneath the surface and nothing was quite what it seemed. Of course, most people didn't care. They liked the status quo. There were no unexpected surprises. Everything was taken care of. No need to worry or think. That was enough for them. And for a long time, it had been enough for her too.

But now?

"Are you feeling revived, my dear?" Mirabelle asked, buttering her bread.

"Yes." Leila smiled, reaching for her soup spoon. "Very revived, thanks."

"Good. Because I have other news." Mirabelle leaned forward and stage-whispered: "About the murder."

Leila steadied herself. "You do?"

Mirabelle nodded. "Officially, Mr. Weatherall had an unfortunate accident. You know, like a lot of people do."

"And the unofficial line?"

"No one from the ship killed him."

"I don't understand."

"They think someone got on board."

Leila felt ice trickle down her bowed spine. "That's impossible, surely?"

Mirabelle arched an eyebrow. "They've been searching the ship. Discreetly, of course. But they haven't found the interloper."

"Perhaps they got away?"

"Perhaps. Or maybe they're hiding."

Leila swallowed. "Surely not. The crew know everyone on this ship. Do you really think a stranger could escape their notice?"

She knew there was a glint in her friend's eyes behind the dark glasses.

"A good point," Mirabelle said, reaching for her wine. "Unless . . ."

"Unless what?"

"A former passenger—one who jumped ship—came back. They would know the ship's layout, routine. They would know how to disguise themselves."

Disguise themselves. Of course. *Donnie Dog.* Jaunty red collar. Lolling pink tongue.

This time, Leila tried to keep her calm. She adjusted her napkin primly and smiled. "Well, I think it's all a little far-fetched. I'm sure they'll find that it's just another crew member."

Mirabelle tensed. She didn't like it when Leila disagreed with her. Never had. It was how their relationship worked. Mirabelle was the one in control. Leila placidly acquiesced.

"Well, we shall see." Mirabelle sniffed, taking a sip of wine. "I'm sure none of us wants a murderer running amok on board. I hope they catch them soon."

Leila smiled. "I'm sure they're following every lead."

MUCH AS SHE wanted to get away, Leila forced herself to join Mirabelle and a couple of the other ladies—Maureen and Barbara—in the Piano Bar for cocktails. Her head was starting to ache, and her stomach cramped with nervous anticipation. Not helped by the talk of the murder. The Creators usually tried to keep such things contained, but they also knew that the ship had a grapevine (of which Mirabelle was the juiciest grape). When it suited them, they let things travel. In a situation like this, it might throw up useful information.

Leila was certain the ever-present servers heard more than they let on and, as discreet as Mirabelle thought she was, her whispers grew more exaggerated the more cocktails she downed. Leila sipped conservatively at her Bloody Mary, making it last, wanting to keep her wits (or what remained of them) about her. *12 a.m. Life Station 1.*

The piano player tinkled out easy-listening and swing versions of the Creators' famous tunes. Leila gritted her teeth and tried not to scream. Finally, the clock ticked around to ten fifteen. She rose, made her apologies, bade the staff good night and walked slowly toward the lifts. Although she wanted to hurry, Leila forced herself to keep to a leisurely pace, to wait patiently for the lift. Nothing must seem amiss. Not tonight.

A murder. A body. An intruder on board. *12 a.m. Life Station 1.*

As she stepped out of the lift onto her floor, Leila spotted Arianne, the cabin maid, walking toward her. Just as she did every night. Good. A witness. It was important that Leila was seen to go to her room. No aberrations from routine.

She smiled widely. "Good night, Arianne."

Arianne smiled back. "Good night, Mrs. Simmonds."

Ritual pleasantries exchanged, Leila walked down the corridor to her cabin—5734. She pressed her card key to the door and it buzzed open. She stepped inside, letting the door shut behind her, and stood for a moment, breathing deeply. Ninety minutes until her assignation.

Leila looked around. The cabin felt smaller, suffocating. Conscious of hidden ears, she walked into the tiny bathroom, brushed her teeth, washed her face and then came back out and shuffled around, opening the wardrobe door, shutting it again and hoping that it would be enough to indicate she had changed into her night-clothes. She was probably being paranoid. They couldn't be listening *all* the time, surely? But it didn't hurt to be overcautious.

Finally, Leila climbed into bed and turned her light off. In the darkness, she could see the glow of the digital alarm clock: 10:45 p.m. Now, she just had to wait until she could make her move.

Time seemed to deliberately drag its feet. Leila tried not to glance at the clock. Despite her nerves and the tension in her stomach, her eyelids felt heavy. No. She mustn't sleep. Stay awake. Stay alert. But age and wine had other ideas. Her eyelids drooped again . . .

HER EYES SHOT back open. They must only have been shut for a few minutes. Leila checked the clock: 11:54 p.m. *No.* She sat up so suddenly her head spun. No time to let it settle. She clambered out of bed and crossed hurriedly to the bathroom, stubbing her toe in the dark, biting back a cry of pain. Quickly, she flicked the light on, shut the door, counted ten excruciating seconds then flushed the cistern.

As quietly as she could, she slipped out of the bathroom. No time to grab her coat. She stuck her feet into her sensible moccasins and let herself out through the cabin door. It was only when she was halfway down the corridor that she realized she had left her card key inside her cabin. She hesitated and then told herself not to be so stupid. One way or another, there was no coming back from this.

Leila trotted as fast as she could along the corridor, her shoes whispering across the thick carpet. Was she too late? Her cabin was on the fifth floor. She had to make it down four sets of stairs to get to Life Station 1. She didn't dare take the lift. Once, as a sprightly twenty-something, she could have jogged down those stairs in less than a minute. Now, her descent was far slower. She couldn't afford to trip or twist her ankle. And the stairs were in semi-darkness, il-luminated only by the soft orange glow of the night lighting.

The ship slept, except the ship never really slept. There were always crew working and watching, cleaning and maintaining. Right on cue, as Leila reached the first-floor atrium, she heard the sound of a vacuum and a uniformed cleaner emerged around a corner. Leila ducked into the small recess behind the staircase. The cleaner, a young woman with short dark hair and pale skin, continued pushing the vacuum rhythmically back and forth, coming closer and closer. If she turned or looked up, she would surely see Leila half crouching in the shadows.

But she didn't. She moved on past, almost close enough to touch, completely oblivious. And then Leila realized why. She had a pair of headphones on, and a small MP3 player tucked into her back pocket. Staff weren't permitted to wear headphones or listen to music while at work. Too much of a distraction. She supposed the young woman thought that no one would see her on the night shift. And fortunately for Leila, she *was* distracted.

The cleaner moved past, humming to herself, and then turned off, down a corridor. Leila let herself breathe and checked her watch. 12 a.m. on the dot. Dammit. She was going to be late. She scurried across the atrium to the outer doors, which led to the deck. She pulled them open and stepped outside.

The breeze had died down. The night was still but cold. Leila shivered. She was wearing only a thin sweater and skirt. No jacket. No room key. No weapon either. Again, the thought that this was madness, dangerous, insane, flitted across her mind. But only briefly.

Her heart pounded, but not with fear, with exhilaration. As she stood on the deck, the stars hovering above, all her senses felt heightened. She could hear the low rumble of the ship's engines, the endless murmur of the waves. She could smell the salt and damp wood of the deck. The hairs on her arms tingled. For the first time in decades, she felt . . . alive.

Her only fear now was that she might be too late. 12:03 a.m. Ahead of her, she could see the sign hanging on the wall. "Life Station 1." But the deck was empty. Had she missed him? Was she too late? Was it a trick? She took out the note from her pocket.

And then she heard a noise. A creak. A figure stepped out from the shadows. Brown fur, jaunty red collar, lolling pink tongue. Donnie Dog.

Donnie walked toward her until he stood within an arm's length. Cheeky Donnie, whom Addison had so adored. But who lurked beneath the motheaten fur?

"You . . . you asked me to meet you," Leila stammered.

Donnie nodded his big head.

"You left me the fossil?"

Another nod.

"Why? Who are you?"

He moved closer. Leila could smell the faint mildewy smell of the costume and something else beneath. Sweat, body odor. Instinctively, she stepped away. Her back was against the deck railing.

"Who are you?" she asked again, her voice a little shaky. "Show me."

Donnie stretched out his arms, reaching for his shaggy head. And then he paused. His big furry paws shot out and he pushed her hard over the deck rail.

Leila toppled backward, arms flailing. Her screams evaporated into the night air. She felt the wind rushing past her, saw the blur of the ship's cabin lights, and then the hard smack of the icy water snatched her breath away. The sea swallowed her. She kicked her feet, fighting against its pull, breaking free of its dark embrace just long enough to see the splash of another body hitting the water, before her head dipped under again.

She fought her way back, kicking as hard as her aged legs allowed. Leila had always been a good swimmer, but this was a world away from a leisurely crawl in the liner's heated pool. Her sodden clothes were dragging her down. Waves washed over her head and the aching cold was paralyzing her limbs. She gasped, sucking in water, and started to cough. It was no good. You couldn't fight the sea. The sea always won.

And then she heard something. The whine of a small engine. A bright light suddenly blinded her. A spotlight, searching the waters. Had the liner deployed a lifeboat to rescue her?

The tug chuntered closer. Leila tried to raise a hand to wave, but her arms were lead. The light drew closer. So close. But it was no good. The cold was shutting her body down. She couldn't feel her limbs. And perhaps it was easier to just . . .

"No you don't."

A man's voice. Strong hands grasped her arms and yanked her out of the water, onto the tug. Leila was dimly aware of someone else climbing in after her. A bearded face loomed into vision and she felt hands wrap her in towels. But her breath was wheezy, her heart trembled in her chest. Too late. She was so weak. Darkness beckoned.

The last voice she heard was a woman's:

"It's okay. It's all going to be okay."

And then, in a sharper tone: "Let's go. Home and dry."

Sounds. Unfamiliar. High-pitched tweeting and a lower, buzzing sound. Leila gradually opened her eyes. A room. Bare white walls, peeling paint. Was this it? Re-education. Perhaps she was being held in some secret room on the ship's lower levels?

No. That wasn't it. There was something else. Something she was missing. The bed, the room. *Movement*, she realized. On board, even on the calmest of seas, there was always a sense of movement. Tiny undulations. The vibration of the great engines. After such a long time, you barely noticed them. But now, Leila felt their absence. Everything here was completely *static*. And those noises? *What were they?*

Leila tried to sit up and fell back again. Her joints felt stiff, and her head was stuffed full of wool. She breathed deeply and almost retched. Smells. Also strange. Not the usual air-freshened smell of the ship, nor the salty sea water. Dust, something vaguely "earthy," and another, more unpleasant smell, like drains. Foreign, strange, unsettling.

She made another attempt to get vertical and this time succeeded. Her vision swam and then settled. She took in her surroundings.

Not a cell, but certainly not a cabin. The room was huge. There were two beds, roughly made with an assortment of blankets and sheets that didn't look like they had ever seen an iron or fabric softener. There was a small dressing table and a lopsided wardrobe. Directly in front of her was a wooden door, slightly ajar, and to her left a window. Not a porthole. A large window letting in strips of light through wooden shutters.

Leila's stomach rolled. *Oh, dear God.* She was in a building. *On land.* Panic overwhelmed her and she fought it down, trying to breathe, to keep calm. Home and dry. Dry land. For the first time in fifty years. And the noises she could hear? Of course. Birds tweeting and bees buzzing. You never heard birds on the ship, or insects. Seagulls, yes, but not songbirds. Yet how could there be songbirds here, on this ravaged land? Wasn't it all poisoned, corrupted, toxic?

Leila swung her legs out of bed. She had been re-dressed: in baggy woolen trousers and a shapeless cotton shirt. The fabric was hard, and it itched. She supposed her other clothes were drying. A pair of rubber flip flops had been laid beside the bed. She slipped her feet into them and walked hesitantly toward the window. She reached for the shutters, feeling a desperate urge to see outside. To see what the world really looked like. And then she heard a sound behind her. The creak of the door opening. Leila spun around.

A woman walked in. Tall and slim, with dark brown hair cropped short into a jagged cut that framed her angular face. She was no delicate beauty—but striking. You could see it in the set of her chin, her fierce gaze. She wore a pair of gray combats, a T-shirt and sneakers. Her arms, poking out of the T-shirt, were muscular. No days spent sipping cocktails by the pool for her. While Leila had felt herself grow soft over the years, like proven dough, this woman looked tough, a little scary even.

And then she smiled, her face relaxing. "Mum? It's me, Addison."

Leila nodded. She knew. A mother always knows. Even after twenty years. Her baby was alive.

"Addison—" she started to say, and then the tears came. Addison crossed the room and drew Leila into her arms. A reversal of roles, Leila thought. Now she was the weak one being supported. They stayed that way for several minutes until Addison drew away.

"I thought you were dead," Leila said. "They told us—"

"They lie," Addison said in a harder tone. "We got away, Mum. We made it to land."

"All this time . . ."

"I'm sorry. I wanted to come back for you, but . . . well, there was a lot to do here. Establishing some sort of community, finding like-minded people, working to rebuild. And the ship doesn't come close to land often. I tracked its progress before we made our escape. Its cycle for drawing near enough to make a crossing possible is roughly six to seven years. I had to wait. And then, I knew that if I didn't get to you before the Retirement Ceremony—" She let the words hang. "So, anyway, Cal, my partner, he took the boat out with me, and I managed to throw a grapple hook up and climb on board."

"All along that was you, in the Donnie suit?"

Addison nodded. Leila stared at her daughter. There was something else: "What about Sam?"

Addison sighed. "He was on deck, sneaking a cigarette. He saw me come aboard. I had to do it, Mum."

Leila felt her heart clench. Her little girl, a killer. But Addison had come back for *her*, she reminded herself.

"Why leave him in the pool?"

Her face hardened. "Because he didn't deserve to be given to the Sea Gods."

Leila nodded slowly. "I understand."

Another sigh, a little more impatient. "I've had to learn to be tough, Mum—to survive. But everything I've done has been for other people, for the greater good."

The greater good. Wasn't that what the Creators always said?

Leila stared at her daughter and tried to contain a small shiver. "Does that include pushing me overboard?"

"I'm sorry. But it was the quickest way. I didn't want you to worry about jumping or get cold feet."

"You could have killed me."

"I knew you were a strong swimmer." A small shrug. "And you were going to be retired in a couple of days. It was a risk worth taking."

There it was again, Leila thought. That hardness in her daughter's tone. It hadn't been there before, she was sure.

Addison smiled. "But it's okay. You're here now. With me. With all of us."

"Yes," Leila said, suddenly feeling unsure.

But where was here, and who was us?

"What's wrong, Mum?"

"Are we safe here? We were told the air was unbreathable, the land was contaminated, what remained of the people, they were . . . monsters?"

Addison shook her head, eyes shining with anger. "It was lies, Mum. All lies. To keep you on board. To keep you under control. To keep them in charge." She held out her hand. "I'll show you."

Leila hesitated and then took her daughter's hand. Addison led her out into a long, light corridor.

"This place used to be a hotel," Addison explained. "But now it's ours."

"And who lives here, exactly?"

"Our community. There's about thirty of us. We work and live together."

"Like a commune?" Leila said.

Addison laughed. "If you want to call it that."

This was all so much to take in, Leila thought. On the ship she had never felt uncertain or stupid. She knew all the routines, all the people. She felt secure. Here, she didn't know *what* she knew anymore.

She followed Addison obediently down a large winding staircase into what she supposed used to be the hotel's reception. It seemed to have been converted into some kind of lounging area. Battered armchairs were arranged around a large makeshift firepit. Blankets and beanbags were scattered across the floor. A man and a woman in torn jeans and grubby sweatshirts, both shaven-headed, reclined on a half-collapsed sofa, sipping from mugs and smoking. They nodded at Addison and Leila as they passed.

"That's Fred and Evie," Addison said. "Their parents died not long after the Event. They learned to fend for themselves. Even developed their own language. Half of the time, the rest of us have no idea what they're saying." She chuckled again, but Leila didn't find it very funny. Just sad.

They crossed the reception to the main double doors. Addison shoved them open, and Leila blinked against the bright sunlight.

"Welcome to our Garden of Eden," Addison said.

They stepped outside. More unfamiliar smells assailed Leila's nostrils. She raised a hand to her eyes and squinted around. Acres of green lawn, but not manicured and mown, as she had expected. Overgrown and untended, the grass thick with weeds. To her left, a few people worked in a large muddy area which she presumed was a vegetable patch. Mangy chickens, pigs and sheep roamed around, uncontained. As well as the aroma of earth and vegetation, she could smell the distinctly un-Eden-like stench of manure.

"We've cultivated some of the grounds to grow vegetables," Addison said. "Plus, we have a few livestock and hope to breed more. We're pretty self-sufficient."

Leila blinked. For the first time in fifty years, she could stand on grass, as she had always dreamed of doing, but her feet felt rooted to the tarmac pathway. It was all so . . . primitive.

"It's lovely," she stuttered.

"Thanks. We've worked hard to get it like this."

Leila glanced toward the high stone walls that surrounded the greenery. "And out there?"

Another chuckle. "Don't worry, Mum. The streets aren't prowled by bloodthirsty zombies. Come on."

Addison turned from the gardens and strode down the pathway toward a pair of high metal gates. Leila followed her. Perhaps there was more, she thought. Addison might be happy in this hippie commune, but maybe there was more civilization beyond.

"Ready?" Addison asked. She pulled the gates open.

Leila stared around. Her heart slid to her toes.

The hotel stood at the top of a hill, offering a panoramic view of the city beyond. Or, what remained of it. Ruins, rubble. Crumbling buildings, gaping windows. Hoardings and billboards overgrown with weeds. Abandoned cars piled at the sides of the road. Rubbish, chaos. Leila spotted a fox or stray cat crawl over a heap of rusted cans, dragging a dead rat.

"This . . . this is—"

"Beautiful. I know." Addison breathed in deeply. "We had imagined what it might be like, but it's so much more."

For a moment, Leila wondered if Addison was joking. And then the realization hit. Addison had never seen the world as it was before. Most of the people here were too young to remember it. And to Addison, whose whole life had been spent confined in the ship, this deconstructed world, this chaos and destruction, *was* beautiful.

Leila looked back toward the ramshackle hotel. No heat or electricity. No running water either, she presumed. She wondered how soon she would miss a hot shower or a manicure or evening cocktails in the Piano Bar.

"Are you all right, Mum?" Addison asked.

Leila swallowed. "Yes. It's just . . . a lot to take in."

Addison took her hand. Leila noticed how rough and calloused her daughter's skin was. "I know it's a big shock, Mum," she said. "But don't worry. You'll soon settle in. And we'll keep you busy."

"Busy?"

"Yes." Addison nodded enthusiastically. "There's always work to do. There are no passengers here. And no one ever retires."

Leila smiled weakly. "Never?"

"Never."

They stared out across the ruined city.

Leila slipped a hand inside her pocket. But these weren't her clothes. The vial was gone.

Never, she thought. *Never ever.*

And suddenly, she felt very tired.

The Block

Introduction

I love Nottingham. It's my hometown. I did all my important growing up there. Renting my first house, getting my first job, falling in love, having my heart broken and meeting my now husband.

It's a great city. Visit, if you ever get the chance. There are some beautiful public spaces, great shops and awesome pubs. The people aren't bad either!

Of course, like most big cities, there are parts that aren't so picturesque.

In 2012, I was working as a dog walker, and I used to walk two very sweet rescue dogs in one of the less affluent areas of the city. Next to the scrubby hillside where I took them to play ball was an abandoned tower block. It was a pretty grim building. Long since empty, most of the windows were broken or boarded up. The bottom of the building was covered in graffiti.

The council had renovated a lot of the other high-rise buildings in Nottingham but this one remained, a dark eyesore, throwing the huddled terraces below into perpetual shadow.

At the time, the block fascinated me. I had no doubt it was a magnet for crime, squatters and drug dealers. But I also thought that it would be a great setting for a horror story. Maybe about a group of kids who decided to break in for a dare and found more than they bargained for.

Originally, I intended "The Block" to be a whole novel—middle-grade or YA fiction. I had been trying to get my adult novels published for years but had been told by one agent that my mix of horror and mystery just wasn't publishable. I'd started to think that I might stand a better chance writing for kids—kids love scary stuff, after all!

I wrote the first three chapters and then for various reasons, not least because I had just found out I was pregnant, the story stalled. I had always planned to go back to it, but then I had my daughter, and finally signed a publishing deal, for my adult novel *The Chalk Man* (proving the agent wrong), and my life changed.

Still, "The Block" remained (a little like the high-rise that inspired it), squatting on my laptop. Every time I skimmed past the title, it bugged me that I hadn't done something with it. But I didn't have time to write a middle-grade novel alongside my other books. And then, one day, I realized that it didn't have to be a full novel. "The Block" could work just as well—perhaps better—as a short story. And so, eight years after conception, I finally finished the story.

Afterward, I found myself curious. I decided to look up the old tower block and see what had happened to it. Unsurprisingly, I found that it is now being redeveloped.

But I also discovered something far more chilling. Not long after I gave up dog walking to have my daughter, the block was the site of a gruesome murder. The victim's headless and armless body was found buried in a shallow grave nearby.

Seven years later, they found his head and arms.

In the scrubland where I used to walk.

Sometimes, fact is more disturbing than fiction.

No one remembered it being built.

People remembered before and after. But nothing in between. As if it just landed one night, planted itself in the ground and took root. A great big mountain of gray concrete, looming up over the back streets of Nottingham.

Tyler had a theory. Back then, there were so many tower blocks going up in the city, people didn't see them after a while. Like the way you stopped noticing burnt-out cars around the Rec. One more, give or take, didn't make much difference.

But then, over the years, all the others were demolished and only the Block remained. People always called it "the Block." Never "the tower block" or "the block of apartments." The Block. Solid, unyielding; an impenetrable shadow over the huddled terraces below.

Tyler's gran said she could remember people living in it. But then Tyler's gran also said she remembered being abducted by aliens and meeting Abraham Lincoln (whoever *he* was), so you couldn't put a lot of stock in that. She was demented and often got confused between real stuff and stuff she saw on TV.

After everything that happened, I sort of knew how she felt.

It was Tyler's idea. Tyler had loads of ideas and nearly all of them involved us doing something we shouldn't.

"We need to get in there," he said as we lay in the scrubby patch of wasteland behind the Block staring up at the gray sky, smoking some dope he'd nicked off his mum. "Get in there and have a look around."

"Why?" Abid asked.

" 'Cos it'd be fun."

I didn't think it would be fun. Looking up at that towering, dark monolith, rows of broken windows like bullet holes in the hide of some massive beast, I thought it looked the furthest thing from fun I could imagine.

But I didn't say anything. I was the new kid in the group, still finding my feet. I wasn't going to argue with Tyler. Or use the word "monolith" in front of him.

Tyler was a tall, skinny kid with a huge afro and a real gold tooth. He lived with his mum and demented gran, just up the street from us. Tyler's dad was in jail and his elder brother got shot when Tyler was a baby. I'd never known anyone with a brother that got shot. Or that had a real gold tooth at thirteen.

Abid and Shannon were the other members of our gang. Abid's mum was a dinner lady at the school and his dad owned a big discount warehouse out on the ring road. Shannon had blonde hair and was kind of pretty. She also had a fat cousin called Courtney who wasn't.

Tyler said Courtney would give you a blow job for a can of Special Brew and a bag of chips. I told him she'd have to lay off the chips for a bit first. He laughed at that, flashing his gold tooth. I guess that was when we became friends.

MUM AND I had only moved to Nottingham a couple of months before. We moved a lot. Because of Dad. He didn't live with us anymore. But, somehow, he always found us.

"So, Danny, what do you think of our new home?" Mum asked, as she pushed open the front door of Number 8 Manvers Street.

I thought it looked just like our old home. Another crappy terrace in another crappy, depressing street. No double glazing. Electric heating. Stained carpets and peeling wallpaper.

"It's fine."

"Well, it's all we can afford for now."

"It's fine, Mum."

"When I get another job and . . ."

"It's *fine*, Mum. It's a frigging *palace*. Okay?"

"Danny, don't you use that language with me—"

I ignored her and walked up the sagging stairs, poked my head into the bathroom, wrinkled up my nose at the avocado suite and then walked back into the front bedroom and sat on the floor. I pulled out a small penknife, rolled up my sleeve and cut a thin line down my forearm. The fresh blood trickled along the tracks of the old scars beneath.

Later that evening we bought fish and chips and ate it sitting on some bits of plastic garden furniture we found in the backyard. We'd left our old furniture in the old house. Mum couldn't buy any more till she got a new line of credit.

The addresses changed. Nothing else did.

"So, you in?" Tyler was staring at me.

I got the feeling I'd missed something. That happened sometimes. I kind of tuned out, or "went away," as Mum called it. "*Uh-oh. Danny's gone away again. Earth to Danny. Earth to Danny.*" I used to think that was kind of funny, when I was about five.

"C'mon, man," Abid said. "It has to be you. You're the smallest."

It used to piss me off that I was always the smallest. But over the years, being so short and thin had come in useful. I could get away fast in a crowd. I could hide in tight spaces. Once, I even managed to squeeze out of a cat-flap when I needed to make a quick getaway from Dad.

"You're not scared, are you?" Shannon flicked her hair over one shoulder and took a drag on the remaining stub of joint.

"'Course not." I didn't even know yet what I was supposed to be "not scared" of.

"So, you'll do it?" Tyler asked.

I hesitated. I wanted to say yes. Didn't want to look chicken in front of them. But on the other hand, I didn't want to commit myself to something I'd regret.

"I . . . err . . . I'm not sure, man."

"Okay. Fair enough." Tyler stood up. "Take a look first and then decide."

IT WAS A tiny gap. A small space where a breezeblock had been removed or fallen out. All the ground- and first-floor windows were bricked up. To stop squatters and druggies getting in. From the second floor upward, the windows were smashed or covered with plywood boards.

Somehow, I'd known that whatever Tyler wanted me to do, it had to do with the Block.

"So, you get in through there, take a rope up to the second floor. Then you drop it out one of the windows and we climb up."

I stared up at the vertical slab of gray concrete. Three floors up was still a good thirty feet.

"It's a long way to climb," I said.

"It's nothing, man. We'll drag over some of them old wheeled trash cans. Climb up from there."

"But what if there's nothing to tie a rope to when I get up there? What if I can't get out?"

Tyler gave me a look and spat on the floor. "If you don't want to do it, just say, right?"

I looked over at Abid. He looked down at his new Adidas sneakers. I could tell he wasn't so keen on the idea now we were actually standing here, in the cold shadow of the Block. The wind sliced around the corners of the building like a knife. Litter scuttled across the ground and piled up against the walls. A collection of wheeled trash cans squatted in one corner of the deserted parking lot.

"I'll do it," Shannon suddenly said.

I stared at her. "You can't."

She stuck out her chin. "Why? Because I'm a girl?"

"No. Because your shoulders are too wide. You'll get stuck." I took a couple of steps forward, crouched down and peered into the small, dark gap. The window was close to the ground. A basement window. Inside, it stank of piss and vomit and something else. Kind of sweet yet sickly too. Disgusting.

"What can you see?" Abid asked.

"Nothing. It's pitch black."

Except that wasn't quite right. There was *something*. I couldn't see it exactly, but I could sense movement, just past the edge of my vision. Rats, probably.

"So?" Tyler sounded impatient. "What d'you say?"

I looked back at him. What did I *say*? There was no way I was going in there. I'd have to be out of my mind. He could find some other moron to do it. It was a bad, bad idea.

"I'll need a decent flashlight," I said.

WE AGREED TO meet at 7 p.m.

I didn't have much trouble getting out. The four of us often hung out down at the Rec on a Saturday night. Mum wasn't as keen about me being out on a school night, but she didn't give me too much crap. Seeing as she was the one messing up my schooling by moving us about all the time, she couldn't really.

Abid was there first. He couldn't help being punctual. Or dressing sharp. He always wore the latest sportswear and pristine white sneakers. His family had money. I didn't know why they still lived around here. I bet they could have afforded somewhere nicer.

Abid never talked about his family. Just like he never said why he hung out with us instead of one of the Asian gangs. Sometimes I saw his mum cleaning graffiti off their door. It was Indian graffiti, so I knew it wasn't racist. I guessed every family had secrets.

"You got the flashlight?" I asked him.

He nodded and pulled a big, heavy-duty number out of his rucksack. He flicked it on. The parking lot lit up like a football stadium.

"Shit, man. Put it away. You want to get us arrested before we even start?"

He turned the flashlight off again. Immediately, shadows crowded in on us. The distant glow of streetlights illuminated the edge of the parking lot, but here, behind the Block, the darkness was complete. It pooled in the corners and swallowed up shapes. I could barely see the gleam of Abid's white Adidas.

"It's creepy here," he muttered.

I opened my mouth to agree. Then someone tapped me on the shoulder and I almost crapped myself.

"Shit!"

Shannon stood behind me. Next to her loomed a vision in a pink Nike tracksuit. Courtney.

"What's she doing here?" Abid asked.

"Lookout. In case the police drive round," Shannon replied.

I supposed it wasn't a bad idea. The police did drive around here sometimes. They used to do it a lot more. Just like the fences used to be fixed to keep people out. But now, no one seemed to bother. It was weird, really. Like everyone had just forgotten about the place. Although I wasn't sure how you could just forget three hundred feet of sheer concrete.

I saw a glint of gold in the darkness and Tyler emerged out of the shadows. He had a thick coil of rope wound around one shoulder.

"Ready for some adventure?" Then he saw Courtney. The grin snapped off. "Who brought that to the party?"

"I did," Shannon said defiantly. "She's our lookout."

"Yeah? For what? More pizza?"

Courtney took out a bit of gum, mashed it into her mouth and chomped wordlessly. I suppose I should have felt sorry for her, but actually she creeped me out a bit, with her blank stare, greasy plaits and flat voice. I don't think she understood she was being insulted. Or maybe she just didn't care.

Shannon looked like she was going to retort, but then Tyler held a hand up. "Fine. Let her be lookout. Let's just get on with it." He looked at me. "You ready?"

I felt as far from ready as I could be. I felt scared. All the way here, I'd kept hoping something would happen that meant we couldn't go ahead with the plan. Even thought about calling the cops myself. But I wasn't a snitch. Dad taught me that, at least.

"Let's do this," I said.

Tyler whacked me on the back. "All right!"

"Stay here. Keep watch," Shannon said to Courtney, like she was talking to a dog.

Courtney nodded, chomped. " 'Kay."

I approached the hole in the bricked-up window. It gaped like a wound. I felt sweat prickle at the back of my neck. Then I crouched down and slid my legs in, one by one, so I was sitting on the edge.

"Once I'm in, chuck me down the flashlight first, then the rope."

Abid nodded, looking even more scared than I felt. Even Tyler looked apprehensive.

"Good luck," Shannon said, and smiled.

No going back now. I swiveled around, squeezed the rest of my body through and let myself fall into the darkness.

The floor was further away than I expected. I hit it off balance and fell sideways. "Oww. Crap."

It was covered in some kind of slimy mush. Like wet, rotten cardboard.

"You okay?" Tyler called down.

"Yeah." I stood, wiping my hands on my jeans. "It's just pretty rank in here."

"You want the flashlight?" Abid asked.

"Nah. I think I'll just stand here in the dark."

A pause. Abid didn't really get sarcasm. Then I heard Tyler say, "Give him the fuckin' flashlight, man."

"Wait," Abid said. "I'm gonna tie it to the rope and lower it down."

Actually, that was a good idea. Abid might not have much of a sense of humor but he always thought things through.

"Here it comes. When you get it, untie it and then I'll chuck down the rest of the rope."

"Okay."

I waited, blinking in the blackness, trying to breathe through my mouth. Somehow, that didn't help. The smell just seemed to stick in my throat.

I heard a scraping, rattling sound and squinted up. Abid had switched the flashlight on and it spun as it came down, fleetingly illuminating patches of flaking cement wall, damp-speckled ceiling and . . . my breath snagged . . . something on the ground. Something that *moved;* something black and shiny, with legs. Lots of legs.

I stumbled backward into the wall. The flashlight banged into my head. I yelped.

"Danny? You okay? What is it?"

Shannon's voice this time. My heart thumped inside my chest. The flashlight continued to spin. I grabbed it, yanked it down and pointed it into the darkness like a weapon. I'd been right about the floor. Covered in rotting bits of cardboard and rubbish. Old shopping bags. Food wrappers. Rusted tins and crushed plastic bottles.

Nothing else. Whatever I'd seen, or thought I'd seen, was gone. Probably just a cockroach, I tried to tell myself. Although it had looked too big for a cockroach. More the size of a rat. Except rats weren't black and shiny. And they only had four legs.

I swallowed.

"Danny?"

"I'm fine," I called up. "Just thought I saw a . . . rat or something."

Or something.

"Well, screw that." Tyler's voice again. "Grab the rope and get going, man. We ain't got all night."

I quickly untied the flashlight. The rope slithered down the wall like a large snake. I shuddered, wished I hadn't thought that. Wished I wasn't here. Wished with all my heart I was sitting with my mum in our crappy front room watching rubbish on the rented TV.

But as Mum would say: "*Wishing is just wasting time. You want something, you've got to go out there and get it.*" Except what had she got? No money, no proper home. Maybe Mum should have had a few more wishes. Or perhaps she did and Dad just knocked them out of her.

I coiled the rope over my shoulder—I had to put the flashlight down for a moment to do it—and felt a momentary shiver of panic.

Black and shiny with legs, Danny. That was no cockroach, and you know it.

I silenced the voice inside my head, grabbed the flashlight and pointed it around, looking for an exit. The beam fell on a battered and graffiti-scarred gray door. It suddenly struck me that if the door was locked, I was trapped. I couldn't climb back up to the window. No way out. Tyler had conveniently forgotten to mention that flaw in his plan.

Too late now. I cursed and walked toward the door. Rubbish crunched under my sneakers. Something rustled behind me. I spun around, waving the flashlight. Nothing but more rubbish and moldy damp walls. I waited, listening. All I could hear was my own raspy breath and blood pounding in my ears. I turned back to the door.

Another sound. Closer. To my left. A kind of *snickering* sound. Like a cross between a rattle and a hiss. This time I spun around so fast I almost dropped the flashlight . . . just as *something* disappeared beneath a pile of crisp packets.

I didn't care what it was anymore. I just wanted to get out of there. I turned and grabbed the door handle. For a moment, I thought it was stuck. I pulled again, harder. This time the door burst open. I staggered out into another dark, smelly space. But normal smells this time. Urine and stale weed.

I slammed the door shut behind me and shone the flashlight around. The bottom of a stairwell. I could see another door to my left (that must lead to the lobby) and in front of me . . . I pointed the flashlight upward . . . cracked concrete steps that wound up into more darkness.

I seriously did not want to go up there. But then . . . I glanced back, thought about that shiny black body and awful, *snickering* sound. No way could I go back in there. I placed my sneaker on the first step. Behind me, something thudded against the closed basement door.

I took the next steps two at a time.

FLOOR 2. EXCEPT someone had graffitied the sign on the door so it read: Floor 2 HELL. Underneath, someone had added, in different spray paint: RUN.

Great. I pushed open the door from the stairwell. It led into a long, narrow corridor, lined with more doors—some closed, some open, some half hanging off their hinges. Jeez. The walls were plastered with even more graffiti. They practically dripped with it. And the smell. The smell was back, the same one as in the basement.

I tried to ignore it and concentrate on what I was supposed to be doing: getting Tyler and the others in here. Which was a stupid idea, I thought again. A frigging stupid, *mental* idea. All I wanted to do was get out. But I couldn't look chicken.

I scanned the doors with the flashlight, trying to decide which one to go through. I decided on the one third to my left. It was kind of hard to work out the geography of the building now I was inside, but it seemed to me that it was the closest one to where I'd got in.

The door was already half open. Feeling my heart start to up its tempo again, I walked forward and pushed it wide, pointing the flashlight inside.

I'm not sure if I was relieved or disappointed. A room. Depressingly familiar. Sagging old sofa. Peeling wallpaper. Stained carpet. No graffiti in here, but something about the room was still off. I scanned around with the flashlight, then realized what it was: ornaments, pictures in frames, even dirty mugs on the coffee table. Whoever had been here had left in a hurry. Again. Depressingly familiar.

I walked over to the window. Fortunately, it wasn't boarded, just broken. I smashed a few sharp shards of glass off with the flashlight. Then heard a voice yell up from below:

"Hey, man, over here."

I peered down. Tyler stood below the window, Shannon and Abid just behind him. Tyler grinned and his gold tooth gleamed.

"You did it."

I held the rope up. "I've still got to find somewhere to tie this."

Abid called up: "What's it like in there?"

I hesitated. Then said, "You'll see."

The sofa was the only heavy thing in the living room. I tied a sturdy knot around one of the feet, wedged it beneath the window and tugged on the rope. I thought it would hold. I threw the rope down.

Tyler shimmied up first, fast and smooth, making it look easy. He clambered into the room and slapped me on the back. Shannon came next, almost as fast and agile. Finally, Abid. Slow, ungainly. At one point, he wobbled so much I thought he was going to fall. But somehow he managed to make it through the window and tumbled to the floor, panting.

Tyler shook his head. "Shit, man. You climb like a girl." Then he glanced at Shannon. "No offense."

She gave him the finger.

Abid stood up, brushing at his jeans. "Got crap all over these now."

"Get over it," Shannon said.

Tyler took out his phone to use as a light and walked around the room. He pulled a face. "What a shithole."

Well, what did you expect? I thought, but didn't say.

He picked up one of the moldy mugs. "Someone just left all their stuff. That's weird, man."

Yeah. I thought about the thing in the basement, the graffiti over the walls. "Weird" was one word. "You should see the rest," I said.

Tyler grinned again. "So, what are we waiting for?"

I let Tyler lead. Even though I'd got everyone in. That was just how it was. I followed, Shannon behind me and Abid at the back. Again. Just how it was.

We checked out a few more of the apartments. All pretty much the same as the first. Dishes left in sinks. Ironing abandoned in baskets, mugs left on tables. Tyler yanked open drawers and wardrobes. Shannon rifled through clothing. Abid stood awkwardly, not touching anything.

I wandered into one of the kitchens, using the flashlight to illuminate my way. I pulled open a few cupboards. Peered inside the fridge. I frowned.

Tyler poked his head in. "Found anything?"

"There's no food," I said.

"What?"

"Nothing. Not in the cupboards or the fridge."

"So?"

"Well, why would you take all your food but leave all your clothes?"

"Maybe they had the munchies. Who gives a shit?" He kicked the fridge door shut. "There ain't nothing worth nicking in here. Let's go."

I sighed. I gave a shit. I didn't like it. But I stood up and followed him out of the apartment.

We continued slowly along the corridor, Tyler roaming his phone light over the graffiti-covered walls. We passed the lifts. The metal doors were bent and buckled, like someone had given them a good kicking. From the inside. A makeshift sign had been stuck on the front:

BROKEN

I didn't like that either.

Suddenly Tyler stopped and I almost walked right into the back of him.

"What?"

He whistled between his teeth.

"Now that is *fucking* weird."

"What?"

"This graffiti, man."

I stared at the wall. Just a mass of colors and letters, sprayed so thick I couldn't make out anything legible.

"D'you see?" he asked.

I squinted harder. "Not really."

"It's just a mess," Shannon said.

"No, it ain't," Tyler said impatiently. "It's just one word. Written over and over." He pointed. "This is an 'H.' Here, 'u n g,' and here 'r y.'"

And now I could see it. I felt a shiver crawl up my spine like something alive.

"Hungry," I whispered.

Empty cupboards. Empty fridge.

Shannon craned her neck, looking around. "Why would you write that?"

"Someone ain't had their Nando's lately." Tyler laughed.

"It's not funny," Abid said quietly.

"Oooh. You scared, Abid?"

"I just don't like this. Like you said, there's nothing worth nicking. We should go," he replied.

"After all the hassle Dan the man went to to get us in."

"It's okay," I said.

"No," Tyler said sharply. "It ain't okay. We ain't finished lookin' around yet. Right?"

Abid pursed his lips. Shannon shrugged. Tyler stared at me. "Right?"

I hesitated. And that was when the noise shuddered through the floor: a massive, mechanical groan from the bowels of the building.

"Shit!" Shannon jumped, hair whipping across her face.

Tyler spun round, phone light ricocheting off the walls. "What the fuck?"

It came again. Like a great metal beast rousing itself into life. This time, followed by another sound—a slow, labored grinding rising up from the floors below.

"It's getting closer," Shannon said.

"But what the fuck *is* it?" Tyler said again, sounding rattled.

Suddenly I knew and my stomach plummeted into my sneakers. *No, not possible.*

Before I could reply, Abid gave a strange little half-laugh.

"It's the lift," he said.

We all turned, slowly.

The grinding, groaning sound grew louder. Then stopped. There was a strange, discordant *ping*.

I thought about that skittering shiny black body in the basement.

"We need to get out of here," I said.

Tyler was still staring at the lift door. "Wait, man."

The door started to slide open, and then stuck. We all stared at the sliver of darkness. From inside, I could hear breathing—a dry, rattling sound.

"I don't like this," Abid whispered.

A hand reached out of the gap. Humanish, but horribly long and skeletal, the skin dry and kind of scaly. Nails like sharp yellow talons scratched at the metal.

And then a voice rasped: "Hungry."

"Fuck!" Tyler muttered. "*Run!*"

We didn't need telling twice. We took off down the corridor, sneakers squealing on the concrete floor. At the end, we rounded the corner into another dark corridor. Doors lined either side. A wall blocked our escape.

"Fuck!" Tyler swore. "It's a fucking dead end."

"Shit," Shannon cursed.

From behind us came the sound of metallic screeching. The lift doors. Whatever was inside was pushing them open.

"What do we do?" Abid asked.

"Hide," I said. Because it was all we could do. Something I had learned all too well.

"Where?" Shannon asked.

"In one of the apartments." I could hear more sounds from the corridor. Rasping and shuffling. I swallowed. "Now."

Tyler turned and aimed his foot at the nearest door. He kicked it open and we all scuttled inside. I closed the door as quietly as I could behind us.

"Now what?" Abid whispered.

I aimed the flashlight around the apartment. The others used their phones. The living room and kitchen looked much the same as the other apartments: tired, dirty and deserted.

"We find somewhere to hide," I said. "If that thing comes in, we let it get into the room and then we run for the door fast as we can and leg it back to the emergency exit."

It was a strategy I'd used before, with Dad.

"That's it?" Tyler asked. "That's your plan?"

"You got a better one?"

He swiveled round. "We need weapons."

"Yeah, well, maybe someone left their AK-47 behind," Shannon deadpanned.

"They left *some* stuff behind, right?" Tyler retorted. "Might be something useful somewhere."

He walked over to the tiny kitchen and began opening cabinet doors. I winced at the sound.

"Yeah!" Tyler turned, holding up a long bread knife. "That's what I'm talking about, man."

"Is there anything else?" Shannon asked, walking over.

"Shouldn't we call someone—the police—for help?" Abid said.

"And tell them what?" Tyler sneered. "We broke into a tower block and now some crazy half-human monster is chasing us? You think they'll send out the squad cars for that?"

He had a point. Abid sighed and joined them, rummaging in the kitchen drawers and cabinets.

I remained by the door. A spyhole was set into it. I stood on my tiptoes and peered out. My heart freewheeled. At the far end of the corridor, I could see the thing from the lift. It was human in shape, but as far from human as I had ever seen, except in movies or Play-

Station games. It was skeletally thin, hunched and scaled. Its face looked almost reptilian, remnants of hair clinging to its skull, and it was swathed in rags of clothing: what might once have been shorts and a ripped T-shirt. At the end of its bony arms, its hands were claws.

I backed away, heart thudding. "It's coming."

"Here."

I turned. Shannon thrust a can into my hand. I looked down. Fly spray. In her other hand, she held a bottle of bleach. Abid held a corkscrew.

"Thanks," I said, wondering what I could do with fly spray.

From outside came the sound of doors thudding open.

"It's looking for us," Shannon murmured.

"We need to get ready," I said.

"Or we could attack it," Tyler said.

We looked at each other, and at our makeshift weapons—a bread knife, a corkscrew, bleach and fly spray. I remembered that I still had my penknife in my pocket, but that was hardly going to do a lot of damage to the thing out there. And besides, I'd never hurt anything but myself with it.

"We go with Danny's plan," Shannon said.

Abid nodded. "I'm good with that."

Tyler rolled his eyes, but didn't argue.

"How will we know when to run?" Abid asked.

"I'll give a signal," I said.

"What?"

Good question.

"I'll shout 'Go!'"

"Original, man," Tyler said.

Another door slammed across the corridor. There wasn't time to retort.

"Hide," I said. "Now."

Abid and Tyler ducked down behind the worktop that divided the kitchen from the living room. Shannon and I crouched behind the tatty sofa. I flicked off the flashlight. They weren't exactly great hiding places, but that wasn't the point. It just needed to be enough for the creature to get into the room, far enough away from the door for us to run out.

"Will this work?" Shannon whispered.

"I don't know," I admitted. "It worked with my dad—but he was usually wasted."

She stared at me, and then the door creaked open.

The creature smelled. Rotten and sour. Its breathing was labored and its words a guttural growl: "Hungry. Hungry."

I held my breath. I heard it shuffle forward. One, two, three steps. Not far enough from the door. Not yet. I peered tentatively around the edge of the sofa. It was dark, but I could just make out the shape of the creature, illuminated by the glow of the city lights through the window. It was never proper dark in the city. The creature stood, almost in the middle of the room. Just a few more steps and I would give the signal.

And then it turned. Not toward Shannon and me. Toward the kitchen where Tyler and Abid were crouching. If it went any further, it would see them and block their route of escape.

"Hungry," it rasped. "*Hungry*."

Fuck.

I had to do something. I stood up.

"Hey!"

The creature turned.

"Over here, fuck face."

I turned on the flashlight. It roared and raised its claws against the beam. I caught a glimpse of something black and shiny with sharp teeth inside its mouth. While it was disorientated, I raised the fly spray and pressed the button, sending the toxic spray straight into the creature's eyes. It let out a wail and staggered away, clutching at its face.

"GO!" I screamed to the others.

Abid and Tyler jumped up and sped toward the door. Shannon

rose. I grabbed her hand and yanked her up. We shot out of the door and I pulled it shut on the hideous thing inside.

"Fuck. Jesus fucking fuck," Tyler panted as we ran back down the corridor.

"Oh man. I think I'm gonna—" Abid suddenly stopped and threw up, all over his neat jeans and pristine white sneakers. "Oh shit," he moaned.

But we didn't have time to deal with it. "We need to get to the exit," I yelled.

Because now I could hear more noises. Things moving inside the other apartments. Awakened. We reached the corner and ran around it. A door burst open right in front of us. Another skeletal, scaly figure lurched out. It wore the remnants of a dress and straggly blonde hair fell to its hunched shoulders.

These were people. People who had lived here until . . .

"Hungry," it groaned. "Hungry."

It opened its mouth. I saw a glossy black head emerge, sharp teeth snapping.

Shannon screamed.

Tyler lunged forward. "Take that, you ugly bitch."

He drove the bread knife into the creature's stomach. It threw back its head and shrieked in pain, grasping at its torso. Shannon fumbled with the bleach cap and then, just as the creature turned toward Tyler, she threw bleach in its face. The creature reeled away, grabbing at its eyes, its wailing cries both inhuman and pitiful.

"Keep going!" Tyler shouted.

We darted past the creature. I could see the lift to our left. Tyler turned toward it.

"No!" I shouted. "The stairs. Take the stairs."

Tyler ran past and reached the door to the stairs. He shoved it open. The stairwell was black. No windows. No city lights, although right now the city felt about a million miles away. Another world.

Tyler, Abid and Shannon pointed their phones downward. My flashlight beam was ailing.

"My battery's almost dead," Abid moaned.

The lights picked out just a few steps at a time. We moved as fast as we could without losing our footing. We were almost at the bottom when I paused. I could hear something. I grabbed Tyler's arm.

He turned. "What?"

"D'you hear that noise?"

He cocked his head. "Nah."

"Listen."

"He's right," Shannon said. "I can hear it too. Like a weird rustling."

Or a *snickering*, I thought. Like lots of shiny, shelled bodies rubbing busily up against each other. Shit.

We descended the remaining stairs more cautiously. At the bottom, we paused again. The rustling, snickering sound was louder now, unmistakable. From here, one door led down, into the basement where I had climbed in. The other door led out into the lobby and the front entrance. The noise wasn't coming from the basement. I walked over to the lobby door and inched it open. I pointed my flashlight through the gap.

"Holy shit," Shannon muttered.

The lobby floor was moving. Like a sea of oil. Dozens of shiny black bodies swarmed around, covering every inch. They looked like beetles but were bigger, the size of rats, with scaled tails and jaws full of sharp teeth. As the light hit them, the noises stopped.

"They know we're here," Tyler whispered.

"Then why aren't they coming for us?" Shannon asked.

The realization chilled me. "They know we have to get past them," I said. "They're waiting."

"What do we do?" Abid groaned. He didn't look good, like he might collapse once the adrenaline stopped pounding round his system. "We can't go back and we can't get past those fucking things." He turned to Tyler. "This is all your fucking fault." And then he started to cry. Big, heaving sobs.

"S'okay," Shannon said, putting an arm around him. "We'll figure it out."

And then she looked at me. Not Tyler. *Me.*

I tried to think. There was no way out from the basement. We had to get across the lobby, to the front door. But how? What did we have? A bread knife, a corkscrew, bleach and fly spray. Tyler and Abid couldn't stab all the beetle creatures. They might not even penetrate the shells. Ditto with the bleach. Which left the fly spray? They *were* insects. But they were big. Too big for the spray to have much effect. Unless . . .

The idea came to me like a bulb lighting up in my head.

Lighting up. That was it.

I turned to Tyler. "You got your lighter?"

"Yeah. But I'm not sure now's the time for a toke, man."

"What about some huffing?" I held up the aerosol can.

Tyler grinned. "With you." He dug in his pocket and pulled out the lighter. "What's the plan?"

"We head down. When we get to the bottom, I'll light the spray and blast them so we can forge a path through."

Tyler looked at the lighter and shook his head. "You can't do it."

I bristled. "I can. I *have* to."

"No." He flicked the lighter and a steady flame shot up. "I'll do it."

"This isn't some dick-waving competition." Shannon scowled.

"I want to do it," Tyler said. "I got you into this. I should get you out." He looked at me pleadingly. "Please."

I sighed. "Okay." I handed the fly spray over.

He edged past me and pushed open the door. We followed closely behind. Every fiber of my being wanted to run away from the swarming beetle creatures, but I forced my legs to keep going.

Tyler nodded. "Ready?"

We all murmured yes, even though we weren't. We would never be ready, but we had no choice.

"One, two, three—" He burst into the lobby, at the same time pressing the button on the fly spray and flicking the lighter. "Yippee-kay-yay, motherfuckers."

A line of flame shot out from the aerosol can and ignited the nearest black bodies. They screamed, hideous high-pitched cries of agony, and the smell of burning flesh filled the air.

Tyler advanced, spraying fire, and the rest of us followed, dodging flames and snapping jaws, kicking out at the scuttling bodies. We had almost made it, when Abid tripped over one of the beetle creatures. He went down fast, corkscrew flying from his fingers. The creature was faster. It scuttled up his legs, hissing and snapping.

Abid screamed. The beetle creature squatted on his chest, feelers stretching toward his open mouth.

Because that was how they got inside. To feed.

"No!" I shouted.

Barely thinking, I pulled out my penknife and drove it down, into the gap between the beetle creature's head and hard exoskeleton. It shrieked, rearing up. I reached down and grabbed its body. It felt hot and slippery, and my stomach lurched in revulsion. But I held tight, hauling it off Abid and throwing it as far away from him as I could. Tyler spun round, lightning fast, and spray-fired at it in mid-air. The creature burst into flames.

I held out my hand to Abid. "Get up."

He grabbed it and scrambled to his feet. "Thanks, man."

Tyler aimed another blast of flames at the scuttling, smoking beetle creatures, which were now retreating, hissing in fear and frustration.

"Keep going!" he yelled. "Get to the door!"

He ignited the aerosol again and we sped past him, crashing into the door. I rattled the handle. Locked. Shit. Why didn't we think? Of course, it was locked. Why the hell did I climb in through the basement?

"The other way!" Shannon screamed.

"What?"

She grabbed my hand. I looked down. A sign on the door read, "Pull."

We both yanked at the handle. The door flew open.

Unlocked. All this time, the front door was unlocked. *Why the hell did I climb in through the basement?*

No time to think about it. We barreled through the door, out into the cold night air, and kept running. We didn't stop until we were on the other side of the parking lot. Only then did I dare to stop and look back, half expecting to see a stream of black bodies scuttling out behind us.

But the parking lot was empty. Inside the Block, flames licked at the door. The place was dry and dusty. Lots of old curtains and non-fire-resistant furniture to catch hold of.

We stood, panting, breathing in the cool night air: it stank of take-aways, overflowing trash cans, car fumes and weed. It had never smelled sweeter.

"Why aren't they following us?" Shannon asked eventually. "Why aren't they escaping?"

"Maybe they can't," Abid said.

"Why?"

"Maybe the Block is like a portal. To another dimension. Maybe those things slipped through, and now they're trapped there." He paused. "Maybe the only way they can survive is inside a human host."

I thought about the half-humans in the apartments, the beetle creature's feelers reaching for Abid's mouth. I shuddered.

"How the hell did you figure that out?" Tyler asked.

Abid shrugged. "I watch a lot of *Doctor Who*."

As if to prove his point, the building seemed to tremble, like there was an earthquake. But the ground felt perfectly stable beneath our feet. As we watched, the Block began to collapse. No explosion, no dust. It just folded in, like water sucked down a plughole. The floors rapidly disappeared, one by one, until, with a small pop, it was gone. Like it had never been.

"What the fuck?" Tyler gasped.

"Told you," Abid said.

We stared at the space where the Block once stood. All that remained was a patch of blackened earth.

A hand grasped my arm. I screamed and spun around.

Courtney stood behind me. Chomping gum.

"Christ," I said. "You scared the shit out of me."

"I waited," she said, in her usual toneless way.

"Right. Thanks."

"You didn't come out," she continued. "So I came looking for you."

"You went inside?" Shannon said.

I realized now that Courtney's hair was loose from her braids and her face was streaked with dirt.

She nodded. "The front door wasn't locked."

"Yeah." I glanced at Tyler. "We got that."

"Are you okay?" Shannon asked her.

Courtney frowned. "Fine."

"You didn't see those . . ." I faltered. "Those *things* inside."

Courtney stared at me blankly. "I didn't see anything."

Shannon and I exchanged glances. She touched my arm. "Leave it," she whispered. "We need to get out of here."

"Yeah."

But something was still bugging me. I glanced back at Courtney. There was something different about her. Not just her hair and the dirt on her face. Her tracksuit. It looked looser. Like she'd lost weight.

Which was crazy. She couldn't have lost weight since we went into the Block.

But she went inside too.

"Where shall we go?" Abid asked.

Tyler grinned at us sheepishly. "What about Maccy D's . . . anyone hungry?"

We all groaned.

"I am," Courtney suddenly said.

Her cheekbones looked razor-sharp beneath her skin. Almost skeletal.

She smiled, teeth flashing. "I'm really, *really* hungry."

Runaway Blues

Introduction

I don't tend to listen to music while I write, but I play it in the car and while I'm out running, and often song titles or lines from songs will spark an idea for a story.

I wrote the first draft of "Runaway Blues" several years ago. I had a lot of My Chemical Romance on my playlist and one of the songs—"Na Na Na"—had stuck in my head. There's a line that mentions taking something from someone's heart and keeping it in a box. Something about that line just resonated. It was kind of creepy.

It will come as no surprise that I was also reading a lot of Stephen King at the time, and "Runaway Blues" is probably my most King-esque short story. I didn't plan it that way, but once you get a voice in your head you just have to go with it. The voice I had in my head for this story was very much Morgan Freeman in *The Shawshank Redemption*. It just seemed to fit.

Unfortunately, once I had the first draft down, I didn't have anywhere to send the story. I was unpublished, a wannabe, and the story wasn't right for some of the women's magazines I had started to sell a few shorts to. So it just sat on my laptop, unedited, incomplete.

I only came back to it when I was thinking about this collection. And the weird thing is, although I remembered the main parts of the story, it had been so long since I wrote it that I had forgotten the payoff. When I reached the final twist, I felt a shiver run down my spine. Damn, I thought. This is actually good! I immediately started knocking it into shape, and I'm pretty pleased with the result.

I hope you get that same shiver down your spine when you read "Runaway Blues." And I hope you enjoy my tribute to Mr. King.

Now, let me tell you about the Fat Man . . .

L *et me tell you about the Fat Man.*

Not his real name, of course. That's just what everyone at the club called him. If you asked me now what his real name was, I could probably tell you. But only because I did a little research to jolt my increasingly unreliable memory.

That's not to say this story has been skewed by those pesky malfunctioning neurons that make me misplace my car keys and go out in mismatching shoes. No. The past I can remember as clear as if it was yesterday. Ironic that it's yesterday I forget.

The Blue Flamingo was the name of the club, if you're asking. Which you're not. But that's kind of how storytelling works, isn't it? Like a one-sided conversation. I ramble on, you listen. And if I lose your interest, well, you can just turn the page or close the book.

You won't, though. You'll want to hear this story. And I need to tell it. Because I've not told anyone else, not in over fifty years. And that's a long time to nurse a horror.

I never even told Stella. Not all of it. Even though she was there the night it started. Sitting in the club, drinking pink Martinis. Just writing it I can almost taste them. Pink Martinis in the Blue Flamingo. Their club specialty. Pink Martinis and the blues.

This was 'seventy-one or two, I guess. Blues clubs weren't really the thing back then. It was all funk and disco. But the Blue Flamingo was a real throwback. Stepping through those black doors, you could believe that you'd been transported back to the 1930s.

The lighting was flatteringly dim. Small candles glowed in pink frosted holders placed upon an array of round tables positioned in front of a small stage. Red tablecloths, white candles. Pink Martinis. Did I mention the pink Martinis? Bursting like little bubbles of sunset on your tongue.

That was what it felt like in that club. Permanent sunset. Sunset that went right on until sunrise with no dark night in between. Many

times, Stella and I had stumbled out of that club into the cold blackness, amazed at the hours lost within those walls.

We'd go most Friday nights. I guess it wasn't fashionable. Most
of our friends went to the funk club up the road—the Hippo. But
Stella and I had always been an old-fashioned couple. She never
wore jeans. Not in all the years I knew her. Blouses and skirts and
real stockings and garters. Right up until the day she died.

I favored suits and hats. Man, I loved a hat. My idols were James
Stewart and Clark Gable. Dean Martin and Frank Sinatra. T-shirts
and bell bottoms never seemed to sit right on me. And I always refused to grow my hair. Stella and I often said we must have been
born in the wrong decade. A miracle we found each other. I believe
in miracles. But if you believe in miracles; if you believe in God and
love, then you must believe in the opposite. In evil.

I remember once reading that "all evil needs to flourish is for
good men to do nothing." Well, that's probably true. But it's also
true that love can make good men do bad things. I prefer to think
that. I prefer to think that the Fat Man wasn't all bad. He just had a
bad case of the blues.

"I GOTTA BAD, bad case of the lovesick blues."

The audience erupted into applause. Not polite applause like a
lot of the bands and singers at the club got. Real, stand-up stuff. A
few people even did stand. I think Stella did; her cheeks flushed, a
few stray tendrils of dark hair coming loose from her ponytail.

"My. Isn't he something?" she gasped.

He really was. Although you'd never know it to look at him.
When the skinny, pale kid with lank brown hair and an ill-fitting
suit had walked meekly on to the stage, shoulders sloped and eyes
planted on the floor, you could almost feel the barely contained con-
tempt ripple through the room. Even the backing band looked kind
of embarrassed.

People exchanged wry smirks. Others sat back in seats; arms

folded. Now, I'm not meaning to sound racist here, and there was always a fair mix of people in the Blue Flamingo, black and white (like Stella and me) although we never got a lot of Asian or Chinese folk. But on stage, well, I'm sorry, it was always black guys, because that's what real jazz is about, isn't it? White boys don't sing the blues.

Certainly not this white boy. Man, he barely looked old enough to shave. He looked like he'd wandered into the wrong club by mistake. In one hand he carried a saxophone and in the other he carried a large hat box. Just plain odd.

As he reached the microphone, one of the regulars, a sweaty, fat guy who drank way too many Martinis and often found himself leaving accompanied by one of the doormen, raised his hands to cup his mouth and called out: "Shouldn't you be at home in bed, boy?"

Not the greatest heckle, but a few people laughed and, now that the dam had been broken, a flood of insults started pouring out.

"Does your mommy know you sneaked out the window?"

"Son, you look paler than the milk you're still sucking from your mommy's titties."

Only the last one got any reaction. But not from the young man. Stella had always been a feisty young woman, imbued with a righteous sense of morality. One of the reasons I fell in love with her. And the knockout legs. As this last insult was hurled, she stood up and spun around, hands on hips, eyes scouring the crowd for the heckler.

"Why don't you just shut up and let the boy play?"

Stella was only a slip of a thing but when she was riled, she was fierce. There was something in her eyes that told you she was not for messing with. The black guy who had shouted out the last insult must have been six foot and two hundred pounds, but he slunk into his seat like a scolded child. Stella glared around once more, then sat down, turned to the stage, and smiled.

The young man smiled back. Or, at least, his lips moved, showing small white teeth and one sparkling gold incisor. Then, he placed the hat box on the floor, flipped the lid and took out a neat brown trilby. A nice hat. I'd have placed money on it being an original from the thirties. Like I said, I love a hat. I have quite a collection myself.

He placed the hat upon his head, casting his pale skin into shadow. He glanced behind him and gave the band a quick nod. Then he looked around the room and drawled, in a voice as rich and deep as molten treacle: "I just want to play some jazz, man."

You felt the air move, as the audience took in a breath. You could feel that voice from the root of your hairs at the base of your neck to the tips of your toenails. Deep, resonant, aged like fine bourbon. The kid looked like a teenager. He spoke like a seventy-year-old black dude.

In the pause generated by those eight words, he raised the saxophone to his lips and started to play. You wouldn't imagine he had enough breath in his shallow frame to generate those notes, but the air swelled with gaudy, lazy chords, people started to sway and click their fingers. A few got up to dance . . . and then he took that sax away from his lips and he started to sing.

We'd heard a lot of guys and girls sing at the Blue Flamingo. Some well-known. Some jobbing musicians trying to make some extra cash. Most played covers because this was a club and people came here for a good time, to sing and dance to songs they knew.

This wasn't a tune anyone knew, but man, it *felt* like you did. It felt like you must have heard that tune a million times. On the radio, blaring out of your open car windows. Familiar but fresh. It was that good. The kid's voice lifted and dipped, and more people started to get up to dance. I could tell Stella wanted to, but it usually took me at least three of the pink Martinis before I'd take to the tiny rectangular dance floor in front of the bar.

Instead, I sat in my seat and tapped my feet, tapped my fingers. You couldn't listen to that tune without tapping something. When he'd finished, the applause started, but the kid had more. He lay down the sax, swapped places with the piano player and started again.

I lost track of the hours and the tunes and the pink Martinis. I'm pretty sure I got up to dance at some point. And later, as the candles dimmed and the notes from the piano became more mournful, I sat down again. Like an unspoken signal, everyone just subsided into their seats and listened.

The kid's voice ached with melancholy; the piano seemed to weep music as he sang his song of the lovesick blues. When he finished, there was a moment before people started to applaud. They were too busy wiping at their eyes.

Later that night, as the tables began to empty and Stella and I gathered our coats and hats, a thin shadow fell over our table. The skinny kid from the stage. Or "the Fat Man," as I had already heard people start to call him because, well, you get it, I'm sure. His step was so quiet we never even heard him walk up.

"I just wanted to thank you, miss," the Fat Man said to Stella. He had taken off his hat and held it in his hands, like a gentleman should when talking to a lady.

She smiled and batted him away with a none too steady hand. "I just don't like bullies."

"We should be thanking you," I said. "That's some voice you've got on you there, son." And yes, I used "son" to assert a little authority in front of Stella, even though I guessed there was barely five or so years between me and the kid.

He smiled back, that gold tooth glinting. "Well, thank you, sir." He held out a hand and introduced himself.

I shook it right back. "Jack Morley, and my fiancée, Stella Grey."

"Nice to meet you both. Could I buy you a drink?"

I glanced over to the bar, where the staff were drying glasses. We might well have lingered a little longer, but for some reason I felt an itch, a tickle at the back of my neck. I couldn't tell you now whether it was a premonition, or just my imagination, but even though the kid seemed pleasant and inoffensive, right then I wanted to get myself and Stella about a million miles away from him.

"I think it might be a little late, and we were just leaving."

I saw Stella give me a look and guessed I'd be in for some earache later.

The Fat Man replacing his hat and tipping it. "Another time maybe."

"Yes, maybe," I said, fully expecting never to see him again. He was good. Brilliant, even. But a novelty. He was a white boy. And the Blue Flamingo wouldn't keep booking a white boy to sing the blues.

THE FAT MAN booked a regular spot every Friday. One of the club's most prized spots. On the first night, Stella and I arrived early, as usual, to find a line all the way down the street.

"I guess word has spread," Stella said with an eye roll.

"Maybe we should go somewhere else?" I suggested. I hated waiting in line and normally we walked right in. I felt a little aggrieved at these part-timers intruding.

"Where?" Stella asked.

Good question. We were hardly dressed for the Hippo. But then, we saw one of the doormen walk toward us.

"Jack Morley and Stella Grey?" he asked.

"Yes."

"You two are on the list. Courtesy of the Fat Man."

He led us to a table right at the front. *Reserved*. We took our seats and man, that did feel kind of special.

After that, when the Fat Man asked to join us for a drink post show, it seemed discourteous to say no. And so it was that every Friday night after he'd performed—each performance even better than the last, if that was possible—he'd come and take a seat with Stella and me.

At first, I wasn't too happy about it. Truth be told, I thought perhaps he had his eye on my fiancée. I think Stella might have thought the same about him too. Stella wasn't a beauty exactly, but she was slim and cute, and did I mention those legs? And while the kid was no looker, he had *that voice*.

Fortunately, my doubts were dispelled one night when Stella asked him if he wrote his songs for anyone in particular.

He reached his bony fingers, delicate like a lady's, into his coat pocket and pulled out his wallet. Unfolding it carefully, he slipped out a photograph.

"This is Veda."

She looked Spanish, or maybe Italian. Of some exotic origin, anyway. Skin a warm honey hue. Long dark hair that cascaded in ringlets around a perfect oval face. And her eyes. Large, tilted and a remarkable emerald green. She was wearing a red dress which clung to her curves like it was melted on. For a moment, even though I loved Stella more than life itself, I was seized by a sharp stab of jealousy. Veda was beautiful. Not pretty or cute. Jaw-droppingly stunning. How had such an odd-looking young man managed to harness such a beauty?

I looked up, into his pale eyes. And I knew he could see what I was thinking. Like he could see all the hurtful thoughts and snide comments in my soul.

"She's gorgeous," Stella said. And I could hear it in her voice too. A tightening. Envy. She had thought she was favoring this young man with her warm smiles and occasional touches upon the arm (oh, I'd noticed). But in reality, he had been humoring *her*. For who would want a thin little thing like Stella when they could have a voluptuous beauty like Veda?

"She's kind too," the Fat Man said. "She bought me this hat, you know?" He picked it up from the table. "It cost her a month's wages, but she knew how much I loved it." He gave a shrug. "I don't know what she sees in me."

But I knew. *He* knew. It was his voice. His beautiful molten voice.

"Oh, don't be so silly," Stella said, a little too brightly. "She's the lucky one."

The Fat Man smiled and accepted the lie. He pressed his fingers to his lips, touched them to the lips of the woman in the photograph and slipped it gently back into his wallet.

"I write all my songs for her," he said. "She brings out the music in me. I write the music and she dances."

"She's a dancer?" Stella asked politely, taking a sip of her drink.

"Yes. She dances beautifully. She wanted to be a ballerina, but she grew a little too tall. She still moves with that grace. Like a swan."

"I've never seen her in here," I said.

He shook his head. "No. Her shifts clash. She works at the Rock Island Diner."

"The place where they dance on the tables?" Stella was unable to contain her disapproval and for perhaps the first time I found myself disliking her a little. Her properness. Her snobbery. Her feeling that she was so much better than all the other girls.

The Fat Man nodded. "It's not the job she wanted, but at least she gets to dance every night. That's all that matters to her. You have to do what you love, right?"

"Right," I said, even though I worked as an accountant and hated it. But it was a good, respectable job and I was saving for our wedding. Doing what you loved. Well, that would be something.

"You know what that place is?" Stella said later, as we walked to catch the bus home. Not a question.

"What place?" I asked carefully.

"The Rock Island Diner."

"Erm, a diner?" I said.

Stella slapped my arm. "Don't play stupid with me, Jack Morley. You know very well what I'm talking about."

I didn't reply. I didn't dare for fear she might hear something in my voice.

"That place is little better than a brothel," she said crisply.

I stared at her in shock. "That's a terrible thing to say."

"Oh, pish. Everyone knows the girls who dance there are sluts. The men slip money in their brassieres *and* their panties, and if they slip them enough, then those girls will do a whole lot more than dance."

"Stella," I said, voice rising. "What's brought this on?"

I'm not sure she knew herself. But she stopped then and bit her lip. "I'm sorry, it's just—he's such a nice young man. Naïve. He adores that girl, but I bet she's there every night doing the dirty on him."

"You don't know that, Stella."

She gave me a flinty stare that chilled me to my very bone. "I know," she said and, for the first time ever, she walked away without kissing me good night.

As it was, I did know places like the Rock Island Diner. Once upon a time, anyway. Not for a long while. And not the place where Veda danced. A little too close to home in more ways than one. And now Stella and I were going strong, well, I didn't exactly need to get my bread buttered elsewhere, if you know what I mean?

So, I still have no idea how I came to be sitting in a booth in a narrow dark room, lit only by fluorescents and beer tabs that Saturday night.

I mean, I know how I got there. I got in my car, drove and parked up in the last space in the parking lot at just gone a quarter past ten. But that wasn't where I was heading. I was heading for the 7-Eleven on Main. A night in with a movie and a few cold beers.

Stella was still being chilly with me. I didn't know why. I'd never told her about the place I visited that time and the girl who danced for me. No way could she have known. But something had riled her and instead of going to the pictures like we often would on a Saturday night, and then maybe for a burger afterward, she had told me she was going out with her girlfriends instead.

I'd sat in my one-bed apartment and stewed for a while. I drank two of the four-pack of beers in the fridge and then I decided that I'd go out and buy some more and watch an action movie that was on the TV. Stella hated action movies, and I pretended I did too, but secretly I quite enjoyed them. Men have a lot of little secrets. Women too, I guess. Sometimes I think it isn't the truths that hold a relationship together but the lies. And only if you never tell.

It wasn't as if the diner was on the way, not really. But somehow, I found myself taking a slightly circuitous route to the store so that I drove right past it. I slowed a little, staring at the tacky neon sign. Even from the road, with the windows on my old Ford Maverick up, I could hear the music pumping out through the door.

I was about to press my foot on the accelerator and drive on past. McQueen and another four-pack were waiting for me. Plus, a pretty decent bourbon at the back of the cabinet. Then, I thought, what the hell? Stella was out with her girlfriends, no doubt flirting with guys. Maybe I should have some fun too.

I guess a lot of mistakes, mishaps and unhappy endings start with a "What the hell?" What's the worst that could happen? What harm could it do? Just to take a look inside. Just to get a glimpse of beautiful Veda in the flesh. It wasn't like I was going to do anything. I loved Stella. I really did. And I wasn't a cheater. No woman would ever say I was.

Anyways, I guess I'm putting off the main point, which is for some goddamn reason I parked my car up and walked into the bar. There were a lot of pretty girls in there, sashaying around the room in skimpy outfits. Little crop tops and tasseled skirts that barely covered their backsides. Those that weren't wandering around, flashing their pert little bottoms, were on the tables, gyrating and twirling. They wore next to nothing. Bare breasts and tiny little thongs. They were smooth too. Hairless all over. They jiggled those boobies and thrust out their crotches and men didn't put money in their brassieres because they weren't wearing any. But they slipped those notes lovingly into their thongs, fingers lingering, so I guess Stella was right about that one.

The hour was pretty late, but the place was jammed. I managed to spy a booth, only just vacated, by the look of the empty glass and full ashtray. I eased myself into it, feeling self-conscious and a little seedy. A drinks menu had been stuck lopsidedly into a plastic holder.

It looked and felt sticky. I was just peeling it apart when a voice spoke from my right.

"What would you like, sir? Drink and a dance?"

I turned. It was Veda. Of course. I should have guessed by the foreign lilt in her voice. She looked even more beautiful in the flesh. Some women don't. Some women who look stunning in photographs look a little odd in real life. The angles and lines that create a beautiful picture can be too much for the eye. Conversely, it's true that a pretty girl can take an awful picture. Stella always looks pinched and harsh in the photos of us together. Eyes too close. Lips a little thin. And that isn't how I remember her. Photos can lie, just like people.

But Veda. I don't think that girl could have looked ugly if she'd tried. Her ringlets fell around her bare shoulders, like some kind of Greek goddess. I found myself staring at her beautiful face, those mesmerizing eyes. And then, I'm not going to lie, my eyes trailed down to her body. Her breasts were full and round. Her stomach was taut and her legs, *man,* they made me want to cry. Even semi-naked, she looked like a dancer. She carried herself with a grace and poise. And dignity too.

"Did you hear me, sir? Drink and a dance?" She leaned in, a little closer, hair almost brushing my face. "You have to buy at least one or they'll kick you out."

Then she smiled, revealing her only flaw. Every woman has one. Strong white teeth but an incisor was missing.

"Oh." I looked down at the menu, feeling flustered and stupid. What the hell was I doing here? I didn't drink these overpriced cocktails with names like "Slippery Nipples" and "Sex on the Beach." I didn't like the trashy music blaring out of the speakers. And Veda was beautiful, but she was not my girlfriend.

"I . . . err . . ." I closed the menu again. "Nothing, thank you. I just realized that I left my wallet at home."

I expected her to be annoyed, but she just laughed. "I'm always doing things like that. My boyfriend, he tells me, you have a head like a sieve, Veda."

Her boyfriend. The Fat Man. I needed to go. I stood and offered a hand. "Well, anyway. Nice to meet you." She shook it. Her hand was slim and petite. "Your boyfriend is a very lucky man."

The smile faltered. She looked down, but not before I caught something in her face. A shadow. Regret? Fear? Perhaps I imagined it. Hindsight makes wise men of us all. But still, something caused me to linger, gazing after her as she walked, swinging her hips, back to the bar.

If I hadn't. If I had grabbed my hat and left right away, I would never have seen him.

There were men working the bar too. No doubt to deal with any rowdy troublemakers pestering the women. This man was not the tallest or the most muscular, but he was beautiful, just like Veda. That might sound odd, but some men *are* beautiful. His skin was darker than Veda's, his hair was thick, and his face was like one of those classical sculptures, all high cheekbones and full lips. You could tell that God had taken his time with this one, as my mother used to say.

As Veda rounded the corner of the bar, he looked up and smiled. She moved toward him. As she did, he said something, and she laughed and touched his arm. It was all there in that laugh, that touch.

The pair of them didn't kiss or embrace, but I knew. Some things you just do. I clutched my hat a little tighter and turned away, heart heavy, cursing myself for coming here. It was none of my business. Nothing to do with my life. But I felt for the Fat Man. I thought about how he had touched his fingers to her photo, how much he loved her.

Even so, I thought, perhaps he could still keep her. As long as he could sing. The barman might have the looks, but the Fat Man had that voice. He could keep her with his voice.

————

A FEW DAYS passed and Stella thawed, as I knew she would. We returned to the Blue Flamingo. But the Fat Man didn't. One week passed, then two and eventually I asked the manager, Marvin, where he was. Had he left? Got a gig somewhere else?

"Oh no," said Marvin. "He's lost his voice. Laryngitis."

It could have been a blues song itself. *I lost my voice then, I lost my girl.* Because that's just what happened. I knew the minute he came back. Something in him had changed. Broken. Like a puppet with its strings cut. He slunk back onto that stage, looking even paler and skinnier. Everyone else thought it was just because of the illness. But I could tell. It wasn't his throat. It was a different kind of sickness. Heart sickness. And there's no cure for that.

When he sang, he didn't play any of the upbeat numbers. He crooned mournful songs of love and loss. And he never wore his hat. He still brought the box and laid it on the stage by his feet. But I never saw him wear the hat that Veda had bought him ever again.

One night, he sat down and told us. How Veda had run off with a guy she worked with at the diner. How she loved the Fat Man, but she was *in love* with Freddie. I guess he wasn't the first man to hear that line, nor would he be the last. And a man knows what that really means. *I love you like a friend, but I want to be fucked by Freddie.*

His words not mine. Bitter words from a bitter man. The Fat Man never used to drink much, normally stuck to Coke and ice. But that night he added bourbon and sank about half a dozen of them.

Stella and I let him talk. There's not much you can say to help a man with a broken heart. All you can do is let him spill. Like crying or bleeding. You got to let it out until it all dries up. Occasionally, we interjected with a platitude, but that's all it was. I wasn't sure he was even listening.

"He turned her head, her pretty little head," he said, voice thick with bourbon and tears. "And if I could find her, if I could just find her, then . . ."

"—you think you could win her back?" Stella said gently, voice a tiny bit slurred. She'd been putting away those pink Martinis pretty fast herself that night.

"No—" He shook his head. "If I could find her . . . I'd kill her."

I'M A LITTLE ashamed to say I'm not a man of reading. Not books or magazines or even newspapers. I didn't much care for the news on the television either. Too much death and doom and gloom. The only time I ever caught up with current events was when I had the radio on in my car.

That's how I heard the news. About the woman's body. Found in the woods off the main road out of town. Her killer had tried to burn her corpse. It's why they didn't identify her right away. That and the fact that she had no head. She'd been decapitated.

Did I make the leap then? I'm not so sure I did. I think I might have felt a tremor of foreboding, something stirring in the back of my mind. I think even then, my memory was starting to falter. I wouldn't always remember conversations or events so clearly.

It was Stella who made the connection. She was always sharper than me and she read lots of crime novels, so perhaps it was only natural that she should have gone straight to the darkest conclusion.

"Did you hear, Jack . . . about the woman who was killed?"

I frowned and then nodded. "Oh, yes. I did. Awful. Horrible. I hope they catch whoever did it."

"*Whoever* did it? Isn't it obvious?"

I hated it when she spoke to me like that. Like I was stupid. *Hasn't your slow old brain got there yet? Do I have to spell everything out for you?*

"Well, I guess it isn't or I'd know what the hell you're talking about," I said, a little more roughly than I normally spoke to Stella.

It didn't faze her, though. She was too caught up in her wild theory. "It's *her*. It's Veda. The Fat Man found her, and he killed her, just like he said he would."

"Stella. That's one heck of an accusation."

"What? You heard him. You heard what he said. About turning her pretty little head. She was *decapitated,* Jack."

She leaned on that word—*decapitated*—with a little too much relish, eyes widening.

"That could mean anything."

"It's her. You mark my words."

"But . . . I mean, how will they identify her? They didn't find her head."

You could almost hear the penny drop with a dull clunk. We both stared at each other.

"The hat box," Stella whispered.

AN UGLY IDEA is like a worm inside your gut. It gnaws and gnaws away at you, and you can't ignore it, much as you'd like to.

We kept on going back to the Blue Flamingo, but we weren't really listening to the music. We were watching the Fat Man. Did he look different? Guilty? Did we expect to see blood on his hands or seeping from the bottom of the hat box?

God. *That damn box*. I'd like to say I prayed for him to open it and prove that there was nothing but a hat inside. I'd like to say that when we talked, I felt sure of his innocence. But I didn't. That's not how human nature works. That's not what the ugly worm wants. The ugly worm wants to see ugly reflected back. I found myself watching the Fat Man to see if he carried the box any differently. Like it weighed more. Like there was something heavier than a hat inside there. I can't say he did, but he did do one thing differently. After the show, before he came to join us, he took the box and put it in his dressing room.

I suppose, if it had just been down to me, I would have let it go.

I would have stopped going to the club and told Stella to forget all about it. But, as with many things, I left it too late, and Stella got in first.

"We have to look."

"What?"

"We have to look in the hat box. We have to know, Jack."

"Stella, I think we've been letting our imaginations run away with us—"

"*No*. This is you all over. You think you can just sweep stuff under the carpet like it never happened."

"Stell—"

"People in love, they can do terrible things. He killed her and he's keeping her head in that hat box. And I want you to look and see."

"But he carries that box with him all the time."

She shook her head, lips pursing. "You know that's not true. After the show he takes it to his dressing room."

"Which is locked, I'm sure."

She smiled smugly and reached into the pocket of her coat. When her hand emerged, she held a small, shiny key between her fingers.

"How did you get that?" I hissed.

"When I said I was going to the Ladies last night, I slipped backstage and stole it."

"Stella!"

She waved a hand. "The manager will have a spare. They'll just think it got lost."

I stared at her. This was a new Stella. A wily, sly Stella. A Stella full of ugly worms. A Stella I wasn't so sweet on.

"Why do you care?" I asked her.

"Why do I care?" She looked at me like she was thinking the same thing. That she didn't know this stranger in front of her. "Jack, he might have murdered that young woman. The question is—why don't *you* care?"

WOMEN HAVE A habit of asking questions a man can't answer. I guess that's why, the next Friday night, I found myself standing outside the Fat Man's dressing room, that shiny silver key clutched in my sweaty palm.

The Fat Man was at the bar, buying a round of pink Martinis. He seemed happier that night, ebullient. He even played a few of the upbeat numbers. Maybe his heart was healing. Maybe he'd found a new girlfriend. Maybe he thought he'd got away with murder.

It was the opportunity I needed. When he marched up to the bar, Stella gave me a look and I knew that this was it. Now or never. I'd have preferred never, but sometimes, well, a man has to do what his woman wants him to do.

And so, I stood, outside that dressing room. If anyone came past or asked me what I was doing, I had planned to tell them the Fat Man had asked me to go and fetch his wallet. But no one wandered past. No one asked. I slipped the key into the lock, hoping against hope that it might stick. But it turned smoothly, and the door eased open.

I stepped inside. The room was cramped, barely bigger than a toilet stall. But it was still the best in the club. The only one a performer had to themselves. I spotted the hat box right away, on the floor beneath the dressing table.

I stared at myself in the speckled mirror. A stocky man in a well-cut suit, hair slicked back, a few lines already creeping in prematurely. Not bad-looking, but hardly handsome. Not a remarkable man. Not an adventurous man. Not the sort of man to do something like this. But here I was.

I crouched down. My heart thumped louder than a bass drum. I lifted the box up and my stomach twisted. Something shifted inside. It felt heavy. Too heavy for a hat. I placed the box on the chipped dressing table. My fingers poised to lift the lid and then my heart almost erupted through my chest as a deep, mellifluous voice said from behind me:

"What you doing in here, Jack?"

I turned. The Fat Man stood in the doorway. He seemed taller, face cast into shadow.

"I—" The words congealed on my tongue.

He smiled, gold tooth glinting. "I know why you're here."

I stared at him. "You do?"

He nodded. "It's the hat, isn't it? Ever since Veda left, you noticed I haven't been wearing my hat."

"Yes," I said, grabbing at the straw.

He moved toward me. I fought the urge to shrink away.

"I should have realized that friends like you—*good friends*—would notice." He nodded slowly. "The truth is, all the time I thought I'd lost her, I couldn't wear that hat. But I couldn't get rid of it either because, in my heart, I always knew she'd come back." He paused. "And I was right."

I stared at him. "Veda came back?"

"Yeah." He laughed and the hairs stood up on my arms, just like when he sang, but for different reasons. "She's out there right now, drinking pink Martinis. Come and see."

He held out his arm. I moved toward the door on legs that felt like lumps of clay and followed him out into the club. I couldn't see Stella, but I saw Veda right away. Sitting at a far table near the edge of the stage, hair pulled back, wearing a sparkly, low-cut dress. Unmistakable. Beautiful. Relief washed over me and, I must admit, a little jealousy too. She had come back. Stunning, gorgeous Veda. And here I was, stuck with plain, faithful little Stella.

"Beautiful, isn't she?" the Fat Man sighed.

I nodded and just managed to stop myself saying, *And alive too.*

"Jack?"

I turned. Stella stood behind me, looking suspicious and annoyed.

"Where did you go?" I asked.

"I went to the Ladies," she said primly. "Did you—"

"Veda's back," I said before she could continue.

She blinked at me. "What?"

The Fat Man looked at her. "I know what you're going to say. You're going to tell me not to trust her because she'll do the same thing again. But she's changed, Stella. She realizes that she needs me now."

"Well." Stella cleared her throat. "That's good."

"I'm happy for you," I said, and I like to think I meant it.

"Thanks, man." The Fat Man glanced at Veda, a strange look on his face. "I know this time she won't ever run away again." Then he turned to Stella and me, grinning widely. "Hey, won't you join us?"

"Thank you," Stella said quickly. "But I'm a little tired. I think we'll take a rain check."

I didn't argue. It felt wrong, after all those ugly thoughts, to intrude on the Fat Man's joy.

"Are you sure?" he asked.

"Yes," I said firmly. "We should be going home."

STELLA DIDN'T SAY a word as we walked down the street. She had been wrong about the Fat Man and Stella hated being wrong. I let her stew. She deserved it.

We were halfway to the bus stop when I stopped dead, the realization striking me. *My hat.* I'd left my hat.

"I have to go back," I said to Stella.

"Why?"

"I left my hat."

She huffed. "For God's sake, Jack. You'd forget your head if it wasn't screwed on."

"I was distracted," I said.

"I bet you were," she said in a mean tone.

"What's that supposed to mean?"

"Like you don't know."

I wasn't in the mood for this right now, so I just said, "I'm going back."

"Can't you get the damn hat tomorrow?"

"It's my favorite hat."

"They'll be closing up."

"They'll let me back in. We're regulars."

She sighed. "Fine. I'll wait here for you."

I jogged back down the street but when I reached the club I could see that the front door was already locked. There was a stage door though, down the alley. That would probably still be open for the staff and performers to leave.

I walked around the side of the club, and sure enough, the stage door was ajar, spilling out voices and light. A white van was parked just outside.

I walked toward it . . . and paused.

There are moments in life—I've had maybe two—where time really does seem to freeze. Like it's holding up a hand and saying *Look, really look. Remember this. Take it all in and never forget. You wanted to know and now you do. How d'you like it, now?*

The Fat Man stood at the rear of the van, smoking and holding the hat box. As I watched, the stage door to the club opened wider and Veda emerged. Not alone. One of the doormen stood behind her, pushing the wheelchair.

A ramp had been set up and he maneuvered Veda down it backward. She sat patiently in the chair, a pale pink blanket covering her from the waist down. As the doorman tilted the chair up at the end of the ramp, it slipped slightly to one side, revealing those long dancer's legs: smooth thighs, toned calves . . . and two ugly stumps where her feet should be.

I stared at the stumps, at the pink, puckered skin. My head spun. I thought about the weight of the box. How something had shifted inside.

But not her head.

I know this time she won't ever run away again.

The Fat Man walked toward Veda, smiling. He placed a hand on her cheek, caressing it. Then he placed the hat box in her lap. She looked down at it and she started to cry.

———

TIME PASSED, AS time is wont to. I never told anyone about what I saw that night. Some horrors are just too great to share. And what did I know, really? Just ugly thoughts.

Stella and I never went back to the Blue Flamingo. Somehow, it had lost its appeal. Soon after, I heard that the Fat Man went away, and never came back.

They identified the woman in the woods as one of the dancers at the Rock Island Diner. They found her head, dumped half a mile away, as if someone had been planning to take it with them and then changed their mind. Crucially, the police had connected the murder with a cold case. Another dancer from a different bar, killed almost five years ago. Also burnt and decapitated. But they never found her head.

Stella was right. People do terrible things in the name of love. But she would never know just how terrible. I made sure of that.

She's been gone almost two years now. I forget sometimes. I wake up and I'm puzzled why her side of the bed is cold, why there's no dent in the pillow or familiar scent. Sometimes, I go out looking for her in my night clothes and the police have to bring me back home. And I remember. And it's like losing her all over again.

I visited a place like the Rock Island Diner once. The girl that danced for me did other things for me too, later that night, in my car. Things I had never done with Stella. Things that felt good at the time but made me feel bad afterward. What if Stella found out? What would I do without her? Stella and I were in love, and this girl, she was just trash.

Well, I knew what you did with trash. You burnt it.

But I kept a memento. I couldn't help myself.

Just like I couldn't help returning to the Rock Island Diner a night or two after I'd met Veda and taking out the trash again.

I open the garage door and walk inside, flicking on the fluorescent lights. My space. Stella never came in here. Not once in the forty-five years we were married. It was where I went when I needed some time. Every man needs some time, just like every man sings his own tune in the end.

I used to come here and tinker with my old Maverick, back when they still let me drive. Nowadays, the place is full of junk, as well as an old armchair I like to sit in and a radio that ran out of batteries a while ago. It's also the place where I keep my hats. Neatly stored in boxes and lined up on a couple of shelves.

Except, there's one box that doesn't contain a hat.

I pick it up now and place it carefully on my workbench. Then I lift the lid and stare inside.

Sometimes I remember she's here and sometimes I forget. The Alzheimer's is cruel like that. It takes away everything. Your memories, your secrets. Even your words.

I'm not a reader, but I always loved to tell a story. These days, I can't remember what I was talking about five minutes ago . . .

Did I ever tell you about the Fat Man?

The Completion

Introduction

During the past three years I've given the apocalypse a lot of thought, not least because I wasn't sure if we were on the cusp of it. As I write this, we still might be.

One of the things that struck me is that filmmakers have got it all wrong. If society collapsed and zombies roamed the streets, we wouldn't go all Mad Max and survivalist. By and large, I reckon people would just get on with it. We'd buy bread and milk and remember to record *Bake Off*. We'd moan about the zombie invasion and lament the days when you could stroll down the road without stepping over the living dead. It's the British way.

At the end of 2020 I was in the throes of helping my mum sell the family home and buy a new retirement apartment. This was during the pandemic, but the housing market was booming—partly because of the cut in stamp duty. Partly because, in the event of an apocalypse, the only things to flourish will be cockroaches and estate agents (sorry, estate agents. It's a joke, okay?).

"Completion" was a word I heard a lot during that period. The sellers were eager to get it done as soon as possible. In fact, I heard the word so many times, it began to take on a more sinister undertone. Almost like a demonic chant: *completion, completion, completion.*

One morning, I found myself writing it down as a title. Just that.

Sometime later, I came back to it and wrote this short story.

It combines a lot of things that were on my mind at the time—the apocalypse, human nature, the devil. You know.

I'm fifty now, and more fatalistic about my own future. Once you accept you have more years behind you than ahead, you have to be. My worries are for my daughter. I've gone from wanting her to have a better future to just wanting her to have a future. But increasingly, I feel that history repeats, and life is cyclical. All I can do for Betty is to try and instill the right values and give her the tools to carve out her own space in the world.

And if the zombie apocalypse happens, remind her to record *Bake Off*.

The day of completion started—as many of Dan Ransom's days did—with a lie.

"Well, that's a good offer, but I'm afraid that the other buyer has also upped what they're willing to pay." He nodded as the purchaser complained down the phone. "Yes, I know. No one wants to get into a situation of gazumping, but I have to put it to the seller." A pause. "Yes, they *are* a cash buyer."

Dan waited, studying his nails—which could do with a manicure—as the purchaser ummed and ahhed and made noises about not going above the asking price.

"I hear you," he said, even though he was barely listening. "So, would you like me to tell the seller that this is your final and best—"

He broke off. No. They didn't want him to do that, as he had known they wouldn't. They increased their offer by £10,000, as he had known they would. Dan grinned and assured them that this would definitely seal the deal. He ended the call and swung his feet off the desk. The space that they had occupied was immediately taken by the pert backside of Holly, another of the agents.

"You're a fucking liar, Ransom."

"Why, thank you."

"There is no higher offer, is there?"

"Well, technically . . ." Dan winked. "There is no other buyer."

She shook her head. "Hell has a seat warmed just for you."

"Nice. I do like a toasty tushy."

She rolled her eyes.

"C'mon, Hol," he cajoled. "It's a little white lie—and they can afford it."

"That's not the point."

He sighed. "The world is heading to hell in a handcart. Frankly, I'm amazed anyone is still buying and selling property. We all ought to be eating babies by now. So, let's not get all high horse about it."

"I'm not. I just think we should still have some integrity."

"Integrity?" He laughed. "It's end of fucking days, Hol. Integrity went out with free healthcare and democracy."

Holly stood up. He'd upset her, and he almost felt bad about it. Dan liked Holly, but sometimes she was just so naïve. He had no idea how she had ended up working as an estate agent—or how the hell she sold anything. Well, actually, that was a lie. She sold stuff because she was hot, even for a thirty-year-old. Audrey Hepburn with breasts and bee-stung lips. She favored pencil skirts and heels, a crisp white blouse unbuttoned just enough . . . *Okay, stop it, Ransom. Do not go there. Do not get distracted. Not today.*

He looked at his watch. An old-fashioned Rotary timepiece he'd got off a client who had passed away. *Literally* got it off him, slipping it off the old codger's wrist moments before the ambulance came to take him away.

He checked it against the time on his laptop. Five minutes off. The lag was getting longer. You couldn't trust GMT anymore. Old watches that were set before time began to slip, or at least before people noticed it, were safer. Unless you didn't care. Most people didn't. Half of the world lived their life five minutes in delay. But things like that niggled Dan. He liked to know he was right. Correct. Or perhaps he just liked to know he had one over on everyone else.

Fortunately, his next client was also a Rotary man. So it wouldn't do to be late. Dan slipped the sales documents into his briefcase and stood.

"Okay. Wish me luck. I'm off to seal the deal with Bragshaw."

Holly's eyes widened. "You finally nailed the old bastard down."

"Yeah. Today is the day." He winked. "Completion."

"Don't count your chickens just yet, son." The dry, raspy drone came from the back of the office.

Dan clicked his tongue against his teeth in annoyance. Jack Holywell.

Jack had worked at Revere's Estate Agents since, well, probably since the dawn of fucking time. He must be way past retirement age by now, but for some reason the "powers that be" kept him on, even though Dan hadn't seen the old fart sell a damn thing the whole time he had worked here. As far as Dan could tell, all he did was sit there like a wilting potted plant that someone had forgotten to water, filling his trash can with tissues full of mucus and occasionally spitting up pearls of "wisdom" like this one.

"And why's that?" Dan asked as politely as he could, which wasn't very polite at all. "I've got all the paperwork. Neither party is using a solicitor. I am authorized to exchange and complete on the same day. It's a done deal."

A raspy chuckle wheezed into a phlegmy cough. "Plenty been there before you and fallen at the final hurdle. Me included."

Dan's eyebrows shot up. "*You?*"

Jack nodded, a sly smile on his crinkled lips. "Thirty years ago. Set off to get the papers signed. Best suit, shoes shined, just like you, son."

Dan bristled at the comparison.

"What happened?" Holly asked.

A shrug. "Bragshaw changed his mind. Said the time wasn't right."

"But why refuse to complete? He'd be liable for costs."

Jack shook his head. "Money doesn't mean anything to him. He's so rich he probably doesn't even know how much money he has." He tapped his nose, bulbous with broken veins. "What Bragshaw *does* like is games."

Dan stared at him. The man's eyes were rheumy and bloodshot, jowls like limp dishrags either side of his dry, flaky lips, which always seemed to have a bit of white spittle lodged at the corner. The suit he wore was fit only for the coffin and his shoes had worn through to the inner.

Disgusting. Decrepit. Nothing like Dan. At twenty-five, Dan considered himself in the prime of his life. For a man. Women were different. They lost their bloom far earlier. That's why Dan preferred them a little . . . fresher.

He straightened his tie and offered a small smile. "Well, luckily, I'm not you, Jack. I will seal this deal today and it will be the biggest sale in the history of Revere's."

And that was the truth, for once. Bragshaw Manor was the largest property in the area. The old house boasted twenty bedrooms, two turrets, five acres of grounds, a lake, a wood and a plethora of tales about the supposed spooks and monsters that lurked within its stone walls. Even now, with a real-life apocalypse upon them, people were still afraid of ghosts.

Dan knew all the stories. He had grown up just down the road from the manor in a cramped terrace with a tiny, cobbled backyard for a garden. Like a lot of local kids, he used to sneak into Bragshaw Woods to play, although they never crossed the boundary fence into the actual gardens, lest they were spotted. Until that day when Alice had said . . .

"*Dan?*" Holly was staring at him in concern. "You okay?"

"Fine." He whacked his smile up to full voltage. "Just thinking how I'm going to spend all that lovely commission."

She rolled her eyes. "On therapy?"

"Oooh." He feigned an arrow to the heart. "Harsh, Hol. Harsh."

He slipped on his best jacket, picked up his briefcase and offered Holly and Jack a small salute. "Later, losers. See you on the other side."

"What if you're already there?" Jack said.

Dan glanced at him. The old man had a strange look on his age-ravaged face. Almost . . . pity? Dan's smile faltered. He turned quickly away.

What if you're already there?

He shook his head

Senile old goat.

BRAGSHAW MANOR SQUATTED, like a huge and particularly ugly vulture, on the outskirts of town. It had all the attributes of a classic haunted house. Like someone had lifted it right out of a clichéd horror movie or an old-fashioned funfair. You half expected the front door to creak open and find a wobbly moving ramp or an arcadia of mirrors inside.

You'd be wrong, of course.

The drive through town had been tiresome—the usual human obstacle course of protestors, vagrants, infected and dead bodies littered Dan's way. He had tutted and checked his watch, narrowly missing a couple of limping infected en route. *Must try harder next time, Ransom.* He didn't know why the government, or whoever was running this shitshow, didn't just come and flame-thrower the lot of them. He supposed it wouldn't look good on the news, or in the polls.

Sometimes, Dan thought he was wasted as an estate agent. He had achieved outstanding grades at school (he had cheated, obviously, but that just showed initiative), he had been to the best universities (expelled from all three, but that was semantics). He should have become a politician. Should have been running this shitshow himself. He felt he had all the necessary qualities—he was a compulsive liar, he had absolutely no morals and would happily dump on anyone to progress his own career. Plus, he was handsome enough to get away with it all.

There was just one problem. His indiscretions. Tastes that some might find unpalatable. Although why people found an attraction to youth unpalatable always baffled him. They worshipped it in every other way. Young, firm flesh sold everything from cars to ice cream. Haggard, middle-aged women spent a fortune trying to reclaim that dewy-skinned look from their teens. They couldn't, of course. They could present a good facade, but that was all it was. Up close, the stretched skin was shiny and unnatural, their wrinkly necks and veiny hands a giveaway of the years. Not lithe, fresh, unsullied. Pure.

He licked his lips and realized he was getting a slight erection. *Not now. Rein it in, Ransom. Professional, remember? Seal the deal.*

He pulled up outside the manor's huge iron gates and wound

down the window to press the intercom. He had barely touched the button when there was a low, grinding groan and the gates swung open. Probably a sensor.

Dan eased the shiny Tesla through, trying to ignore the slight frisson of unease that always skittered down his spine as the ominous dark bulk of the manor loomed up ahead. Behind him, the gates clanged shut with a sobering finality.

"Are you chicken, Danny Boy?"

The tic in his eye twitched. Stupid. It was just a house. A creepy old house, but just a house, nonetheless. And he wasn't a kid anymore. There was nothing to fear here. No monsters or boogeymen, vampires, or werewolves. Just an old man with a big pot of money.

He pulled up on the weed-strewn gravel outside the main entrance. Half a dozen steps led up to a huge wooden door framed with ivy. At the bottom of the steps, two leering gargoyles perched on stone pillars.

"Soooo creepy."

He checked himself in the rearview mirror. Grinned. His teeth gleamed, white and even. Veneers, of course. The fake tan looked subtle and healthy. Dark hair cut into a fashionable short style. Someone had once told him he looked a little like that old actor— what was his name? Tom something or other. In his heyday, of course.

He winked at himself. *Looking good, Ransom.* Then he sprang out of the car, feeling hyped with nervous energy. Today was the day. The day he showed everyone at Revere's who the boss really was. The biggest mansion, the biggest sale, and the biggest commission anyone in the agency had ever scored. If this didn't line him up for a partnership, he didn't know what the hell would.

"Just keep cool, Ransom," he murmured to himself. "Strike the right note. Professional, friendly, not desperate. Don't act desperate."

Bragshaw didn't like desperate. Dan had got that from the old man the first time he'd met him, almost two months ago. The guy might be ancient, but he wasn't stupid or soft. Some old people were kind of squishy, like their brains had gone to mush along with their gums and muscle tone. They couldn't see or hear you properly and their marbles, if not lost, were certainly scattered far and wide. Much as they were distasteful to Dan, they were good clients. Easy to con.

Bragshaw wasn't like that. He was tough. Like beaten leather. Weathered skin stretched taut over sharp bones. Bald skull speckled with age spots, but the old man was still upright and surprisingly tall, blue eyes scalpel-sharp. When his bony fingers gripped yours, you sensed he could crush your bones like a vise if he so wished.

Dan could tell he didn't suffer fools. Flattery wouldn't work, nor charm. With Bragshaw, it was all about the business. No pleasantries. Don't veer off topic unless he drove the conversation that way. Be honest or, at least, *appear* to be honest. Dan was good at that.

He reached for the heavy brass knocker and rapped three times. Then he stood back, blinking hard to dispel the annoying twitch. He was just thinking he should knock again when the door swung open. Dan hesitated and then peered around it. No one stood on the other side. *O-kay.* Probably more sensors.

He stepped into the hallway. The door slammed shut behind him and he jumped. *Christ.* His nerves were hotwired today. *Calm it down, Ransom.* He stared around. The hallway was huge. Flagstones on the floor. A massive winding staircase in front of him. Oil paintings of whey-faced men and women in medieval garb glowered down from wood-paneled walls. Dan rolled his eyes. Sooner this old heap was converted into modern apartments and this crap plasterboarded over, the better.

"Mr. Ransom?"

He spun round.

Olive, Bragshaw's secretary, stood behind him. Dan fought back a shudder of revulsion. As ancient as Bragshaw himself, the old hag was reed-thin, her back bent with osteoporosis. She walked with a cane and stared up through small, half-moon glasses. With her straggly white hair and whiskered chin, she reminded Dan of the Evil Queen when she transformed into a witch in *Snow White*. All she needed was a poisoned apple.

He gathered himself. "Good to see you again, ma'am."

Olive regarded him for a moment as if she knew he was lying and then turned away. "Follow me."

Dan had expected to turn right. That was the way he had gone last time, to Bragshaw's office. He had sat on a creaky leather chair and the old man had sat behind a wide oak desk, more of the omni-present medieval folk glaring down at them from the walls.

"Tell me, boy," Bragshaw had said, eyeing him intently. "Why should I let you sell my home?"

Dan had considered any number of lies, but eventually he said simply, "Why not, sir?"

A raspy chuckle had scuttled from Bragshaw's cracked lips. "Why not indeed?"

He'd continued to regard Dan as if he were an interesting insect trapped under glass. "You know, many of your *type* have tried to persuade me to sell this place. Investors, developers, rich old men with beautiful young whores for wives. What makes you different?"

"Well"—Dan had leaned forward—"the buyer I have lined up is prepared to pay way more than any previous offer you've received and their plans . . ."

Bragshaw had waved a gnarled and knotted hand, looking bored. "I don't care about them. Tell me about *you*."

Dan had paused. *Him*. Okay. He wasn't used to that. Or rather, the problem was, which *him*? There were so many. The confident salesman, the sensitive young suitor, the sympathetic shoulder to cry on. Oh, and his favorite—the vulnerable man-child sharing his deep-est secret.

That one always worked. Well, nearly always. He'd had one fail-ure. Holly. She was a little old for his tastes, but she was undeniably hot. And her obvious disdain for him just made her hotter. He had thought that his "confession" would help win his way into her lacy black underpants. But she had simply smiled and said, "Your time will come, Dan." And that was it. Leaving him there, like a fucking limp dick. Frigid bitch. And to think he had been prepared to do *her* a favor. He had consoled himself with the fact that she was undoubtedly a lesbian.

"Mr. Ransom?" Bragshaw had prompted.

Dan had cleared his throat. "Well, sir, the truth is . . . I would do anything to get a deal. I have lied, cheated, betrayed people, even taken bribes. But that's because I want to be the best at what I do. Sometimes, you have to crack a few skulls to get the crown."

Bagshaw had laughed heartily. Dan had half expected to see dust billow out of his mouth. He had found himself praying that the old bastard didn't keel over and die right there and then, before they agreed to the sale.

Fortunately, Bragshaw had straightened and looked him in the eye. "I like you, boy," he said, even though his tone suggested otherwise. "You may have this sale. Talk to your buyers and tell them I accept their offer."

Dan's heart had leaped. "You do? I mean, thank you, sir. That's great to hear. I'll just need to leave these documents."

He had opened his briefcase. Bragshaw had continued to stare at him. "You'd really do anything for a sale?"

Dan grinned as he pulled out a sheaf of papers. "I'd slit my own grandmother's throat, sir."

"Do you *have* a grandmother?"

Dan winked. "Not since I slit her throat, sir."

"What about a sister?"

The smile lost its grip. Dan's eyelid fluttered.

"Are you chicken, Danny Boy? Dare you."

"No." He cleared his throat. "I don't have a sister."

"What about Alice?"

Alice. The tic fluttered harder. As a child he had had terrible tics. They worsened after . . .

Bragshaw smiled. "Think about it, son."

Then he had waved a hand. Dan was dismissed.

He had risen from the deep leather seat and walked down the dark hallway feeling a little unnerved, discombobulated. Unusual for him. Sister. *Of course* he didn't have a sister. He had shaken his head. *And who the fuck was Alice?*

OLIVE LED HIM down a long corridor. Doors on either side. More pictures. Dark. Really dark. Eventually, they reached another heavy wooden door. The old hag raised her hand and, once again, the door swung open. He really needed to get himself some of those sensors for his new place, Dan thought. He had his eye on a nice sprawling penthouse in one of the more exclusive gated communities. A place that would really impress the ladies. The *young* ladies.

"Just through here, Mr. Ransom."

"Okey-dokey."

Olive stood aside as he walked through. Another office, even bigger than the last one. Dusty, dimly lit, worn books lining every wall. The desk in the center was made of some kind of granite or quartz and either side of it two stone pillars held flaming torches.

Rich people, Dan thought. *More fucking money than sense, or style.*

But there was something else. Something vaguely familiar about this room. The stone, the books, the torches. He shook his head. The tic twitched.

"Take a seat, Mr. Ransom."

He jolted. Olive had disappeared. Bragshaw sat on a chair behind the desk. He must have been there when Dan came in. Perhaps the darkness had concealed him. *Fuck.* This was getting weirder by the minute.

Think about the money. The penthouse apartment. The girls. Lots of girls. He saw himself leading them in, their eyes wide. *All his. Oh yes.*

Dan smiled. "This is an impressive space, Mr. Bragshaw."

"Oh, this," Bragshaw said dismissively. "This is just the chamber."

"The chamber?"

"That's right. The chamber before the temple."

Dan stared at him "You have a temple? We really should have added that to the details. I could have got you another hundred grand."

Bragshaw smiled. "You really are a base creature, aren't you, Mr. Ransom?"

Dan blinked. Was he being insulted? Hard to tell. Best to ignore it for now. He reached into his briefcase and took out the contract. He laid it on the desk.

"So, shall we proceed to business?"

"First, a drink, Mr. Ransom."

"Oh, I don't drink when I'm working."

Truth was, Dan didn't really drink at all. He didn't like the woozy feeling, the way that alcohol seemed to dredge up unwanted memories. Sorrows float, as they say.

But Bragshaw was already up and walking across to the bookcase.

"I insist, Mr. Ransom. A drink to seal the deal."

Dan cleared his throat. Seal the deal. "Of course. Why not?"

Bragshaw chuckled his dusty chuckle again. "Why not, Danny Boy?"

Dan felt something uncoil in his mind. Something long forgotten, shaking off dirt. "What did you call me?"

"Danny Boy, like the song." Bragshaw glanced back over his bony shoulder. "No one ever call you that before, Mr. Ransom?"

"Are you chicken, Danny Boy? Dare you."

"No." He swallowed. "I don't think so, sir."

"Right."

Bragshaw pressed a book and a section of the bookcase swung around, presenting a small bar upon which sat a chunky crystal decanter filled with dark, reddish-brown liquid and two cut-crystal glasses. Bragshaw uncorked the decanter and poured two large measures. He brought them over and placed one glass in front of Dan. The other he held aloft.

"To completion." He tipped it up and threw the drink back in one go, slamming the glass down on the desk.

Dan picked up his own glass . . . and paused. The liquid smelled odd. Sweet and musty. Not bourbon or wine. He wasn't sure what it was. Perhaps some sort of cognac?

Bragshaw watched him. "Is there a problem, Mr. Ransom?"

"Oh. No."

The deal. The money. The penthouse. The girls.

"To completion."

Dan raised the glass and took a sip. He grimaced. His stomach rolled. And then—*whatever it took*—he followed Bragshaw's lead and downed the drink in one.

Done deal.

He smirked and reached to put the glass back on the desk. It slipped from his fingers. Darkness swallowed him.

THEY SHOULDN'T BE out this late. October, not long till Halloween, and their parents had told them to come home while it was still light. But they had been playing in the woods and lost track of time, as kids do.

On his own, Dan would never have ventured into Bragshaw Woods. They were private property. They weren't supposed to play there, although a lot of kids did. But with Alice he felt fearless.

She was twelve, two years older than him. Dark-haired, elfin-faced, beautiful and brave. He was sallow-faced, skinny and weak. Alice led the escapades. He followed. He would have followed his sister anywhere. Alice was the only person he truly loved.

That afternoon they had climbed trees, made dens, skimmed

stones across the dirty lake, invented games . . . and then, Alice had said the words he could never resist:

"I dare you."

Dan shook his head. "No."

"C'mon. There's no one there."

Dan had looked up at the old manor house. *Monster mansion. Amityville. Dracula's castle. The* Addams Family *home.*

"What if we get caught?"

"We won't. I told you. We'll just sneak into the grounds, take a few photos and then go home."

Dan hesitated.

"Are you chicken, *Danny Boy*?"

That did it. No one called him chicken or, worse, *Danny Boy*. He hated that nickname.

"Okay," he muttered. "But promise you'll be quick? It's getting dark."

"Okay."

But she didn't promise.

They emerged from the tangled undergrowth and ducked under the wire fence. Up ahead, manicured lawns led up to the manor. No lights were on in the house. So, hopefully, Alice was right and no one was home, unless they just liked the dark. Alice was already halfway across the lawn. She stood in the center and held up her phone. Dan tiptoed tentatively after her.

"Can you make it quick?"

She tutted. "Stop being such a wuss."

She snapped a few photos and started to walk around the side of the house. Dan didn't want to follow her. But he didn't want to stay where he was either. Despite the dark windows, he felt the distinct and unpleasant weight of eyes upon him. Reluctantly, he scuttled after his sister.

At the front of the house, stone steps led up to a massive wooden front door with a heavy iron knocker in the center. Ugly gargoyles snarled from atop pillars either side of the steps. Alice took some photos of them and then leaned and wrapped her arm around one to take a selfie.

"These are soooo creepy," she said with delight.

They were. Dan could almost imagine one of them springing to life as Alice leaned in close, opening its ugly beaked mouth and snapping her head off without even blinking. He pushed the thought away.

"Can we go now?" he asked, hating how pathetic he sounded. "It's getting dark."

"Soon."

Alice hopped up another step, just one away from the front door. She glanced back, eyes gleaming in the twilight. "Dare me?"

"No," he said firmly, panic rising in his chest. "I don't."

"Too late."

She reached for the heavy knocker. But as she did, something strange happened. The door swung open. Alice looked at the door, then back at Dan, then back at the door, then back at Dan. She grinned.

"Don't—" Dan started to say, but she was already gone.

Dan stared after her from the bottom of the steps, the tic in his eye fluttering furiously. The gargoyles leered at him. *Chicken, Danny boy?*

Perhaps she would come back out. Any second now. Any minute. Soon. But the doorway remained empty, the darkness within taunting him.

He should have run. Gone back home for help. But he didn't. He didn't want a beating off their dad, for one thing. And also, something about that half-open door was kind of tempting. Despite the knocking in his knees and the trembling in his gut, Dan crept slowly up the steps and, with a deep breath, like he was about to jump off a cliff, he followed his sister inside.

"Alice?"

The hallway was huge and dimly lit. Ahead of him, a massive staircase wound up into blackness. Either side, pale figures in medieval garb glowered down from the wood-paneled walls. Like they were poised to leap from the picture frames and attack him. Dan backed away.

"Alice?" he hissed. "Where are you?"

No reply. But he thought he could hear *something*. Voices, a low murmuring. Coming from a corridor to his left. He stumbled down it, calling his sister's name. Light was leaking from a door left ajar at the far end. He reached it and paused, debating with himself. *Are you chicken?* And then he clutched the handle and pushed it open.

An office of some sort. Dusty old books lined the walls. In the center was a huge stone desk. But that wasn't what drew Dan's attention. It was the noise—*chanting,* he realized—and the flickering light coming from a corner of the room where a section of the bookcase had been slid aside. He padded toward it. Tentatively, he peered through the gap, and gasped.

A vast, domed temple. Like something out of Greek mythology. Tall stone pillars stretched up to a high, vaulted ceiling. Flaming torches were fixed to the walls. At the front, a hunched figure in dark crimson robes sat upon a throne of yellowed skulls. *Bragshaw*. Rows of black-robed worshippers knelt before him and chanted:

"Completion, completion, completion."

In the center of it all, a huge wicker basket hung, like a giant birdcage, over a massive pit of fire. And inside the cage . . .

"ALICE!"

Dan's eyes shot open. He stared around wildly. Had he been drugged, dreaming?

Alice. The temple. The cage.

"Welcome back, Mr. Ransom."

Comprehension rushed at him like a rocket. He looked up.

Hands chained above his head. He looked down. Naked. Flames licking at the wicker cage beneath his bare feet.

"What the fuck is going on here?" He yanked at the chains. "Get me out of this fucking cage."

Bragshaw eyed him with amusement from his throne of skulls. "But, Mr. Ransom, this is what you came here for. Completion."

And now Dan could hear the robed worshippers chanting again: *Completion, completion, completion.*

This was happening. This was real.

Sweat trickled from his temples and underarms. Even his fucking butt crack was slick with it. He could feel the heat from the fire scorching the balls of his feet. He hopped on his toes.

"Look, I know I said I'd do anything to get this sale, but don't you think this is a bit much?" He attempted a laugh. It sounded more like a sob.

Bragshaw chuckled. "It's quaint that you think this is still about a property, Mr. Ransom."

"Then tell me what it *is* about?"

"Completion is about transferring ownership. But not of bricks and mortar. Ownership of *humanity*."

"Humanity?"

Bragshaw spread out his arms. "Look at the world. A plague is sweeping it. Infection, societal collapse, war, death. How do you think that all started?"

Dan blinked. "Bats?"

Another chuckle. "*I* started it, Mr. Ransom, all those years ago, with the first blood sacrifice—your sister. And now *you* are going to help me complete it. The end of the world as you know it."

Dan felt the cage lurch. It dipped closer to the flames.

"*Wait!*" he cried. "People know I'm here. My agency. Holly. They'll miss me."

Bragshaw's lip curled. "Will they though?"

He beckoned to one of the chanting figures. They rose and

walked over to stand beside him. Then they let their hood fall, revealing long dark hair, pale skin, bee-stung lips. Dan's heart plummeted to his crisping toes.

Holly smiled. "Hello, Ransom."

He stared at her. "Seriously, Hol? You're down with this shit?"

"Very much so."

He tried a different tack. "Look, I know we've had our disagreements, but I'm not that bad. Help me out here. Please?"

"The way you helped your sister?"

"What?"

"Alice. Your sister. You ran away. Left her to die. Never told a soul."

"How do you—"

"I know everything. That was my job, Dan. To find someone like you."

He turned back to Bragshaw. "Is that what this is about? Retribution? Salvation? You want me to confess, beg for forgiveness. I did a bad thing. I know. So bad I literally wiped it from my memory. I'm sorry. There."

Bragshaw sighed. "You give yourself too much credit, Mr. Ransom. This isn't about you. Or even your sister, although it has a certain serendipity. *You* are simply the sacrifice."

The cage lurched and dipped again. The flames licked at the wicker. Dan danced on his tiptoes. *Think, Ransom. Think.* There had to be a way out of this. *Had* to be.

And then, something struck him. "Don't sacrifices have to be pure?"

"Exactly," Bragshaw said. "Which is why you are perfect. A virgin."

Dan stared at him. He started to laugh. "Oh, man. Have you guys made a boo-boo."

"I'm sorry?"

"You will be."

Bragshaw scowled. "For a man about to be burnt to death you seem remarkably cocky, Mr. Ransom."

Dan smiled. "You're not going to burn me to death. Not if you want your completion to succeed."

"I don't understand."

"I'm not a virgin."

"Nice try, Ransom," Holly said. "You told me. You confessed. How all of this cocky arrogance was a front. How you were terrified of intimacy. Scared you wouldn't be able to perform. That's why you had never had sex."

Dan chuckled. "And honestly, Hol, I didn't expect you to fall for it so fucking hard."

Her face darkened. "What the hell d'you mean?"

"It was a *ploy,* to get you to sleep with me. It's what I do. The whole drunk confession thing. Pretending to be a virgin, vulnerable, embarrassed. It's all just an act to get laid."

Holly glared at him. "You're a liar, Ransom."

He shook his head. "No. I *was* a liar, and you sucked it up." He winked at her. "A shame you didn't literally suck it up, of course."

Holly glanced back at Bragshaw, looking panicked. "He's lying. To save his skin."

Bragshaw looked at Dan, frowning. "You're *not* a virgin?"

"Fuck, no."

"You mustn't listen to him—" Holly started to say.

Bagshaw raised a bony hand to silence her. "Olive?" he called.

A second robed figure emerged from the crowd. She dropped her hood. The old hag.

Bragshaw nodded at her. "Tell me. Where lies the truth?"

Olive stared at Dan. She stretched out a bony finger and pointed. He felt something prickle in his mind.

"With him, master."

Bragshaw sighed heavily. "You made a mistake, Holly."

"I'm sorry," she whispered. "It won't happen again."

"No. It won't."

Bragshaw turned, remarkably quickly, and grabbed her around the neck. Holly's face turned red then puce. She scrabbled at Bragshaw's hands, but Dan had been right: those bony fingers were strong, like a vise. Holly's eyeballs bulged, the veins in her neck stood out. Bone cracked, sinew squelched and then—*POP!* Holly's lovely head shot right off.

It bounced down the steps and came to rest at the bottom, almond eyes staring up at Dan in bemusement. Her decapitated body remained standing for a moment, blood spurting from its neck, and then it got with the program and collapsed gracelessly to the floor. Dan thought he caught a glimpse of lacy underpants through her parted robe. Nice.

Bragshaw shook his head regretfully. "Children. They always disappoint you."

Dan swallowed. "O-kay. Well, this is a bit awkward. But, as I'm of no further use to you, then I suppose you can just let me go."

"I'm afraid not," Bragshaw replied. "We'll need to burn you anyway. To dispose of the evidence. You understand."

"NO!!" Dan screamed. "WAIT! I *am* useful. I mean, I can be."

"In what way?"

Dan summoned up his best full-wattage smile. "You need a virgin? Fresh, untainted flesh?"

"Yes?"

"I can get you a virgin. More than one, if you want. It's what you might call my special talent." He nodded at the crone. "Ask your friend over there."

Bragshaw glanced at Olive. She nodded. "He's a vile creature, but he does speak the truth."

"Harsh," Dan muttered.

Bragshaw regarded him for what seemed like an interminable amount of time. Dan's whole body felt like it was slowly crisping, like a chicken on a rotisserie. He'd never realized before that his eyeballs could sweat.

Finally, Bragshaw said, "If I let you go, Mr. Ransom, how do I know I can trust you?"

Dan tried to prop his feet on the edges of the cage, but now his balls were scorching.

"Okay . . . Jesus . . . well, I'd kind of like to survive this whole end-of-the-world scenario. So, if I get you your unpopped cherry, how about you set me up in a nice penthouse somewhere, plenty of ready cash, safe from all the damnation and pestilence shit? That would work for me. Both of us get what we want, right?"

"That can be arranged."

"We have a deal then?"

Another long pause. Then Bragshaw nodded. "We do."

"Excellent." Dan rattled at his chains. "So, d'you think you could get me out of this thing?" He pulled a face. "No offense, but wicker is *so* 1973."

THE OFFICE WAS quiet. A half-empty coffee cup still sat in front of Holly's chair. Shame, Dan thought. Losing her head like that, although decent of Bragshaw to let him keep it as a souvenir. It was going to look good above his bed.

He walked over to his desk. A voice spoke up from the corner. Jack.

"So, how did it go with Bragshaw?"

"He, err, changed his mind."

"Ah . . . well, I hate to say I told you so."

Dan looked over at him. "Do you? Really?"

A flash of yellow teeth. "Don't take it too hard, son. You're young. There'll be other deals."

Actually, there wouldn't, Dan thought. Because he'd just made the biggest—and most final—deal mankind would ever see. Huge, massive, apocalyptic even.

He sat down and propped his feet up on his desk. "You're right, Jack." He grinned. "After all, it's not the end of the world."

The Lion at the Gate

Introduction

When I first met my husband, Neil, we lived in a not-so-great area of Nottingham. We didn't have much cash, and it was all we could afford. Same for most people. At the time, I used to regularly drive along a road called Woodborough Road into the city.

If you know Nottingham, you'll know Woodborough Road. Even if you don't know Nottingham, you'll probably know of a road like it.

Woodborough Road is a long road lined with a mixture of once-grand old houses, run-down terraces and council flats. The sort of road that's fine on the surface, pleasant even. But look closer and you'll notice the disrepair: the overgrown gardens, dogs barking behind locked gates, the smell of weed from open windows. At night, there are stretches where you walk a little faster, clutching your key between your fingers.

One morning I was driving along Woodborough Road and something caught my eye—a large piece of graffiti on the back gate of one of the houses. It wasn't unusual to see graffiti along here, but this piece was out of the ordinary: a massive lion's head with a huge Technicolor mane and black eyes.

Striking, psychedelic and creepy as hell.

Unsurprisingly, it stuck with me. Every morning when I drove past I found myself looking out for the lion. And then, a weird thing happened. Overnight, the lion changed. The mane was now blue instead of multicolored and the angle of the head was slightly different. There also seemed to be flecks of white in the pupils, making them glint with a fierce light.

I supposed the artist had gone back and decided to revise the artwork. But I couldn't shake the feeling that somehow the lion had changed *itself*.

This new lion remained in place for a few weeks until one day I drove past and it was gone. Not even a mark on the gate to show it had ever been there. I felt kind of sad. Obviously, the council must have cleaned the graffiti away . . . but a small part of me couldn't help picturing the great lion pulling itself free from the gate with a huge roar and setting off to prowl around the city.

I never saw the lion again. But if you're ever in Nottingham, driving along the Woodborough Road, keep a lookout. You never know. The lion might be back. Just don't get too close. I have a feeling it bites.

Stiff saw it first. He was good at spotting stuff. Usually stuff that would get us into trouble.

It wasn't like he deliberately went out looking for it. But trouble always seemed to find him. And Stiff couldn't look away. Like a magpie spotting something shiny or a moth throwing itself into the flame.

The day he saw the lion, we were on our way to school. Late. My fault. It usually was. Even if I got up early, some shit would happen that would stop me leaving on time.

I guess that's why I always felt responsible. Because if we hadn't been late, we'd never have taken the cut-through and Stiff would never have seen it.

And maybe, just maybe, they'd all be alive.

But then, as my nan used to say (before she went completely doolally): "Easy to smell the shit when you're stood in it. The secret is not to stand in the shit."

'Course, by that point, she was usually lying in hers, so I guess we all end up in the shit eventually.

"C'MON," CARL PANTED. "We've only got eleven minutes and thirty-five seconds and we've still got point-nine of a mile to go."

He hitched his schoolbag over his shoulder and adopted the half-scuttle, half-jog that passed for a run. Carl was a stout kid. Not fat but stocky. He looked like the sort of kid who would smash heads first and ask questions later. But that was crap. Carl was clever. Like genius clever. He could do math and equations in his head like fucking Stephen Hawking. But he was also soft when it came to normal world stuff. "*Soft as mushy peas,*" Fallow said.

Fallow was not soft. Fallow was hard and sharp, with a temper to match. You had to watch yourself with Fallow. A wrong word could easily end up in a black eye. But he looked out for his friends. And Stiff, Carl and me were his friends. Fuck knows why.

"Shit," he cursed now. "We're not gonna make it."

He was right. No way were we going to get to school on time. Farthing, our freshman Form Tutor, would cream his cords over *that*. He was just waiting for an excuse to give us an exclusion. Most of the teachers at school were okay, but Farthing was a real twat. He got off on making kids' lives that bit worse. And mine wasn't exactly a fairy tale to start with.

"We could always cut through the Oaks," Stiff said. And giggled.

Stiff giggled at all sorts of stuff. For no reason. That was how he got his nickname. Because he was always corpsing. Stiff, geddit?

We all stopped and looked at him. Corporation Oaks. That was what it said on the flaking, moss-crusted street sign, but everyone called it the Oaks, on account—amazingly—of all the oak trees that lined the road, so tall they cast the street into a kind of perpetual twilight.

It was a weird road, because you couldn't drive along it, even though it was wide enough. There were concrete bollards, top and bottom. At the end, before you got to the next street, was a patch of scraggy wasteland. A lot of druggies, tramps and alkies hung around there. Prostitutes too. A couple of years back, some kid got murdered. That's why we weren't supposed to walk that way.

It must have been a posh street once. The houses were huge; three-story Victorian ones with high gates, long gardens and great big windows. They were all divided up into apartments now. But it never looked like anyone was living in them. A lot of the windows were shuttered or boarded up. In winter, even when it was dark, you never saw any lights illuminating the black rectangles of glass.

"We're not supposed to go that way," I said.

Fallow sneered. "Are you feeble, man? It's quicker."

"By about seven minutes and twenty-five seconds," Carl added unhelpfully.

I looked at Stiff, who was silent. Like he knew already he had made a bad call.

I wavered. "I dunno."

"Fine," Fallow said. "Do what you want. It's your crazy mum's fault we're late."

I wanted to defend my mum, but he was right. She was crazy.

Fallow turned, leapfrogged one of the bollards and marched up the middle of the road. Stiff followed. Carl looked at me, shrugged and trotted after them. I stood, staring up at the twisted oaks and looming houses. *Welcome to the jungle,* a low voice in my brain whispered.

I sighed, adjusted my rucksack and shouted:

"Wait up."

IT WAS LATE October. The leaves had lost their fragile grip on the trees. The bare branches made spiky silhouettes against the gray clouds, like someone had snipped jagged strips out of the sky.

Either side, the houses stood silent and still. On our street, the houses were always alive with noise and movement. Washing fluttered on makeshift lines, radios blared, front doors opened and slammed with kids running in and out. And usually, somewhere, there was the sound of sirens. Here, you could barely hear the hum of traffic at the end of the road. Everything was muffled. Dead.

The four of us were quiet too. We walked quickly, but we didn't run. Like it felt wrong to shout or leg it along here, a bit like in the school corridors.

I tried to adopt a casual "who gives a crap?" swagger, like Fallow. But even he was having trouble holding it. Something about the road. It kind of weighed down on you, like a heavy fog or that weird feeling you got in your chest when it was about to thunder.

I was relieved to see we were almost at the end of the road, just a couple more houses to pass, when Stiff said: "Whoa. Look at that."

I wish we hadn't. I wish we had said, *For fuck's sake, Stiff, we haven't got time,* put our heads down and hurried past.

But we didn't. Like lemmings, we all turned and looked.

It was a lion.

Not a real lion. Obviously. That would be stupid. This was Nottingham, not Africa. We didn't even have a zoo. At least, not a proper one. Just one of those baby ones with goats and sheep you could feed (except they always ate the paper bags the food came in, or your clothes if you got too close).

This lion was spray-painted, like graffiti, on a wooden gate in front of one of the houses. It was just the lion's face and it was huge, covering the whole gate, which had to be about six feet high. The colors were weird too. Purple and green with flecks of orange and red. Its mane was a heaving, twisted mass of blues and muddy browns, woven like dreadlocks. And the eyes were black. No irises. Blind, yet it still felt like it was staring right at you.

"What the fuck is *that*?" Fallow muttered.

"A lion," I said.

"Yeah, I know it's a *lion,* but it's a fucking weird-looking lion."

He dumped his bag on the ground and took a couple of steps toward it.

I looked up at the house. I could only see the top half, above the wall. Pitted dark stone, half shrouded in dead ivy; splintered wooden window frames, like rotting black bones. I looked back at the lion.

A voice growled in my head. Low, guttural, threatening.

I BITE, SONNY BOY.

I jumped and glanced behind me, half expecting to see someone standing there. But there was no one, except Stiff and Carl. Stiff looked nervous. Carl was frowning, like he was trying to work something out.

Fallow took another step toward the lion. The voice growled again:

I BITE. AND YOU'LL TASTE SWEET. SWEET AS CHEEKS.

Fallow stretched out a hand to touch the wood. I wanted to tell him to stop, to move away. But, just as I opened my mouth, he leaped back, clutching his hand.

"Owww. *Shit!*"

"What is it? What happened?"

Fallow held up his finger. "Fucking splinter."

I could see a sliver of black wood embedded in his index finger. He yanked it out. Blood bloomed, ripe and red, on his fingertip.

"Shit!" He glared at the lion and spat on the ground. "Fuck this." He snatched his bag up, face dark. "C'mon. Let's get out of here."

He strode off. The rest of us stumbled after him. When Fallow got one of his moods on, you were safer to stay in his wake. Stiff looked guilty, like the splinter had been his fault (which it had, kind of). Carl was mumbling to himself.

"What d'you say?" I asked him.

"Dimensions," he muttered.

"What?"

"Seven by five. Six by three. It's not right. Not the right dimensions."

Carl came out with weird shit sometimes. It was his mad, mathematical brain.

"You've lost me, man," I said.

But it was like he hadn't heard me. As though he was furiously scribbling equations on some mental chalk board in his head.

I left him to it and fell in step beside him. As we reached the bollards, I glanced back. The lion stared out from the gate. But something looked different. Something around the nose, the mouth. Then I realized.

It was obviously just a trick of the light . . . but it looked like it was snarling.

I DIDN'T MEAN to go back. If you'd asked me, I would have said it was the furthest thing from my mind. I mean, I had enough problems. There was Mum, for a start. I loved my mum. I'd never known my dad and she was all I had. But Mum was sick. Not outward sick, not even cancer sick. But in her head sick. It wasn't her body that hurt, it was her brain. I guess a doctor would have said she was depressed. But she wouldn't see a doctor and I was scared shitless that if she did, Social Services would take me away, put me in some care home or something. And everyone knew what happened in those places.

So, Mum and me, we tried to deal with it on our own. I mean, some days she would be okay. She'd get up, get dressed. For a while she even managed to get herself to work. But the last year or so, the good days had dropped right off. She'd lost the job she had cleaning at the council offices. Instead, she did casual work, cleaning for a friend of a friend.

She spent more time lying in bed with the curtains pulled. On those days, I would get myself up, go to school, make dinner then watch some TV or play on my PlayStation for a while before bed. That wasn't so bad.

The bad ones were the manic days. The ones where she was all bright and brittle. You never knew what she'd do when she was like that. Once, I woke up to find her trying to put a plastic bag over my head. Another, she stood in the kitchen slicing at her arm with a razor. Still smiling. Always smiling. Although, after a while, it looked more like a snarl.

This morning, a Sunday, I came downstairs to find her cleaning. She'd taken down all the curtains. All the cutlery was in the sink. The cushions had been thrown off the sofas.

"What are you doing, Mum?"

"Cleaning off all the pawprints, sweetheart."

"What?"

"The filthy beastie has been in here."

"The filthy beastie?"

"It sneaks in while we're sleeping and makes everything dirty, sweetheart. It's full of fleas and disease, so I have to make sure everything is clean."

"Right."

"You haven't touched it, have you, Jay? Have you showered this morning? Did you clean your ears? It can get inside your ears, you know. All the way to your brain."

She advanced toward me, hands sheathed in yellow rubber gloves, brandishing a Brillo pad and a bottle of bleach.

I backed away. "Tell you what, Mum. Why don't I go get you some more cleaning stuff? You don't want to run out."

She paused. Her smile brightened. "Good boy. That's a good idea."

She turned back to the patch of carpet she was scrubbing. There was now a huge white threadbare patch on the gray pile.

I scurried out of the door. Once I was outside, I grabbed my bike and sped off down the road. I wasn't sure where I meant to go. When Mum was like this, I just needed to get away. Maybe to the shops, or the Rec.

I certainly didn't intend to cycle the opposite way, down Woodborough Road to the Oaks. But somehow, that's where I found myself. I paused at the bottom of the street, staring up. As always, it was silent and dark. I mean, I suppose that wasn't so weird. It was early on a Sunday and most people would still be in bed. Still, I couldn't quite contain a shiver. I rubbed my arms. Stupid. In my haste to get out of the house, I'd forgotten my hoodie.

The next thing I did was even more stupid. I climbed off my bike and wheeled it between the bollards, up the Oaks. I walked steadily, not fast, not slow, trying to ignore the creeping feeling at the back of my neck, the sort you got when invisible eyes were crawling all over you. Two thirds of the way up, I stopped.

The lion was still there. No one had scrubbed it off or painted over it—and normally the council were shit hot at cleaning up graffiti.

Something about it was different, though. The colors. They looked brighter. Not as dark and sludgy. There were flecks of light in those huge dark eyes. And the mouth. No trick of the light. The mouth had definitely changed. Before, it had been closed. Now, one corner of the lip curled up, revealing a glimpse of sharp, yellow teeth.

Obviously, rationally, I knew that whoever had painted it must have changed it. *Irrationally,* I couldn't shake the image of the lion moving, stretching, yawning.

I forced myself to walk closer. In my head, a voice growled: *WHAT DO WE HAVE HERE? A FILTHY LITTLE BEASTIE.*

No, I thought. I'm not. And you're just a painting. Just a stupid bit of graffiti. And, to prove it, I reached out a hand and touched the wood . . .

Except . . .

I snatched my hand back

No, no, no.

It wasn't wood.

It felt like . . .

Fur.

"I NEED TO talk to you."

Carl didn't look up. He sat on his bed, in his pajamas, intent on some ancient game on his Xbox. Carl liked playing old games. Something about coding. Fuck knows. A plate of uneaten toast sat next to him. There were more plates, smeared with leftover food, on the desk by his bed and on the floor. Dirty cutlery too. *Filthy.* I almost stood on a bread knife lying on the carpet.

"What are you doing here?" he said, and decapitated a badly pixelated zombie.

"Your mum let me in. Said you'd been stuck up here all morning. And to tell you to eat your breakfast."

Carl stared at the screen. "I'm busy."

"It's about the lion."

"What lion?"

"The lion at the gate."

I saw his hand waver, just a fraction. Blood spatter filled the screen.

"Shit!" He threw down the controller in disgust. "Look what you made me do."

I grabbed the controller, yanked it out of the Xbox and lobbed it across the room. "Boo-fucking-hoo."

Carl stared at me. His big, round face looked bewildered and hurt. I felt bad. I lost my temper sometimes. I shouldn't. I sat on the bed. "Sorry. I'm sorry. But it's important. What did you mean about the dimensions?"

"It was nothing."

"No. It meant something."

He sighed. "The dimensions of the painting are seven foot by five foot."

"And?"

"The gate is six foot by three foot."

"I don't understand?"

"The lion is bigger than the gate."

"You're fucking with me."

"No."

"That's impossible."

"I know."

"You must be wrong. I mean, you didn't actually measure it."

"I didn't need to."

I stared at him. He shook his head. "Fine. I'll show you." He slid off the bed and padded over to his desk. "I need a tape measure."

He fumbled in the drawers. I waited a beat and then I crouched down, picked up the bread knife and slid it into my pocket.

WE CYCLED BACK to Woodborough Road. Carl's bike was a lot newer and cooler than mine. But then, Carl's mum and dad had more money than the rest of us. They lived on a new estate, in a big house with a proper garden and shit. They both had cars and Carl always had the latest phone and sneakers. Carl was a friend, but sometimes I felt jealous of his life; resentful of the fact that he just took all this stuff for granted. Occasionally, even though it felt shit to admit it, I kind of hated him.

We reached the Oaks and wheeled our bikes up to the gate. We laid them down on the ground and stared at the lion. In the short time I'd been away it had changed again. The colors seemed even brighter. The light in the dark chasms of its eyes gleamed. The lips revealed more teeth.

I BITE. REMEMBER. I BITE.

"It looks different," Carl said.

"I know."

He frowned and took out his tape measure. "I need you to hold one end."

I didn't really want to get close to the lion again, but I obliged. We measured the gate first. I was the tallest, so I stretched up to reach the top. Carl knelt at the bottom, on the dusty ground.

"Six foot," he said, and showed me.

We measured side to side, the lion's mane just above our heads.

"Three foot. Now the lion."

I took the end of the tape measure and stretched it to the top of the lion's head. I stood on tiptoes. I strained. I couldn't reach. It didn't make sense. I knew what my eyes were telling me. But I also knew that there was no way I could reach the tip of that twisty, dreadlocked mane.

"See," Carl said. "That's already way over six foot five and you haven't reached the top."

I lowered the tape measure, heart thudding. He was right.

"Sideways," I said, feeling a bit irritated at his smugness.

We stretched the tape measure from jaw to jaw.

"Five foot."

"Fuck!"

Carl grinned triumphantly. Suddenly cocky.

TASTY, SWEETCHEEKS.

He reached out to pat the wood.

"I told you. Wrong—"

I wanted to warn him. But it happened so quickly. The roar rose in my head. Carl's grin morphed into a scream.

"MY ARM!!"

But his arm wasn't there. It was in the lion's jaws. Up to the elbow and being dragged in even further. I could see blood oozing out of the wood, and I could hear an awful, hideous crunching sound as the bones were pulverized.

"Jay, help me!"

I grabbed his other arm, tried to yank him back. But it was no good. Then I remembered the knife. I pulled it out of my pocket and stabbed at the lion. I gouged at its eyes, its snout. But it was difficult because Carl kept writhing around screaming and, in my fear and frenzy, I wasn't sure if I was stabbing at the lion or Carl anymore.

Finally, the screams and the roars subsided. I stepped away. Carl slid slowly down the gate. His arm was a mangled mess. His chest and face were a mass of blood. One eye was gone.

I stared at him. At the blood. Pooling on the ground, dripping from the lion's jaws.

RUN, LITTLE BEASTIE. RUN.

I ran, the roars still echoing in my ears.

THEY FOUND CARL's body the next day. What was left of it. All the newspapers said he had been stabbed, mutilated. They didn't say anything about being savaged and half eaten. But I suppose they were trying to cover that bit up.

They came to talk to me, of course. I was the last person to see him alive. I told them I had called for him that day, we'd rode around on our bikes and then gone our separate ways. I didn't know what he was doing on Corporation Oaks. My mum told me never to go up there.

They asked me if I had ever argued with Carl and if I owned a knife. I told them no, he was my friend. And no, I didn't carry a knife.

I'd thrown it in the canal by then, still slimy with his blood.

FOR A COUPLE of weeks afterward, when we walked past the end of the Oaks, the road was bustling with activity. Almost like a normal street. Except the people walking around, talking and squinting at the ground, wore police uniforms and weird white suits.

"I bet some fucking pedo did it," Fallow muttered as we stood and watched.

"Or some nut job out of the hospital," Stiff giggled.

I stayed silent. I couldn't tell Fallow or Stiff what had really happened. They'd have thought *I* was a nut job.

Afterward, I would think that maybe I *should* have said something. Warned them. And maybe, a couple of weeks later, when they suggested we go back and see where it had happened, faces glowing with morbid glee, I should have tried harder to talk them out of it. But I didn't.

LET THEM SEE, a low voice in my head had purred. *FILTHY LITTLE BEASTIES.*

POLICE TAPE FLUTTERED in the breeze like leftover party decorations. A few people had laid flowers. They were mostly wilted and dying.

As we walked along the Oaks, the same oppressive heaviness bore down on me. Like the trees and houses were closing in. I could hear a different sound in my head now. Not roaring. A slow, steady rustling. Several times I glanced behind me, as if I might spot something creeping through the overgrown grass verges.

The houses looked as dead and empty as ever. I supposed the

police must have knocked on doors, talked to people. Yet, for some reason, I felt that these doors had never been opened. Not to the police. Not to anyone.

We approached the gate. Stiff pointed at a large, rusty-looking stain on the ground.

"Shit. Blood."

Fallow whistled. "That's a fuckload of blood. But then, he *was* a fat bastard."

Stiff chortled. I thought how much he annoyed me sometimes. Fallow too. They hadn't said a kind word about Carl since he died. Just made stupid jokes.

I walked past them. I stared at the gate.

The lion was gone.

That wasn't a surprise. I'd half expected the gate to have been scrubbed clean.

The surprise was what was in its place.

A twisted mass of green, yellow, orange and brown. It curled around and around. Like a giant kaleidoscope. Hypnotic. Somewhere amid the mass of tensed coils, two red eyes burned.

"What the fuck is *that*?" Fallow said from behind me.

"A snake," I said.

SOFTLY, SOFTLY, SQUEEZY MONKEY.

My fingers clenched and unclenched.

"A constrictor."

Gloria

Introduction

Some characters stick with you.

Not necessarily the main ones.

Or the good guys.

Often, it's the side characters. The ones who still have a story to tell.

Like Gloria.

Gloria first appeared in my second novel, *The Hiding Place*. A delicate, blonde debt collector, she was terrifying, comic and a lot of fun to write. Despite some of her more unpleasant tendencies, I had a huge soft spot for Gloria, and always felt that there was a possibility that she might one day return (no spoilers).

When I was struggling to write the book that never was, I decided to bring Gloria back. And I was right—she really did have a lot more to give. Her parts were the only ones I enjoyed writing during that tough time. When that book eventually got put to one side, my editor, Max, suggested that perhaps I could still use them in one of my short stories.

It was a great idea. I took those sections out and started to shape them into another outing for Gloria. As the idea developed, I thought it might be fun for Gloria to meet a character from one of my other books. I've always said my books exist in the same universe, and a chance encounter between these two—a hardened mercenary and a girl with a strange gift—seemed perfect. I hope you agree.

It felt good to have Gloria back.

I have a feeling we've not seen the last of her.

She was dyeing her hair in the hotel bathroom when the phone pinged. She cursed, but quickly wrapped a towel around her head and snatched it up from the toilet lid. She glanced at the text.

"New job?"

No niceties. Straight to business.

"What sort?" she typed back.

"Clean-up."

She sucked air between her teeth. Clean-ups were her least favorite type of job. Once, she would have said they were beneath her. But times changed. So did the people in charge. Gloria had been out of the game for a while and was still working her way back up the food chain. She was one of the few with both the stomach and the skills for such jobs. And they paid well.

"Where?" she typed.

An address in north London popped up. About a four-hour drive away.

"OK."

She finished her hair then dumped the stained towels into a black trash bag. She stuffed this into the larger of her two suitcases, which contained several changes of clothes, and selected a T-shirt and jeans. A slimmer case contained a number of uniforms, folded neatly. Gloria picked out the one that was appropriate for today: a green tunic with "CCS" embroidered on the chest.

After drying her newly auburn hair and putting it up into a neat bun, she tidied the room, wiped down the surfaces for prints and left it, possibly looking a little cleaner than it had been when she arrived.

On her way out, she dropped her room card into the express check-out box in the lobby. Yesterday evening, when Gloria had arrived at the hotel, the receptionist had greeted a woman with a strange smile and white hair. This afternoon, a different receptionist

would barely notice a woman with red hair checking out. This satisfied.

The man on the desk glanced up briefly and uttered a perfunc-
tory "Goodbye."

Gloria chirped, "Thank you," cheerily and headed out of the
double doors, her smile snapping off.

She had parked her van in a far corner, away from the CCTV and
other prying eyes. It contained the rest of the things she needed for
her job: a selection of magnetic car signs—*Carli's Elderly Care.*
Fuzzy Bear Nursery. Babs Builders. Dotty's Dog Walking—as well
as cleaning equipment, a toolbox, a chainsaw, protective clothing
and, stored safely in a compartment beneath the floor, a handgun.
Gloria loaded her cases in the back and applied today's signs to the
van: *Carrie's Cleaning Services.* Then she climbed into the driver's
side.

Before she pulled off, she checked herself in the rearview mirror.
It was fair to say that she wasn't the beauty she had once been. Before, she had turned heads. Now, she drew glances for different reasons.

The once-dazzling smile was lopsided, dragged down by nerve
damage on one side of her face. A brutal indentation crossed her
forehead like a lobotomy scar. She had sacrificed two fingers on her
left hand and her beautiful blonde hair, which the doctors had shorn
to stitch her skull back together, had grown back pure white.

Gloria didn't remember much about the fall. She had been on a
job—debt recovery—and it had led her to an old, abandoned mine.
Something had gone wrong. She had plunged through a sinkhole
and been left for dead, buried under rubble for days. Somehow, incredibly, she had clawed her way out and been discovered at the side
of a country lane by a passing car. The driver had taken her to the
hospital, where the doctors had told her that it was a "miracle" she
was alive. If you could call it that. Often, Gloria felt as if she had
returned from somewhere, but not all the way.

Still, the new red hair suited her, and already she felt the familiar anticipation in her stomach. Even though it was her least favorite type of job, she always got a buzz from her work.

Gloria tilted her head and smiled her warped half-smile.

It felt good to be back.

SHE ARRIVED AT the dingy basement apartment just as the sun started to dip below the horizon. A key had been left for her, wedged with putty into the bottom of a drainpipe.

Gloria let herself in, walked into the living area and stared around the room. Plastic sheets covered the floor, but the blood spatter had still made it high up the walls. The sheets themselves were awash with more dried blood and other fluids. The victim, or what remained of her, lay in the middle.

Nasty. Very nasty. Gloria had seen some pretty stomach-churning crime scenes, many of her own making. But this was something else. She stepped carefully around the body. She didn't let herself wonder what kind of person could do this, or whether the woman had suffered. Obviously, she had. Gloria didn't like what she was seeing, but she wasn't paid to like what had happened here. She was paid to deal with it. And unfortunately, that meant things were about to get even nastier.

Gloria opened her case and took out the chainsaw.

It took her five hours to break the body down into manageable parts, stuff them into heavy black sacks and scrub and bleach the whole room.

Finally, sweat-drenched and filthy, Gloria looked around, satisfied. This was grunt work, but it was well-paid grunt work. She changed out of her bloody overalls, stuffed those in the sacks and slipped on a spare set. Then she heaved the black sacks out of the apartment, back up the steps and into her van. To anyone watching, she was just a cleaner taking away bags of rubbish. Finally, van loaded, property secured, she made a call. A transfer of money was paid, and Gloria drove off.

She knew a builder who was happy to accommodate certain things—usually bodies—that needed to disappear. Within an hour, the sacks were submerged beneath concrete, more money had exchanged hands, along with some pleasantries, and Gloria was back on the road.

Scary, how easy it was to make someone disappear.

Gloria yawned. She ached and she was hungry. She needed to find somewhere to get some food and recharge. A service station would do. Gloria liked service stations. They were convenient and comfortingly impersonal, full of transient people. There was a pleasure to be taken in impermanence. A feeling of not being here or there. More and more since the fall, Gloria felt that this *in between* place was where she resided now.

She pulled into a Welcome Break she had frequented in the past. In a secluded corner of the parking lot, she changed the signs on her van again. Now they read: *Office Management Solutions*. A title vague enough to mean whatever you wanted it to without actually meaning anything at all.

In the back of the van, she changed into a smartish suit, put her hair up and slipped on some clear-lensed glasses. Then she climbed out, walked across the parking lot and into the fast-food restaurant. She ordered a burger and a coffee and ate her late dinner at a corner table.

People came and went—workmen in fluorescent jackets, young couples, worn-down-looking families with screaming kids. No one took any notice of her. No one looked at anyone. Human interaction as fast and disposable as the food.

Gloria was about to finish her coffee and move on when she heard the voice:

Did it hurt?

She turned. The voice had sounded close, intimate, like someone had bent and whispered in her ear. But there was no one there, and all the surrounding tables were empty.

Gloria frowned and reached for her cup.

Did it hurt? When you fell?

She jumped, the coffee cup wobbling in her hand. She put it down with a clatter and looked around. The restaurant had emptied out since her arrival. It was getting late now. Only a few patrons remained: an elderly couple, a workman, a young man in a cheap suit staring at his phone (a sales rep, she guessed) and a few tables away . . . a girl.

Around eight or nine. Slight, with dark hair pulled back into a messy ponytail. Her face was thin and drawn, dark circles shadowing her eyes. She sat alone, although a cup across from her suggested an adult was nearby, perhaps in the toilets.

The girl stared at Gloria, her blue gaze unwavering. No one looked at Gloria like that. Even before she fell. Gloria felt a strange schism run through her—and then realized it was a shiver. What the hell?

She pushed her coffee cup aside and stood, meaning to walk out of the restaurant. But then she paused. *No one looked at her like that.* And she had a sudden urge to know why this girl did.

She walked over to her. "Didn't your mummy tell you it's rude to stare?"

The girl had the good grace to blush. "I'm sorry."

"Don't be." Gloria pulled out the chair opposite the girl and sat down. "You asked me a question."

The girl's eyes widened. "You *heard* me?"

Gloria nodded. "Cute trick."

"It's not a trick."

Gloria regarded the girl curiously. She had seen a lot of crazy things in her life. The idea that this little girl possessed some kind of—what did they call it?—telekinesis, wasn't the craziest. But it wasn't far off.

"What's your name? Carrie?"

The girl jutted out her chin. Attitude. Gloria liked it. "Alice," she said.

"Is that your real name?"

"Is Gloria yours?"

Gloria stared at her—and then laughed. "You're good."

They regarded each other with a cautious respect.

"You do that a lot?" Gloria asked. "Get inside people's heads?"

"No . . . Fra— . . . *Mum* wouldn't like it."

Gloria noted the stumble. "You asked if it hurt. What did you mean?"

"You fell," Alice said.

"I was in an accident. I almost died. But I came back."

Alice tilted her head. "Did you?"

Damn it. There it was again, that whisper of ice.

"You're saying I'm a ghost?"

"I don't know what you are."

Gloria barked out a short laugh. "You probably don't want to, sweetie."

Most of Gloria's life had been a gradual erosion of her own humanity. She had hurt, maimed and killed and felt no or little remorse. It wasn't that the emotion was missing in her. She was aware of it. But compassion and morality are partly learned behaviors. If no one teaches them to you at the start of your development, they never grow and blossom. Like an unused limb, they wither, blacken and fall away.

Gloria couldn't blame her parents, not really. They hadn't been cruel, but neither had they been kind. Maybe she should blame the gymnastic coach who fingered her from age eight. Or the boyfriend who had raped her at knifepoint. Perhaps the reason she liked hurting others was because it helped to ease her own hurt inside. Or perhaps in each man that she tortured she saw a little of her abusers.

Gloria wasn't sure that, after thirty-nine years, the origin story was relevant now. She was who she was.

Gloria.

But that wasn't even her name. Just the title of an old song.

"How do you know this stuff?" she asked Alice.

The girl shrugged. "I just do. Sometimes, I . . . I visit this place—the beach."

"The beach? Sounds nice."

"It's not. I think it's . . . somewhere in between."

Gloria frowned. "In between what?"

"This place and there."

"Helpful. Where's 'there'?"

"Across the dark water."

Gloria swallowed. The dark water. So dark. So cold.

"You don't remember?" Alice asked.

"No." More sharply. Because it was a lie.

Gloria remembered falling. She remembered the cold. Such cold. It seeped inside and wrapped itself around her bones. She remembered thinking that she was ready to welcome death. But death never came. Even he had rejected her. Instead, as she lay there, an eager and willing corpse, something else had crept in.

Gloria had once read about an insect that would lay its eggs inside another, bigger insect. When they hatched, the young would slowly devour their host from within so that eventually there was nothing left but a shell.

She wondered if this was what had happened to her. Something else jostled for precedence in her mind. She could feel its weight, hear it whisper. She had come back, but she had brought something with her. And now, bit by bit, more of her "self" was being eaten away. But did it really matter? Could she really mourn a self that had been rotten from the start? And once all the rot was eaten out, what would be left?

Alice lifted a rucksack onto her lap. Purple, with flowers on it. Something rattled inside. *Clickety-click.* Alice took out a smooth, shiny pebble.

She held it out to Gloria. "Here."

Gloria took the white-and-brown stone and turned it over in her hand.

"What do I want a pebble for?" she asked.

"To help you remember."

"Maybe I don't want to."

"Maybe you came back for a reason—" The girl's face suddenly tensed.

"Excuse me, but who the hell are you?" a voice demanded.

Gloria turned. A stringy woman with dark hair and a sharp face stood by the table, glaring at her. Not angry, she thought. Scared. As the woman took in Gloria's face, Gloria saw her flinch. She stood. "I was just going."

"Why were you talking to my daughter?" the woman snapped.

Gloria held up the pebble. "Your daughter dropped this."

The woman recoiled. "Take it. Take it and leave us alone."

"Fine." Gloria slipped the pebble into her pocket and smiled at the woman. Then she glanced at Alice.

"Stay safe—and don't talk to strangers."

GLORIA WALKED BACK to her van and climbed in. The encounter with the girl had unnerved her. She needed to relax. She selected some music from her iPod—an eighties compilation—and checked Google for the nearest motels. It told her there was one at the next service station, thirty-five minutes away.

She stuck the van into gear and was about to pull out of the parking space when she saw Alice and her mother emerge from the restaurant. They were followed almost immediately by the sales rep who had been sitting nearby. Gloria frowned. Coincidence, perhaps.

She watched the mother and daughter walk over to a battered silver car and climb in. The sales rep turned right and got into an equally battered-looking green VW.

Gloria felt her antennae twitch. Sales reps usually drove new cars. Okay, so maybe she had pegged his occupation wrong. But still. Something felt off. The mother reversed out of her space and drove toward the exit. Seconds later, the rep followed. Gloria stared after them, biting her lip. It was none of her business. The girl and her mother were strangers.

She chewed her lip harder, till she tasted blood. The taste was pleasurable. She licked her lips. Then she quickly rubbed at them with her sleeve, pulled out of her space with a squeal of tires and accelerated after the green car.

After ten miles Gloria was damn sure the rep was following Alice and her mother. He was good, staying just far enough back, always a car behind, but still never too far that he let them out of sight. However, he was so intent on not being spotted that he hadn't noticed he too was being tailed.

Alice and her mother passed the motel Gloria had been considering and drove farther on until the sign for another motel and rest stop drew into view on their left. The woman signaled and turned onto the off-ramp. So did the green car. Gloria hung back behind a blue camper van and then pulled off the highway after them.

The woman followed the signs for the motel. The green car drove past, toward the rest area and gas station. Gloria frowned. Perhaps she'd been wrong. Too many years of thinking the worst of people had raised her suspicion levels to near-paranoia. In which case, she might as well just bed down here tonight and forget about the girl and the rep.

On the other hand, her instincts were seldom wrong. Gloria followed the green car into the rest-stop parking lot and pulled into a space a few rows down. Her antennae tweaked again. The rep had chosen a space a fair distance back from the entrance to the rest stop, even though there were plenty free. He had tucked his car into a far corner, in the shadow of a large tree and, more crucially, just a short walk away from the motel. Gloria's hands tightened on the wheel. It was what she would have done.

She turned the engine off and waited. After a few minutes, the rep climbed out of his car and walked to the trunk. Gloria reached into the glovebox and took out a small pair of high-powered binoculars.

She focused them on the rep. Up close, he was younger than she had first thought. Maybe mid-twenties, chin speckled with faint stubble, cheeks scattered with the remnants of teenage acne. *This is how it starts,* Gloria thought. Not the first job, or the second. Those you can forget, put behind you. The third and fourth are what mark this as your career. A life lived on the edges, in the shadows, on the dark, unlit roads. A life that usually ended suddenly, bloodily.

The rep slipped off his suit jacket and took out a dark hoodie, which he pulled on over his shirt. Next, a grubby windbreaker. He affixed something to his lapel, a name badge. Gloria zoomed in. She couldn't quite make out the name, but she recognized the logo of the budget motel. The one Alice and her mother were staying at. *Of course.* The rep reached into the trunk again and slipped something into his pocket. Gloria adjusted the binoculars. A handgun. Modified, by the looks of it. She clicked her tongue against her teeth. Sometimes, she hated being right.

Finally, the rep grabbed a flashlight, then he slammed the trunk shut and walked across the parking lot. Gloria watched him for a moment. Who wanted to kill a young mother and her daughter? Normally, she didn't ask why. People killed for many reasons. Some personal. Some business. She had never really questioned it, nor had second thoughts about her own role in things.

Gloria had always found it hard to *feel* for people. She lacked empathy, which was why she was good at what she did. Since the fall, it was something more. Some days, she felt like she was re-learning how to be human. But tonight, talking to the girl, she had felt something inside her stirring . . .

Did it hurt?

Fuck it. This was not her problem. Gloria turned on the ignition. Then turned it off again.

The rep was young. But so was Alice. Sometimes you had to

make hard choices. Of course, the easy choice would be to walk away. Someone would die tonight. People died every night.

The only question here was who?

And that was up to her.

THE BUDGET MOTEL had only two stories. There would be card keys to grant access to the bedrooms. At the far end of the ground floor was an emergency fire exit. The only other way out or in. In the small reception, a bored young woman sat at a desk, yawning and staring at her smartphone.

Gloria watched as the rep walked in and greeted her. The woman put down her phone and smiled. There was a conversation. Gloria could see the young woman laugh, obviously flirting a little. Then she rose, walked into the back office and re-emerged in a coat with a bag slung over her shoulder. The rep waved goodbye and took her place at the desk. He sat back in the chair, took out his phone, assuming the same position as the woman had. After a few minutes, a red Toyota pulled slowly past the motel, tooted its horn and drove away.

The rep raised a hand. And then his demeanor abruptly changed. He put down the phone, sat up straighter and pulled his chair up to the desk. He bent over the computer and started tapping at keys. He was searching for the room the girl and her mother were staying in, Gloria thought. Had he been given their names? Or was he just looking for the most recent check-in?

Either way, now was her moment.

Gloria pocketed her binoculars, walked across the parking lot and pushed open the doors to reception. The rep looked up, startled. It was late, and quiet. He had obviously counted on being alone.

He forced a smile. "Hi. Can I help—"

His words faltered as Gloria stepped into the light. She knew full well the bright spotlights in the reception area were harsh and unforgiving, illuminating every scar and mutilation in all its raw ugliness.

She smiled sweetly back. "You might want to pop that jaw shut before someone dislocates it."

Then she pulled up a chair and sat down opposite him, neatly crossing her legs.

The rep—"Gary Brown," his name tag read—cleared his throat. "Sorry. Would you like to book a room?"

"No."

"Oh."

"I would like to save you, Gary."

He frowned. "I'm sorry?"

"You will be if you don't listen to me. Very carefully." She leaned forward. "Don't do it, sweetie."

He swallowed, eyes flicking around nervously. "Do what?"

"Kill the woman and the girl."

His face fell. "I have no idea what you're talking about."

Gloria waved a hand. "Don't bullshit me. I know why you're here. I know what you're planning, and I'm telling you—it's a big mistake. Huge."

"You're crazy."

"Quite possibly. But I used to be like you. Well, a better-dressed and more intelligent version. But I know how this starts. And I know how it ends for most people in this business. However much money they are paying you, whatever they have over you, it's not worth it."

A hesitation as he decided whether to keep up the denials. Then his eyes hardened. "You don't know that. You don't know me."

"Trust me—I know. That's why I'm going to give you a chance. Get up, walk out of here and leave with your soul still mostly intact."

A sneering grin. "Maybe I don't have a soul. Maybe this is what I am—a killer."

"Really?" Gloria raised an eyebrow. "You ever kill a woman before, or a child?"

She saw his Adam's apple bob.

"No. And I don't think you have it in you, Gary. Not when it really comes down to it. Even if you do, it will haunt you. You'll see their faces. Every night. You'll remember their eyes when you snatched their lives away from them. But that's the good bit. The worst is when that stops. When you stop feeling. When you start to go numb from the inside out. But just occasionally, you feel this burn where your heart used to be, like a phantom limb."

He stared at her. Gloria let her words sink in and then stood.

"I'm going to leave, Gary. Give you a bit of time to think about it. Two minutes, shall we say? Be smart. I promise, if you do, I won't hurt you."

Gloria strode across reception and out of the door. She didn't look back. She walked briskly to the car, let herself in and sat, waiting.

Precisely one minute and twelve seconds later she saw Gary cross the parking lot. He reached his car. The driver's door opened. Gary slipped inside and sat down.

Gloria leaned forward and pressed the barrel of the gun against his head.

His wide eyes met hers in the rearview mirror.

"You . . . you promised you wouldn't kill me."

Gloria smiled at him from the backseat.

"No, hun. I promised I wouldn't hurt you."

She pulled the trigger.

THE CALL CAME in the early hours. They often did. Gloria was awake, as she often was. Sleep did not come easily to her and, when it did, it brought wraiths and demons.

She had left Gary's body in the trunk of his car. It would be some time before he was discovered. He should have realized she couldn't let him live. He might go back for Alice and her mother. Gloria had just needed to get him out of the motel so she could kill him somewhere quietly.

Gloria yawned then reached for her phone and read the text message.

Another clean-up job for the same client. She thought about the remains of the last victim. Nasty.

She typed: "Another female?"

The reply came: "Possibly two. Any problem with that?"

Any problem? A good question.

Gloria stared at the phone. Was this the part in the story where there came a reckoning? Pick a side. Dark or light. Red pill or blue pill. Heaven or hell. Good or evil.

She reached for the pebble on the bedside table, feeling its smooth, cool weight.

Maybe you came back for a reason.

And maybe redemption was overrated.

After a moment, Gloria replied.

I'm Not Ted

Introduction

Sometimes, it's just a line.

Often, you have no idea where it came from.

But it seems like the start of something.

I'm Not Ted.

It just popped into my head.

I don't know any Teds.

I wasn't thinking about Teds.

But still, there it was—*I'm Not Ted.*

A story waiting to be told. Who was Ted? Why was he in denial? Where was the real Ted?

I needed to know. I needed the rest of the story—and so I wrote it.

This one is short and sweet. To that end, so is the introduction.

And if you do happen to know a Ted, please say hi!

"I'm not Ted."

"Of course you are, sir." The security guard jabbed a plump finger at his clipboard. "You're on my list. See."

I saw. It wasn't much of a list. Just one name. In capitals. Underscored. *TED 1509*.

Beside it, a time had been jotted down: *12 noon*. I glanced at the clock. Four minutes past. I was late. And, of course, I wasn't Ted.

"I think you must be mistaken."

"Oh no, sir."

"Oh, yes."

"The department doesn't tolerate mistakes."

The department? What the hell? I looked around. We were standing in a large foyer. Huge. All gray and black chrome. Even the floor. Large monitors were set into the walls. They all showed the same thing. Three words. *The Elevation Department*.

Weird didn't really cover it.

I cleared my throat. "Where am I, exactly?"

"The Elevation Department, sir."

"I can see that. What *is* the Elevation Department?"

"It's where you're elevated, sir."

"To where?"

"The next level."

"Which is?"

"The level up from this."

"And what happens there?"

"I don't know, sir. I've never been elevated."

We stared at each other. The guard wore a blue uniform with gold cuffs. The embroidery looked like tiny wings. His face was bland and forgettable. If I blinked too long, I'd probably struggle to recognize him again.

"O-kay," I said, refusing to be beaten. "How did I get here?"

"You arrived."

"From?"

"Well, wherever you came from, sir."

"Which is?"

"You don't know where you came from?"

A fair point. I tried to remember. I had been . . . at home. I had a vague impression of an apartment, somewhere. I was lying on a sofa. There was a cat. Tabby, hard green eyes. But everything was murky, indistinct. I couldn't remember where the apartment was or even who *I* was. But I still felt pretty certain who I *wasn't*.

"Look, why do you think I'm Ted?"

The guard looked at me strangely. "Well, it says right here, for a start."

He leaned forward and tapped my chest. Fingernails clicked on laminate. I glanced down. A security pass was secured to the pocket of my suit. I hadn't put it there. I was pretty sure I didn't own a suit. I was more a jeans and T-shirts kind of guy. I reached down and unclipped the pass. The face looking back at me was definitely my face. But different. I looked kind of pissed. Like my evil twin.

Underneath the photograph: *TED 1509.*

I looked back up at the guard. This was something of a conundrum. I mean, I still knew I wasn't Ted. But why did I have his pass? And suit. And . . . I patted my pockets and produced a set of car keys.

The guard frowned. "Oh, goodness. Has no one parked your car for you, sir? I'm so sorry." He clicked his fingers.

I turned. Through the plate glass that formed the front of the building, I could see a red Ferrari parked outside at a rakish angle. The license plate read, somewhat predictably: *TED 1509.*

A Ferrari? I'd always dreamed of owning a Ferrari, but my meager salary would only stretch to a moped. A jolt, as I realized I had remembered something else: I was poor. Great.

Out of nowhere, a skinny youth in a white shirt and black trousers appeared.

"Roy, could you park Ted's car for him," the guard instructed.

"Certainly."

Roy held out his hand. I looked helplessly at the keys and then handed them over.

"That's not my car," I said.

Roy looked confused. "I'm sorry, sir?"

"Just go and park it," the guard said.

Roy scurried off.

This couldn't go on. I had to get out of here.

"Look," I said patiently. "I need to speak to the person in charge."

The guard shuffled uncomfortably. "That could be difficult."

"Why? Isn't he here?"

"Oh, he's here."

"So—go get him."

"I can't."

I sighed. "Is anyone actually in charge here?"

"Yes . . ." A pained look. "You are, sir."

WE GLIDED UPWARD in a sleek black elevator lit with tiny spots on the ceiling and walls that looked like stars. Like we were in our own mini universe. Music played in the background. That sort of ambient, ethereal music you get in spas, or rehab.

"You do understand I'm not Ted," I said.

The guard kept his eyes on the floor, numbers ticking past.

"I thought you'd like to see your living quarters before you start work," he said.

"What exactly does Ted do here?"

"He runs the department."

"Which involves?"

"Elevation."

Of course it fucking does.

I stared at the numbers. They went all the way up to 111. At 110, we stopped. The door slid open.

"Whoa!"

I stared around. A massive open-plan space spread out before me. High ceilings, expensive furniture arranged around a roaring fire. In one corner, a spiral staircase wound up to another level. A sleek chrome kitchen took up one end of the room and floor-to-ceiling windows offered a breathtaking 360-degree view of pure blue skies and fluffy white clouds. *Just how fucking high up were we?*

"Is everything to your liking?" the guard asked.

"This is crazy."

I walked across the living area, ran a hand over the soft brown leather sofa, imagined lying on it, chilling with a drink and . . . something orange flitted past the corner of my eye. I spun round. A long tail disappeared behind one of the stylish armchairs.

The guard frowned. "Is something wrong, sir?"

"Did you see that cat?"

"Cat?"

"Yeah. It just ran past."

I hurried over to the armchair and peered behind it. No cat. I looked around. No sign of a cat, not even a ginger hair. I frowned. That was weird. Well, even *more* weird.

"Why don't I show you the rest of the apartment?" the guard said hurriedly.

"How much more is there?" I asked.

"Five bedrooms, four bathrooms, plus the gym, cinema room, sauna, library, oh, and the *pièce de résistance*—the heated rooftop pool and bar area."

"Rooftop pool?" I barked out a short laugh. "Yeah, I'd like to see that."

"Just this way."

I followed him across the polished floor to the spiral staircase. It curved up past the windows to another door at the top. The guard dutifully held it open, and I stepped outside.

Stunning didn't cover it. A massive swimming pool (at least thirty meters) ran almost the length of the roof. The azure water sparkled in the sun. Arranged around it were half a dozen sun loungers and umbrellas. To my right, a small area had been converted into a roof-top garden with trailing plants and comfortable sofas. At the far end, a bar had been set up, behind which a smartly dressed barman stood, expertly juggling a silver cocktail shaker. The sound of rattling ice filled the air.

"I had James make you up a Margarita," the guard said. "I know it's your favorite."

It was. I guessed it was Ted's too. Somewhat dazed, I walked over to James, who held out my drink. I took a sip. It was the best Margarita I had ever tasted.

I looked up, only now noticing that the whole of the roof was covered by a huge glass dome.

"What's that for?"

"Well, it's actually rather chilly up here without it," the guard said. "We are very, very high."

"Top of the world, Ma," I said with a small giggle. Damn. That Margarita was strong.

"Indeed, sir."

And then my elation began to sink. This was wrong. I shouldn't be here. I put the drink down.

"While this is all very nice, I mean, *more* than nice"—I smiled regretfully—"there's just one problem."

"And that is, sir?"

"I'm still not Ted."

A small nod. "I wondered if you might say that, sir." A sigh. "Well, if you're sure, we should proceed downstairs."

"Right away? I can't catch a few rays first?"

"I'm afraid not. Not if you insist that you are not Ted."

"Fine." I reached for the Margarita and threw the last bit back, grimacing slightly. Damn strong. "Okay. Lead the way."

We descended the staircase. For the last time, I guessed. I felt a small ache of longing. If only I *were* Ted, all of this could be mine. And to all intents and purposes, I *was* Ted. I had his card. His car keys. His face. I mean, I could live pretty convincingly as Ted. Except? There was just *something* stopping me. Call it a conscience. Or perhaps just a fear of getting caught. Which, for most people, is one and the same thing.

We reached the expansive living area. I paused. Something was different. A figure stood by the windows, looking out. In silhouette from where we stood. Another member of staff, perhaps?

"Ah, Alesha," the guard said. "I don't think we'll be requiring you to join us after all."

"Oh, that's a shame." A female voice. Low and mellifluous. Enchanting. I felt something stir in my stomach.

The figure turned and walked toward us. I gasped.

She was the most beautiful woman I had ever seen. All my fantasies and daydreams wrapped into one perfect form.

Long dark hair flowed in waves around her shoulders. Her face was a perfect heart, wide green eyes, full pink lips. She was curvaceous, not skinny, with long brown legs beneath cropped shorts, and a thin vest on top. In one hand she held a book. *Catch-22.* My favorite.

I swallowed. "Nice to meet you, Alesha."

She chuckled. "A little formal, aren't we, Ted?"

"I'm sorry? Do I know you?" I glanced nervously at the guard for help.

He cleared his throat. "Alesha is your wife, sir."

I almost choked. "My *wife*?"

"One of them—"

"*One?*"

"Well, one of *Ted's* wives. The others are in the sauna, I believe." Ted. You dog.

"Anyway"—the guard smiled curtly—"as you are not Ted, I should escort you from the premises—" He held out an arm.

"Wait!"

He raised an eyebrow. "Yes, sir?"

"I was just kidding."

"Kidding?"

"Yes. This was all just a test—and you passed."

"I did?"

"I *am* Ted. Have been all along. I was just playing with you."

"I see." The guard flipped a page on his clipboard. "Well, in that case, I will just need you to sign this document, confirming that."

He held out the clipboard and proffered a pen. I hesitated.

"If I sign, that's it? I'm Ted. No one else can come along and claim to be Ted?"

"No, sir. Once you sign, it's final."

I snatched the pen and signed quickly. *Ted.* I handed the pen back and smiled. "All done."

"Yes, sir. You are."

I stared at the guard. Something had happened to his face. The amiable smile was gone. He looked less plump and shiny. More worn. Lines crept around his eyes and lips. His skin sagged. I turned back toward Alesha. But she had disappeared. In her place, a mangy cat sat, licking its balls.

"What's going on?" I demanded.

"I'm sorry, sir," the guard croaked. "It seems you are not suitable for elevation after all."

"Yes, I am." Panic gripped me. "I really am. I—*oh, my freaking God!*"

The guard had started to disintegrate. Features running, melting like wax. All around me everything was crumbling, falling apart: furniture, walls, reality. The floor beneath my feet sagged and suddenly I was falling. Falling and falling through freezing blue skies.

I tried to scream, but my voice, like the rest of me, was swallowed into the icy abyss.

THE MOOD IN the Control Room was somber.

The operator sighed. "You know, I really thought he was going to make it this time."

"Well, he did get one stage further," her assistant replied. "Last time, we lost him when the lift opened."

"True." The operator slipped on a pair of glasses. "But he's running out of chances to be elevated."

"There's still time."

"Maybe." The operator looked doubtful. "But, to be on the safe side, you should let the Demotion Department know. So they can prepare."

Her assistant looked pained. "Demotion? Are you sure?"

The operator nodded. "We don't have any choice. If he can't pass the temptation test, he can't be elevated."

She leaned forward and pressed an intercom button: "Okay. Ground crew, set him up again. Enter Ted—"

"I'm not Ted."

"Of course you are, sir." The security guard jabbed a plump finger at his clipboard. "You're on my list. See."

I saw. It wasn't much of a list. Just one name. In capitals. Underscored. *TED 1510*.

Final Course

Introduction

Four years ago, my family and I moved from Nottingham to rural East Sussex.

It was something of a culture shock. No streetlights, takeouts or taxis. Just fields, forests, sheep and narrow country lanes. So *many* winding country lanes. Rough, potholed, barely wide enough for one car.

What the hell do I do if I meet a car coming the other way? I thought. I soon found out—reverse, reverse, reverse, onto the grass or a farm track if there's one nearby. Then pray for your wing mirrors!

And then there's the wildlife: pheasants that amble down the middle of the lanes and refuse to fly away, rabbits and foxes darting in front of the car. At night, you need to watch out for herds of deer who tend to leap out suddenly from the undergrowth.

There's also something very eerie about country lanes in the dark. No other vehicles, no people or lights. Just the trees forming twisted canopies overhead and the odd ramshackle farmhouse. There's a real sense of isolation, of being totally alone in the world.

What if it was always like this? I thought one evening as I drove Betty back from a swimming lesson in a nearby town. Perpetual dark?

I had been asked to contribute a short story to a new Subterranean Press anthology in the US and I had been toying with an idea about a dinner party at the end of the world. What could be more apocalyptic than the world being mysteriously cast into darkness?

And what if the darkness brought something with it? Something that thrived in the never-ending night.

"Are we almost there yet?" Betty asked from the backseat.

Good first line, I thought.

So, tell me—are you afraid of the darkness?

"Daddy, I'm scared."

"Don't be. There's nothing to be scared of."

"There's something inside."

"It's just the dark."

"I don't like it."

"It's okay. The dark can't hurt you."

"Promise?"

"Promise."

"Now open your eyes."

You are cordially invited to the 20th anniversary
reunion of the Infamous Five.
Bring scones, jam and lashings of booze!

~~~~~~~~~~

Date: Saturday, 26 October
Venue: Berskow Manor, Barley Mow Lane, Hambleton
Dinner Theme: End of the World as We Know It

"**A**re we nearly there yet?"

Some things never changed.

The skies could fall. Oceans boil. Eternal darkness descend upon the Earth . . . but somewhere along a journey a child will sigh, kick their feet against the back of your seat and mutter those immortal words, closely followed by:

"I'm bored."

"It's not much farther."

"How much farther is 'not much farther'?"

Tom glanced at the clock: 1:37 p.m. They had set off just before ten. Before, it could easily take over four hours to drive from the Midlands to Sussex. But there was less traffic on the roads these days. People didn't like to travel too far in the darkness. Not least because the demise of GPS meant no one knew where the hell they were going anymore.

"Half an hour. Maybe less."

He raised his eyes to the rearview mirror. Millie sat in the back, idly staring out of the window.

"Want some music on?"

"*Your* music?"

Only eight, and already Daddy's music was deserving of derision. They grew up so fast.

"No, you can choose."

She debated. "Okay. Can we listen to *Mary Poppins*?"

He groaned. "Really? Again?"

"You said I could choose."

"I know, but I was hoping you might choose Metallica."

"Da-ad."

"Metallica can be 'feel good' too."

"Yeah, right."

He sighed. "Okay."

He turned on the CD player and Julie Andrews's twee tones floated through the car, singing about a spoonful of sugar helping the medicine go down. Good old Mary, able to sort out everyone's troubles with a saccharine song and a talking umbrella. Back in the days when the world wasn't supercalifragilisticly fucked and the scariest thing lurking in the shadows was Dick Van Dyke with a British accent.

He tried to tune the songs out as he navigated the winding lane. The headlights illuminated only small patches of the road ahead of them. In places where the darkness was thicker, swirling in the car's beams like inky fog, he could barely see more than a few feet. He kept his speed low, hands gripping the wheel tightly, alert for anything else moving in the blackness.

He knew it was a risk to have accepted the invitation. Traveling itself was a risk, and he and Harry had hardly been the closest of friends at uni. Harry Fenton was one of those privileged young men that Tom, with his working-class background, found it difficult *not* to despise. Popular, sporty, good-looking (in the ruddy-cheeked, thoughtless way that all the upper class seemed to share), Harry Fenton glided through life effortlessly, his path gilded with money and good fortune. Tom was pretty sure that if Harry stood in front of the sea long enough, it would part for him.

Tom had always tried to quell his resentment for the sake of the group, but after they left university, while he kept in intermittent touch with Alex, Michael and Josh, he deliberately let his contact with Harry slide.

And now he had accepted an invitation to stay at Harry's country pile. Hypocritical, he knew. But needs must, and he needed to get Millie out of the city. Things were getting worse every day. Riots, looting, burning cars on almost every street corner. That was the problem with scared people. Ultimately, they became more dangerous than the thing they were afraid of.

Well, almost.

The countryside was safer. Everyone said so. Plus, Harry had told them that they were welcome to stay as long as they liked.

"I've got plenty of spare rooms, two massive generators, a wind turbine, electric fences. I'm completely self-sufficient out here."

Of course. Good old Harry. *Student most likely to land on his feet during an apocalypse.*

A white wooden sign drew into view. *Hambleton, 1 mile.* Tom signaled left and pulled onto an even narrower lane, not wide enough even to fit two cars, which was a pain in the backside because a large stag was blocking the road ahead. He hit the brakes.

"Shit!"

"What is it?" Millie asked.

"A deer—a stag."

It was a beautiful creature. At least six foot tall, with a proud head and elegant furred antlers. It stood for a moment, regarding the car. No fear. Not of them, anyway. And then it bounded over the hedge and into the field. A thunder of hooves and the rest of the herd followed, bursting from the hedgerow and springing delicately across the road, a dozen or more. And finally, a straggler. Older, slower. It stopped in the road, panting, disorientated. *Run,* Tom thought. *Run.* But the deer just stared around, eyes terrified orbs.

"Daddy?"

"Shhh."

The shadow swooped from their right. Black, amorphous. The deer screamed, hideously human. Something wet spattered the windshield. Tom hit the full beams, illuminating a vague blur of tentacles and bulbous eyes. The creature hissed at the light and retreated, dragging its prey back into the darkness.

Tom let out a breath. He glanced in the rearview mirror. "You okay?"

Millie nodded. "I'm hungry."

Tom flicked on the windshield wipers and pressed his foot down on the accelerator. In the distance, illuminated by floodlights, he could just see a glowing specter of gray stone. Berskow Manor.

"Almost there."

THEY WERE THE last to arrive. Tom pulled in through the electric gates and trundled along a winding private road to find four other cars parked outside the turreted building on an expansive gravel driveway. He guessed that the battered Defender was Harry's, the Land Rover belonged to Michael and his wife, Amanda, the Volvo was probably Alex's and the yellow Mini had to be Josh and his partner, Lee. Tom pulled up alongside the Mini.

"We're here," he said to Millie.

"Cool."

The floodlights provided a wide area of illumination around the building. Coming from the grid-dependent, power-rationed cities, such a wanton use of light seemed excessive. The have-watts and the have-nots. He tried to stamp on the green worm of envy wriggling in his gut, climbed out of the car and opened Millie's door.

The October air was brisk and fresh. Fresher than in the city, he thought. But then, anything was an improvement on the smell of burning rubber. He breathed it in, relishing the clean feeling in his lungs. This was the right thing. A good thing, he told himself again.

The door to Berskow Manor swung open.

"Tom!"

Tom stared at Harry Fenton. When he had checked up on him on social media, he had looked pretty much the same as he remembered. But those must have been old photos. Because this was not that Harry. Gone were the polo shirts, smart jeans and loafers. Gone was the floppy, foppish side parting. This Harry wore his dirty blond hair long, tied back in a scruffy ponytail. He sported baggy jeans, a loose burlap shirt and battered Converse on his feet. A stud glinted in his nose. If old Harry could have walked straight off the pages of

Tatler, this one could have stage-dived right off the cover of *Kerrang!*

"Hi," Tom stuttered.

"Man, it's so good to see you."

Even the plum wedged in his mouth had softened. Before Tom could move or stop him, Harry stepped forward and embraced him in a tight, incense-scented hug. Tom resisted the urge to squirm. Harry released him with a warm smile and turned his attention to Millie.

"And this must be your little girl?"

"I'm not little. I'm eight," Millie said.

Harry chuckled. "Sorry, my bad." He held out his hand. "Good to meet you."

Millie continued to stare at him through her red, heart-shaped dark glasses, arms at her side.

"She's a little shy," Tom said.

"Sure." Harry lowered his hand again, still staring at her. "Cool glasses, kiddo."

"THE REST OF the gang are already here."

Tom and Millie followed Harry across the huge hallway. Tom had been half hoping that, inside, the manor might be slowly falling into a state of disrepair. But his mean side was disappointed. The hall was shabby, certainly, but still beautiful. Huge lamps lent the space a warm glow. The stone-flagged floor was softened by a worn but obviously expensive Persian rug. In front of them, a wide staircase wound up to the second floor and a giant chandelier drooped sparkling crystals overhead.

He felt a cool hand creep into his. "It's huge," Millie whispered, and he knew she was conscious of her voice echoing off the walls.

"It's an old manor," he told her. "They built them big back in the day."

"Yeah," Harry said. "I rattle around here, to be honest. In fact, I've sealed the whole east wing off. No point heating and lighting it when I never use it, right?"

He gave a small laugh. "That's why it's so great to have you guys here. Add a bit of life." He glanced down at Millie again. "I've often felt this place could do with a few children running up and down the halls."

For a moment, a sadness seemed to sweep across his chiseled features. Then, he gathered himself. "So, anyway, the others are just through here, in the drawing room."

Tom could hear the sound of conversation drifting from the open door. Or, more to the point, he could hear the sound of Josh's voice regaling the others with a lewd and no doubt imaginatively embellished story.

Harry led them through into another beautiful room. Tasteful art and carelessly scattered shabby-chic furniture. Although Tom noted a few bare patches on the walls where pictures had obviously been taken down. Maybe the family money wasn't stretching quite as far as Harry made out.

He turned his attention to the five people standing around, a little awkwardly, holding drinks. Tom hadn't seen them in twenty years. Not in person. As Harry had proved, pictures on Facebook and Twitter aren't the same as seeing people in the flesh. Normally, you could add ten pounds, a few chins and a lot of laughter lines.

And then, sometimes, it's the familiarity of old friends that's as shocking as the changes. Josh stood, center stage, a glass of champagne in his hand. He may have lost the glossy mane of dark hair which had earned him the nickname "Boy Josh" at uni, but he was still just as striking, with a shaven head, dressed (almost) in a fitted black shirt, undone to his skinny jeans.

His partner, Lee, looked younger by a good decade and the total opposite to Josh's overt flamboyance. His curly brown hair was unkempt. He was unshaven and dressed in baggy cords, a shapeless sweater over his shirt. Rather than champagne or wine, he clutched a pint of beer. Tom had never met the young man before but found himself instantly warming to him.

Michael and Amanda stood, as always, shoulder to shoulder, stiffly clutching glasses of wine. At uni they had been inseparable. The "Siamese Twins," people often called them, which was a little creepy, as they were the sort of couple who could, actually, have been brother and sister. They shared the same short stature, thick dark hair and striking blue eyes. Both looked a little stockier than before, although that might just be the matching padded windbreakers, but otherwise they had barely changed. Again, kind of creepy.

Last, but by no means least, his eyes came to rest on Alex. He wished she had aged badly. But Alex never did anything badly. He remembered her sashaying around campus in ripped fishnets, Docs and baggy sweaters that hung off her shoulder, revealing a tantalizing glimpse of scarlet bra strap. She had worn her thick brown hair in semi-dreadlocks and Tom used to dream of it brushing his face as she kissed him.

It never happened. And now the dreadlocks were gone. So was the long hair. She sported a sharp pixie cut that suited her small features, and wore skinny jeans, heavy boots and a loose, striped sweater. His heart did a little forward roll.

"Hi, everyone, look who's here," Harry said.

Josh whirled around. "Tommy. Darling." He grinned, revealing an expensive row of gleaming veneers.

Josh—student most likely to look fabulous at the end of days.

"I always knew you'd grow into those features. Come here."

Tom didn't really have a choice, as Josh swooped in and enveloped him in a waft of skinny limbs and expensive aftershave. Lee held back, then sauntered over and proffered a hand. "Good to meet you."

Tom shook his hand. "You, too. Josh, you haven't changed a bit."

"Liar, but I'll take it!"

Michael and Amanda walked up together. "Lovely to see you, Tom."

They exchanged air kisses. Tom noted a large silver crucifix glinting around Amanda's neck.

"Hey-up, Tom," another voice said.

The warm burr of the Midlands accent still did something to him. Alex pressed her body to his and softly kissed his cheek. He felt it flame red.

"I, err, like the hair," he said. "It suits you."

She grinned. "Which is what men say when they mean they preferred it long."

"No, really. It's nice."

They stared at each other, and then Tom felt a small tug on his hand.

"Oh," he said. "And this is my daughter, Millie."

Millie edged out from where she had been lurking behind him.

Alex's smile faltered only slightly. "Hi, Millie," she said.

Tom waited, holding Millie's hand, looking around at the rest of the group.

Michael broke first. "What's with the glasses?"

"I love them," Josh said blithely. "A real fashion statement."

"Really?" Amanda asked, voice tight. "Is that what they are?"

Tom met her gaze. "Actually, no. Millie is blind."

He felt the atmosphere in the room change. A stalling of the conviviality.

"And you brought her *here*?" Amanda spluttered.

Michael laid a hand on her arm. "Mandy—"

She shook him off and turned to Harry. "Did you know?"

"No, but . . . Millie is welcome here. You all are."

"She's *blind*. You know what that means. You know what they're saying."

"Hysterical claptrap," Josh said. "I thought you and Michael knew better than to listen to that nonsense."

Michael colored. "You still should have told us, Tom."

"She's just a little girl," Tom said. "She deserves to be safe too."

"Safe?" Amanda looked around at them all and clutched her crucifix. "None of us are safe now."

THEY UNPACKED. MILLIE remained silent. The bedroom was large and airy, but cobwebs collected dust in the corners of the high ceiling and there were more bare patches on the walls. Still, the huge king-size bed looked comfortable. Tom would have collapsed in it right away, but he wasn't sure they were stopping that long. He had a feeling—well, more a certainty—that, downstairs, he and Millie were the subject of heated discussion.

He had hoped that the suspicion and intolerance might have been confined to the more ignorant members of society. But he should have remembered that liberalism was just a veneer, the first thing to fall away when the world went to shit; when darkness fell.

History had an unfortunate habit of repeating itself, over and over again. Human beings didn't learn, or rather, they conveniently forgot. The massacre of the Jews in Nazi Germany, the wall between Mexico and the US, the hostility toward refugees in the UK. It didn't take much for society to fold in and start devouring itself. Usually at the expense of the most vulnerable.

People always needed someone to blame, a scapegoat, especially when they were facing things they didn't understand. Things that had the politicians blustering and the scientists scratching their huge, intelligent heads. The sun hadn't gone out, the Earth still turned, flowers still grew and the temperatures hadn't plummeted.

But the Earth had gone dark. For almost a year now.

The power shortages and managed electricity cuts came first. "Just like the seventies," people who remembered the seventies grumbled. Government infomercials advised people about preserving power, safe use of candles, remembering to wear fluorescent clothing when traveling to school or work. Sales of solar panels plummeted, and, in response to public demand, wind turbines began to sprout up everywhere. As did the religious loons declaring the end of days. *We're all doomed.*

Still, people could have coped with that. People *were* coping with that.

But then, with the descent of darkness, came something else.

"We are going to stay, aren't we?" Millie asked him.

"Yes, it will all be fine."

"That lady didn't sound fine."

"Don't worry about her." He sat on the end of the bed next to her. "You know what we talked about? About fear?"

She nodded. "It can make people do stupid things, things they wouldn't do if they weren't afraid."

"That's right."

"Like Jonas at school, who called me names. And Mrs. Masters—who didn't want me to come into class anymore."

He felt his throat tighten.

For the safety of the rest of the children. Obviously, it's just a precaution.

And that was how it started. Exclusion. Isolation. Suspicion. Whispers between parents at the school gates, unfounded stories in the press, Twitter hysteria-mongering.

They act like magnets to those creatures. They can communicate with them. I'm not prejudiced but . . . we can't trust them, they need to be contained, monitored.

Next came the name-calling in the street. Attacks. The mobs with their burning torches. And he only wished that statement was metaphorical.

"You said we'd be safe here?" Millie said.

"We are. We will. It will all be—"

"Fine?"

A knock at the door. Tom rose and pulled it open.

Harry stood there with a tray, upon which he had placed a flute of champagne, a glass of orange juice and a plate of cookies. Iced party rings, bourbons, custard creams. Tom felt his stomach gurgle.

"I come bearing gifts." He laughed weakly.

"Thanks," Tom said.

Harry put the tray down on the chest of drawers by the door. "I'm so sorry about before."

"Not your fault."

"But I invited you here. You're all my guests. I didn't realize that Amanda would be so, well, you know—"

"Bigoted? Offensive?"

Harry shrugged, ran a hand through his hair. "I don't know what to say . . . you know what she was like at uni."

Tom did. Michael, like Harry, came from a well-off farming family. Traditional, conservative. Despite that, Michael was a decent enough bloke; easy-going and good-hearted . . . until he met Amanda. A horsey type of girl, brought up in a strictly Christian household, she set her sights upon Michael, and the pair quickly became inseparable. Michael started attending her church, spouting all sorts of religious nonsense, spent less time with Josh, whom he had always got on well with. Tom had never liked her and had always hoped that Michael would grow out of his infatuation. Sadly, it never happened.

"Anyway, I hope you're not changing your mind about staying," Harry said. "It really is good to see you and . . . I think it would be good for Millie here."

"What about the others?"

"We've always got over our differences in the past. The Infamous Five, remember?"

He clapped Tom on the shoulder. Tom smiled.

"Right," he said.

But they weren't. That was the problem. They hadn't been for a very long time.

Harry was staring at Millie again.

"Does she always wear the glasses?"

"I have to," Millie said.

"It's too dangerous otherwise," Tom said.

Harry nodded. "Of course. I understand."

But he didn't.

"Anyway," Harry continued. "I said I'd give the others a tour of the place before dinner, if you fancy it?"

"Well, we're a bit tired—"

"I'd like it," Millie said suddenly.

Tom glanced at her. "Well, okay, if you're sure?"

"I am."

"Right then. Count us in."

"Great. Catch you back in the Grand Hall at five."

Grand frigging Hall, Tom thought as he pushed the door closed. Right.

FIVE OF THEM were waiting in the "Grand Hall" when Tom and Millie came downstairs: Harry, Josh and Lee, Alex and Michael.

"No Amanda?" Tom asked.

Michael cleared his throat. "She's got a bit of a headache."

"Right. Shame."

For a moment, there was an awkward pause, and then Michael said: "It really is good to see you again, Tom—and your daughter."

Hardly convincing, but at least he was trying. Tom smiled back. "Thanks."

"So, Lord of the Manor, are you going to show us around your ancestral money pit or what?" Josh drawled.

For a fraction of a second, Harry's grin faltered. He shot Josh a look, one Tom couldn't quite read. Then the grin was back up to full wattage.

"Of course. This way."

They filed behind him like day-trippers following a tour guide. Grand room followed grand room. Tom described them to Millie in a low whisper, trying not to let the bitterness creep into his voice, consoling himself by noting more bare patches on the walls. Still, it was insane that just one person lived here.

"How do you manage?" Alex asked Harry, as if reading his mind. "Do you have staff?"

"Well, I have a girl and her mother who come from the village to clean and help with the cooking."

A girl and her mother. Too inconsequential to name.

"No Mrs. Fenton going insane in the attic?" Josh asked as they climbed the grand staircase.

"No," Harry said evenly. "Just the odd rat." He smiled. "Come on—you must see the observatory in the west turret."

Observatory. Of course.

Harry led them along the landing, past the bedrooms and then up a winding staircase. At the top they found themselves in a glass dome. Tom imagined that, once, you would have been able to see for miles. Possibly all the way to the coast. Not anymore. Darkness caressed the panes and, below, charcoal countryside petered out into densely shadowed woodland. To their left, a short distance away, a white wind turbine slowly turned. Below it were two more hulking structures.

"What are those?" Josh asked.

"One houses the generators—main and backup; the other is just an old barn."

"How much land do you have?" Michael asked.

"Around ten acres."

"You've never farmed it?"

"I'm not much of a farmer, I'm afraid."

"I thought you said your family were farmers," Josh said. "Or don't you like getting your hands dirty?"

Tom glanced at him. Josh could be provocative, but he seemed to be deliberately needling Harry today. He wondered why.

"We have lots of farms nearby," Harry said pleasantly. "And they need the income. I think it's important to help others in these dark times, don't you?"

"Oh, absolutely," Josh said. "That's why I took in Lee, out of pity for the poor thing."

"I'm eternally grateful," Lee deadpanned.

"You have electric fences around the whole estate?" Alex asked, peering through the glass.

"Entirely. Nothing gets in here," Harry said. "Nothing." He looked around at them meaningfully.

"Does anything try?" Alex asked.

"Occasionally I have to scrape a mess off one of the electric fences. But that's another beauty of the countryside. We're far more prepared for this type of thing. Used to dealing with vermin."

"Any guns?"

"A couple of shotguns. For what it's worth. Bullets don't have much effect on the buggers."

"What about looters?" Michael said. "After all, you do hear about gangs coming over from London, killing landowners for their homes."

Harry offered a steely smile. "Like I said, nothing gets in here."

"Are you two still in London?" Alex turned to Josh and Lee. "I heard things are getting pretty bad?"

"Oh, you'll never drag Josh out of London," Lee said.

"Unless it's by my cold, dead hands," Josh added. Then he glanced at Tom and colored. "Oh God. Sorry, I didn't think . . ."

"It's okay."

Alex laid a hand on his arm. "We were sorry to hear about your wife."

"Thank you."

Harry offered his best sympathetic smile, blue eyes crinkling around the corners, like a favorite uncle. "Well, it's getting a bit chilly up here. Let's go back downstairs and warm up."

They filed back down the stairs to the first floor. Tom went last, leading Millie carefully by the hand.

"What's that way?" Lee asked, gesturing down the landing, to where the corridor ended abruptly in a sturdy-looking door.

"Oh, that's the east wing," Harry said. "It's just used for storage.

I keep it shut up to save heating and lighting the whole pile. No point wasting energy."

Just what he had told Tom before. Except it hadn't stopped him illuminating the rest of the place like a fairground, Tom thought. There was something else. The door. It wasn't the same as the others in the house. It was new. Tom frowned. If the east wing was just used for storage, why put on a new door?

They reached the staircase. Millie was very quiet. Tom let the others go ahead and then asked quietly: "You okay?"

She shook her head. "They're lying."

"Who?"

"All of them."

THE HUMAN MIND has a wonderful ability to put aside things that it doesn't want to think about, to neatly store away troublesome thoughts and concentrate upon the moment.

There were plenty of moments over the last year when Tom had found that useful. His wife's death. Fleeing their home. The things that had happened since. Survival.

And then, sometimes, your brain gets a worm. Much like an ear worm. A train of thought that just won't go away, however hard you try.

The door. The bare patches on the walls. They're lying.

Something here was wrong, in a way he couldn't quite put his finger on.

Millie dozed on the king-size bed. Tom had been convinced that, the moment he got a chance for a nap, he would join her. But he had been lying here for the best part of an hour now, trying to get to sleep. His brain worm refused to let him.

He sat up and swung his legs off the bed. His throat felt dry and scratchy from the dust in the room. He needed a glass of water (*and a snoop around,* a small voice whispered).

With a final glance at Millie—he wouldn't be long, he promised himself—he padded across the room and slipped out of the door.

He walked back along the landing. The others had also retired to their rooms to rest and get ready for dinner. He wondered if Amanda's headache would be better by then. He hoped not. He hoped it turned into a migraine.

He paused at the top of the staircase and stared down the corridor, toward the door that barred the way to the east wing. He walked over to it and tried the handle. Locked. Why lock the door if the east wing was only used for storage? You didn't lock a door on junk. You didn't lock a door to save on heating and lighting.

He turned and walked down the stairs. Maybe he was just being paranoid. Maybe the events of the last months had made him overly suspicious of people and their motives. The problem with darkness was, once you let it in, it lurked in the corners of your mind, filling them with shadows.

He reached the hall—sorry, the *Grand* Hall—and turned left, toward the kitchen. He half expected to find Harry, in an apron, busily preparing food. But the large space was empty. Pans filled with chopped vegetables sat on the stove. French loafs were laid out, ready to be cut. There was a little detritus of food preparation, but mostly it was clean and tidy. Organized, Tom thought. Everything about this reunion was meticulously organized. So, why did that just add to his uneasy feeling?

He pulled open cupboards, found a glass and walked to the sink to fill it. Cookbooks lined the windowsill in front of him. *Vegan and Vegetarian Recipes*. No surprise there. But also *Cooking for Your Family* and *Healthy Food for Kids*. He frowned. Harry didn't have a family, or kids. But perhaps the books had belonged to his parents—or their chef. He reached out and opened one. The inside page was inscribed:

To Lucy, love Dave.

Dave and Lucy. He couldn't remember what Harry's parents were called, but he felt pretty sure it wasn't Dave and Lucy. He closed the book carefully and put it back on the windowsill. A door creaked behind him. He jumped and whirled round.

Alex and Lee stood in the doorway. Alex looked worried. Lee looked more disheveled than ever.

"Christ! You made me jump."

"Sorry," Lee said. "What are you doing in here?"

"Getting a glass of water. What about you two?"

They exchanged a look, and it struck Tom what was wrong with this picture. Alex and Lee. But what about . . .

"Where's Josh?"

"That's the thing," Alex said. "We can't find him."

THEIR FEET CRUNCHED on gravel. They wore thick jackets and clutched heavy-duty flashlights. Darkness pooled at the edge of the spotlit area. Despite Harry's assurances about the electric fences, Tom felt the hairs on the nape of his neck bristle.

"We went back to our room to have a shower," Lee said. "Josh said he was just going outside for a cigarette. I lay down for a nap. I woke up to find someone knocking on the door. I thought it might be Josh, but when I opened it, it was Alex."

"I wanted to borrow a charger for my phone," she explained.

"How long has he been missing?"

"Over an hour."

"Perhaps he's just stretching his legs, getting some fresh air?"

Lee gave him a look. "This is Josh. A man who regards a Marlboro Light as a health kick."

True.

"Plus, no one just goes for a stroll to stretch their legs. Not these days," Alex added.

Also true.

They rounded the corner of the house to a courtyard area. In one corner stood a dilapidated block of wooden sheds that Tom presumed had once been stables, the first sign of disrepair around the place. But then, horses were not exactly a useful commodity these days. They didn't produce things, you couldn't eat them, although that hadn't deterred some people. They were an expensive luxury that most people could no longer afford. Many had been left to run wild. Ahead of them, where the land rose, the huge wind turbine sliced at the air. Beneath it, a modern steel building that Tom presumed housed the generators. A little further back was the old barn, all shuttered up.

"Are you sure he came out here?"

"We checked everywhere inside," Lee said.

"Except for the mysterious east wing," Alex added. "But that was still locked."

They looked back at the house. Tom spotted something he hadn't noticed before: the first-floor shutters on this side of the building—the east wing—were all closed. He felt that primeval shudder of fear again.

"Did you ask Harry?"

Lee hesitated, then said, "Josh doesn't really trust Harry."

"Why?"

"Back in uni, he found out that Harry's background wasn't quite as upper crust as he made out. His parents had money, but the whole 'Lord of the Manor' thing was a bit of an exaggeration."

Tom thought about the cookbooks again. *Dave and Lucy.*

"What were Harry's parents called?" he asked Alex.

Her forehead creased. "Julian and Annette, I think. Why?"

"When I was in the kitchen, I found a cookbook inscribed 'To Lucy, love Dave.' A family cookbook. And did you notice the bare patches on the walls?"

"I did," Lee said. "Like paintings had been taken down."

"Or photos? There are no photos of Harry, or anyone, in the house, or not that I could see."

"So, what are you saying?" Alex asked. "This house doesn't belong to Harry?"

"And if so," Tom said, "where are the owners?"

"And where's Josh?" Lee added.

They stared back at the house. Then they turned the other way, toward the hulking old barn.

"Only two places we haven't looked," Tom said. "And one's locked. C'mon."

They traipsed through overgrown grass toward the dilapidated old structure, flashlights illuminating a narrow path. The turbine whirring overhead made it difficult to hear anything. But Tom's nose was working overtime. A smell. Actually, more of a stench. Rich, tangy, metallic. Getting stronger and stronger as they approached the barn doors.

"Jesus!" Alex pulled her coat up over her nose. "I can't go in there."

Tom looked at Lee. He was a greener shade of pale, but he nodded resolutely. Tom shoved the barn doors open.

Inside, it was dark, but just normal dark. Tom tried to breathe through his mouth, but the smell seemed to clog in his throat, making him want to gag. Beside him, Lee pulled up his sweater to cover his lower face. They pointed their flashlights around. Rusting machinery, rotting wooden beams, moldy hay and in front of them: the source of the smell. Two dead and decomposing horses, their carcasses busy with a shifting mass of white maggots, wriggling in the ruined flesh.

"Fuck!"

Lee turned away and promptly threw up. Tom managed to wrestle the contents of his stomach down, but he had a feeling that it was only a temporary reprieve. He walked carefully around the dead animals, trying not to step in putrescent flesh or bodily fluids. There were two stalls toward the back of the barn. He approached them with growing trepidation. Lee straightened and followed, making muffled noises of disgust.

Tom peered into the first stall. A mass of rotting black and yellow fur that he guessed had once been the family dogs. He backed out again. A heavy dread weighted his limbs. Horses, dogs and one more stall left for a full house. He turned slowly and trained his flashlight inside. Then he reeled away again. This time his stomach had its way. He vomited cookies and cheap champagne all over the rotting hay.

He heard movement behind him and turned, gasping for breath. "Don't."

Lee looked at him through red-rimmed eyes. "Not—"

Tom shook his head. "But I think I found Dave and Lucy." He swallowed bitter bile, wishing he could erase the image that had branded itself onto his brain. "And their children."

LIGHTS BLARED FROM the house. As they entered the Grand Hall, Tom could hear classical music tinkling out from the dining room. The three of them looked at each other.

"I say we leave right now," Tom said.

"I can't," Lee said. "I have to find Josh."

"Besides," Alex added, "we need Harry to open the electric gates."

"Did I hear my name?"

They turned. Harry walked into the Grand Hall wearing a formal dress suit, his shaggy blond hair loose around his shoulders.

He smiled. "Guys, you're not dressed for dinner? What gives?"

Lee stared at him. "Where's Josh?"

"Josh? I've no idea. I thought he was with you."

"No," Alex said. "We've been out looking for him."

"We went to the barn," Tom said.

"Ah." Harry's smile slipped. He nodded. "Okay. Look, I can explain—"

"There are *rotting bodies* in your barn, Harry!" Tom's voice rose in anger. "At a wild guess, the rotting bodies of the family who lived in this house. How do you explain that? You fancied being the lord of a real manor, so you killed them for it?"

Harry's eyes widened. "Jesus! No! Christ." He ran a hand through his hair. "Okay, I admit I may have exaggerated about my past. And yes, I have recently been 'between properties.' But this place was empty when I got here. I *found* the bodies in the barn. They'd shot the animals, their kids and themselves. They were already dead. What was I to do?"

"Bury them?" Lee said coldly.

"You're right. Yes, I should have, but I just couldn't bring myself to touch them. It was all so horrible . . ." He sighed. "Look, I made a bad call, but please don't let this ruin our night."

Tom barked out a laugh. "No. Why should a few rotting corpses ruin dinner?"

Harry gave him a keener look. "These are different times, Tom. Don't tell me those are the first dead bodies you've seen. Don't tell me you haven't had to make some hard decisions, to look after yourself and your loved ones. All of you."

Tom wanted to retort but found he couldn't reply. Neither Lee nor Alex would meet his eyes.

Harry nodded. "I saw an opportunity and I took it, before someone else did. We all do what we have to in order to survive. So, why don't we sit down for dinner and talk about this, like grown-ups? I have a proposition I want to discuss with you. The others are waiting in the dining room. Michael, Amanda, Millie . . ."

"Millie?" Tom advanced toward him, fists clenched. "If you've hurt Millie—"

Harry held his hands up. "For God's sake. I found her wandering the corridors upstairs, looking for you. She was upset, so I suggested she join us downstairs to wait for you. I thought I was looking out for her."

Tom's cheeks flamed with anger and shame. He shouldn't have left her. Not here. Not in this house.

Harry turned to Lee. "I don't know where Josh is, but he was quite drunk. Alex, remember that time at uni he wandered off after a party and we found him the next afternoon, asleep in the middle of a merry-go-round?"

Alex nodded reluctantly. "Yeah."

"Please, guys," Harry said. "Just hear what I have to say and then, if you still want to leave, I'll open the gates for you and you can be on your way."

Tom smiled thinly. "What a generous, unconditional offer."

"Do we have a choice?" Lee asked.

Harry grinned his big, shit-sucker grin. "Not really."

THE TABLE WAS dressed in crisp white linen. Crystal glasses gleamed. Overhead, another chandelier dripped with sparkling glass, although Tom was pleased to see that, next to it, there was a large discolored patch on the ceiling stippled with lines and sagging a little. The cracks were showing, he thought, quite literally.

Amanda and Michael sat at the far end of the table, Michael in a suit and Amanda wrapped in some sort of patterned curtain. Millie sat beside them, in her glittery party dress. The one they had chosen because every little girl loves sequins, even ones who can't see them. Tom's heart swelled.

Don't tell me you haven't had to make some hard decisions, to look after yourself and your loved ones.

"Millie!"

"Daddy!"

She pushed her chair back and ran to him. "I woke up and you weren't there."

"I know, and I'm sorry. But I'm here now. It's all fine."

"Nice of you to join us," Amanda said coolly.

"We're not stopping," Tom said.

"Oh, don't be like that," Harry said. "Come on, help yourselves to a drink."

The three of them sat stiffly and pulled out chairs. Tom sat beside Millie.

"What's going on, Daddy?"

"I think we're about to find out, sweetheart."

Lee poured himself a hefty red wine and passed the bottle to

Tom. He hesitated and then did the same. Alex held out her glass. He filled it with a slightly shaking hand. A few red splotches hit the white linen.

Harry gazed around the table benevolently and raised his glass. "First, I would like to propose a toast."

Alex rolled her eyes. "For Christ's sake!"

"To the Infamous Five, back together at long last. Here's to our future adventures."

Amanda raised her glass. Michael followed. Tom, Alex and Lee looked back at Harry, glasses resolutely lowered.

If Harry was disappointed at the lack of enthusiasm, he didn't let it dent his sales patter.

"Okay, I have a confession to make. I have an ulterior motive for inviting you all here tonight . . . to this beautiful house, in this beautiful setting and, most importantly, free and safe from the troubles of the cities." He looked around the table, face a picture of practiced sincerity. "We have an opportunity here. To create a sanctuary. Not just for us, but others who would like to join us."

"What are you suggesting? Some kind of cult, with you as our wondrous leader?" Lee asked.

Harry's eyes gleamed. "Not exactly. Sanctuary comes at a price."

And there it was, Tom thought. "You want people to pay to come here?"

"Of course. Look at this place. We have the land, this huge house. We're secure, self-sufficient. We can build, expand. I'm thinking another turbine, indoor pools, a spa. A place people can quite literally escape to from the horror of the cities. A safe place. Sanctuary. That's what I plan to call it: The Sanctuary."

"You're crazy," Tom muttered. "What makes you think people will come?"

"You did."

"And who's going to build all these amazing things?" Lee asked. "Who's going to run it—you?"

"That's where you all come in. Lee—you and Josh have experience in advertising. You can get the word out through social media. Alex, with your architectural experience, you can help with the development of the building, and Michael and Amanda, well, they have offered a very generous investment."

All eyes turned.

"You knew about this?" Tom said. "Before?"

Michael looked down. Amanda held Tom's gaze. "Yes, we were in touch with Harry before we came, and we think it's an excellent idea. Someone should make something out of all this."

"Commercializing the apocalypse," Lee said drily.

"Someone has to."

"Isn't the whole point of an apocalypse that money and possessions are all useless?" Tom said.

"Only for the losers," Amanda said. "There are always people who survive and profit from a disaster. The ones with the money, the land. We'll be in charge."

"And what about what's out there? In the dark? Are you going to be in charge of that too?"

"Like Harry said, we're protected here."

Tom snorted. "Right. Just like the family in the barn. Did Harry mention them? The former occupants of this house. They felt so safe and protected they killed themselves and their children."

Tom waited for the look of horror, confusion, shock on Michael's and Amanda's faces. It didn't come. They looked down at their napkins. Realization dawned.

"You knew about that too," he said flatly. "You knew and you didn't care."

"They were already dead," Amanda said.

"Jesus!"

"Don't judge me, Tom. You came here too. With your daughter. Without even considering the rest of us."

"She's right," Michael said. "Let's not pretend we just wanted to catch up. I'm sure most of us would happily have never set eyes on each other again. We're all here to escape from something, aren't we?"

Tom reached for his wine. Another splotch of red hit the table. He frowned. Brighter red.

Lee shoved his chair back. "I'm going to find Josh. Then we're leaving."

Another splotch. And another. Not wine.

"Shit," Alex said, as one drop hit the table near her. "Is that . . . blood?"

They all looked up. The stained patch on the ceiling had darkened. As they watched, it bubbled and swelled and more drops of red fell, hitting the table below.

Lee's face paled. "Oh God."

"Harry?" Tom asked steadily. "What's above here?"

Harry tipped back his wine. "The east wing. Used to be the children's rooms. But I really wouldn't advise you to look in there."

Tom grabbed him by the arm and forced him to his feet.

"Show us. Now!"

THEY FILED UP the stairs, Harry in the lead, followed by Lee then Alex, Michael and Amanda. Tom brought up the rear, holding tightly to Millie's hand.

"Stay back, keep safe. Remember what I told you?"

She nodded. "Yes, Daddy."

"What is all this, Harry?" Amanda huffed. "I thought you said the east wing was used for storage?"

"It is. I just didn't mention *what* was stored there." He sighed. "I wasn't lying when I said the fences keep everything out. But sometimes it can take a minute for the generator to kick in when the power goes. I think that's when it happened."

"When what happened?" Michael asked.

They reached the first floor. The door to the east wing was ajar. Darkness swelled ominously inside. Noises came from within. Faint, wet, squelching sounds.

"*When what happened?*" Michael asked again.

Harry shook his head. "Bloody creature got inside. Damned if I know how, and damned if I can get rid of it."

Like he was having a problem with rats or mice.

"One of *them* is in there?" Tom clarified.

"Afraid so. I didn't realize until I moved in, and by then, it was too late. Obviously, I can't let it out, so I've tried to keep it contained. But I'm running out of ideas. And food—it prefers fresh, you see."

"Jesus!" Tom exclaimed. "You've been feeding it?"

"I started with some stray dogs. Then there was the occasional trespasser, lurking around the lanes." Harry stuck his hands in his pockets and stared down the corridor. "I really didn't expect Josh to be next. Shame. He must have found the spare key."

"Christ, no." Lee moved forward. Tom laid a hand on his arm. "Don't. You saw the blood. It's too late."

"I'm not leaving him in there. With *that*."

"Lee—"

Lee yanked his arm free and walked to the door. He pushed it fully open. The corridor beyond bristled with tenebrosity. The noises were louder now. A hideous slurping. Lee turned on his flashlight and stepped inside.

"Shut the door," Amanda said.

"And shut him in?"

"If he wants to commit suicide, that's his choice."

"LEE!" Tom called.

But it was too late. As Lee crossed the threshold, the shadows rippled. Black tentacles whipped out and wrapped around his body. Lee tried to turn, dropping the flashlight, grappling with the tentacles, struggling to escape. It was no good. The tentacles wound around his neck, squeezing tighter and tighter. There was a pop, a sound that made Tom think of the time he ran over a pigeon, and Lee's head flew off like a cork shooting from a bottle.

"Shut the door!" Amanda screamed.

This time, Tom obliged. He ran forward and yanked the door

shut. Something silver fell to the ground. A key. He snatched it up and fumbled it into the lock. Behind the door, in the corridor, he could hear the creature eating, absorbing Lee. It couldn't help it. It was just an animal. Just trying to survive, like they all were. The sounds still sickened him.

He turned back to the group. All of them looked shaken and shell-shocked, apart from Harry, who stood with his hands in his pockets, looking contrite but composed. Tom fought the urge to smash a fist into his face and pummel it into putty.

"What the hell have you done?"

"I'm sorry. This wasn't supposed to happen."

"Right. And what exactly *did* you expect to happen?"

"It's just a small setback—"

"A small setback?" Michael spluttered. "This . . . this ruins everything. How can we create a sanctuary here with *that* in there?"

"Just hear me out," Harry said. "I told you, I invited you here for a reason."

"What? To become the next course?" Tom said.

"Not quite." Harry regarded Tom coolly. "Didn't you wonder why I invited *you*? After all, we were never close. Never stayed in touch."

"I don't care," Tom said.

But he did. He should have.

Harry took a step toward him. "I *knew* Millie was blind, Tom. I did my research on all of you."

Tom felt something curdle in his stomach.

"So?"

"So, I did a lot of reading about the empathy the blind have with the darkness and the creatures that live in it. Particularly those born blind. Their connection seems to be the strongest."

"I've told you, it's all rubbish. Hysteria. Superstitious scaremongering."

"Is it?" Harry smiled unpleasantly. "Millie was a pupil at Elmwood Primary. The school wanted to exclude her as a precaution.

You refused. The school was attacked by several creatures while the children were in the playground. Millie was the only one to survive. Untouched."

"She was lucky."

"I don't believe in luck. I believe Millie can save us."

"You're crazy."

"If she can communicate with what's in there and get it out, we'll all be safe."

Tom glanced at Amanda and Michael. "You're surely not buying this?"

Michael shook his head helplessly. "We've left everything. Harry promised us a fresh start here. Peace, security. What choice do we have?"

"You're not using Millie as some sort of guinea pig." He grabbed Millie's hand. "We're leaving."

Cold metal grazed his neck.

"No. You're not."

Tom swiveled his head. Alex stood beside him, holding a small handgun. His heart crumbled.

"And what did he promise you?"

She shrugged. "Like Harry said, we've all done things to survive. You think you have it tough? Do you know how hard it is for a single woman out there? It doesn't take much for men's veneer of civilization to slip. I need this."

Something clicked in Tom's mind.

"Earlier, you said the door to the east wing was still locked. But it can't have been if Josh was inside. You knew he was in there."

"Josh shouldn't have gone poking around in stuff. He brought it on himself."

"How compassionate."

"Practical. Now, it seems to me we have a situation here, and if you and Millie can help to get us out of it, then that would be a good thing for everyone."

"Please, Alex," Tom begged. "She's all I have."

"We all have to make sacrifices."

"No one is going to *sacrifice* Millie," Harry said. "We just want her to help us."

"You're like a bunch of scared peasants wanting to burn the witch to save the rest of the village," Tom said. "I won't let you hurt my daughter."

"Fine." Alex cocked the gun. Tom tensed.

And then a small voice said: "It's okay, Daddy." Millie let go of his hand and stepped forward. "I'll do it."

He looked down at her, tears in his eyes. "You can't."

"I know what to do."

"It's dangerous."

"I can handle it."

"Are you sure?"

"Yes."

"Good girl," Harry said.

Tom stared at him. "Remember, you asked for this."

"And I *always* get what I ask for."

"Oh, you will." Tom smiled. "Millie, take off your glasses."

IT WAS DONE *in seconds. Just like at school. Just like the other times it had been necessary.*

People thought they understood the darkness. But they didn't. They didn't understand how it had found a home inside Millie. Ever since the first day it fell. Even before it birthed the creatures. It filled her. It spoke to her. It protected her and gave her strength.

But it needed to feed.

MILLIE'S EYES BULGED, tumescent black orbs. They swelled and swirled, pregnant with blackness, and then they burst. The darkness poured from her sockets, surging forward, wrapping itself around Harry, Michael and Amanda so fast they couldn't even scream.

It squeezed tight, caressing them like lovers' fingers, probing their soft flesh, plunging into inviting moist orifices, pushing into the deepest parts of their bodies, filling every organ and artery and then, in one quick moment, as though dissatisfied with what it had found, it split its hosts open like rotten fruit, tearing them asunder, body parts flying across the landing.

Alex tried to run, but the wispy tentacles flicked out and snagged her feet, dragging her backward. More found her arms, stretching her into a human star shape. The gun slipped from her fingers. Panic lit her eyes.

"Tom! Please! Help me!"

He regarded her sadly. "I'd like to."

"Please, Tom! I know you still care about me."

"I do . . . but we all have to make sacrifices."

Four wet snaps and her arms and legs were torn from her body. Her limbless torso hit the floor with a thud. Momentarily, her head snapped from side to side, mouth open in a blood-choked scream, and then the tentacles reached forward, ripped it off and tossed it carelessly over the banisters.

"Millie," Tom said. "That's enough."

The darkness slowly retreated, seeping back inside her. Millie blinked a few times, as though dislodging a stray eyelash. Then she placed the glasses back over her eyes.

Tom stared around at what remained of his old friends. Reunions, he thought. They always got messy.

"Did I do good?"

Tom pulled up the bedcovers, tucking his daughter in.

"You did good, sweetheart."

"Those people were bad."

"Yes. We did the right thing."

"Like with Mummy."

He sighed. "Mummy didn't understand your gift. We couldn't let her take you away."

"And my friends at school?"

"They shouldn't have picked on you, called you names."

"And the other people—"

"We've talked about this. Sometimes, if people won't help, you have to hurt them."

Millie yawned. "I'm tired."

"It's been a long day. You should get some sleep now. Ready?"

She laid her head down on the pillow, slipped off her glasses and Tom deftly placed the sleeping mask over her eyes, securing it tightly.

"Are we there yet?" she whispered dozily.

Tom considered, thinking about the house, the grounds. Harry was right. It was beautiful, secure. You could charge people to come here. And if some disappeared, well, nothing was completely perfect. Not even *Mary Poppins*.

"Yes." He kissed her on the forehead. "I think we are."

The Copy Shop

Introduction

"We can copy almost anything," the tatty sign outside the printer's proclaimed.

Anything? I thought as I drove past. *Now, that's interesting.*

Before I signed my publishing deal, I worked as a dog walker. I might have mentioned it. I mention it a lot because I think it's important to know that you don't have to work in the media or have a fancy degree to become an author. I don't even have an A level to my name.

Anyway, in my spare time, and to supplement my meager earnings, I wrote short stories to sell to a woman's weekly magazine. The stories had to be no longer than 2,000 words and had to have a twist in the tale. If accepted, the magazine paid around £300—a *massive* amount to me at the time. To put it in perspective, £300 was the equivalent of thirty hours, or a whole week, of dog walking.

When my first story was accepted, I was absolutely thrilled—and not just because it helped to pay off my overdraft. It was the first time that a story I'd written had been published. Someone had paid me real money for something I had made up. When you've faced rejection after rejection, those small breaks mean a lot. I was finally worthy!

Of course, not every story got picked up by the magazine. Some of my ideas were just a bit too weird for the target market.

"The Copy Shop" was one of those that fell by the wayside.

Inspired by the run-down printer's and its bold claim, it's a tale of a broken vase, a stale marriage and a conundrum: can a copy ever be as good as the original?

Why don't you decide?

Like many things, it started by accident.

A clumsy swipe with the duster and my favorite vase hit the floor. *Smash*.

Not the prettiest vase, or even valuable, but a present from a late, dear friend.

"It was an ugly old thing, anyway," Alan said as I carefully swept up the pieces with a dustpan and brush. "Don't know why you didn't throw it out years ago."

I gave him a look as he shuffled past in in his holey slippers and stained shirt, flies undone, again.

"Neither do I," I muttered.

"What?" he asked.

I shook my head. "Nothing."

I didn't throw out the vase. I glued it together: badly, inexpertly, and then perched it on top of the TV cabinet. Where Alan could stare at it every evening.

"Oh my. What happened to your vase?"

Trust Melinda to notice. Melinda was my neighbor. The perfect neighbor. Perfect house. Perfect husband. Perfect hair. Perfect figure. She often invited herself around for coffee. Usually so she could point out my many imperfections.

"I broke it," I said.

"Well, can't you buy another?"

"A friend made it. I can't just replace it."

Melinda wrinkled her nose. "Well, you should do something, darling. It's a terrible mess."

Good old Melinda. Blunt as a butter knife. I glanced over at Frankenvase. She was right, though. My repair job wasn't pretty.

And Alan was always telling me I was too sentimental. Holding on to things I should really let go of.

"Maybe I *should* throw it away."

"Oh no. No need for that."

Melinda snapped open her handbag. Melinda always carried a handbag. Usually large. Always expensive.

She pulled out a card and handed it to me. "Give these people a call."

I regarded the card curiously. "The Copy Shop? What are they? Some sort of restorer?"

"More like . . . reproductions."

"I don't know. A copy? It wouldn't be the same."

She rested one red-taloned hand on my arm. "Trust me, Fran. I've used them lots of times. They do a remarkable job."

I considered. "So it would be just like the original?"

"*Better* than the original."

I STOOD OUTSIDE the shop, clutching the broken vase in a shopping bag padded with newspaper.

Bloody Melinda. I didn't want to be here. The shop was on the other side of town, which had meant two buses and a long walk. But Melinda could be incredibly persuasive. If I didn't take her "advice," I'd never hear the end of it.

With a sigh, I pushed open the door and stepped inside.

A pretty blonde girl—no more than twenty—stood behind the counter.

"Hello. Can I help you?"

"I hope so. I have this vase I need . . . well, copying, I suppose."

I pulled the vase out of the bag and placed it on the counter. The girl glanced at it and said crisply, "I'll just get the manager."

She sashayed into the back room, and a moment later a man emerged. Small and neat with a shiny bald head and sharp blue eyes.

He picked up the vase and turned it over in clean, smooth hands. "Yes. I think we can definitely improve upon this." He looked at me. "Is it valuable?"

"Sentimental value."

"The most important sort." He smiled. "If you leave it with us, we can have your vase ready by tomorrow."

"That quickly?"

"We pride ourselves on our quick turnaround."

"Right."

"There is just one thing."

A catch. Always a catch.

"Yes?"

"I'm afraid we're not able to return the original. Is that a problem?"

I considered for a moment. The vase was ruined anyway.

"No. I suppose not."

"YOU'RE LATE," ALAN grumbled when I returned home at just past five-thirty.

"Well, I missed the bus and the traffic was . . ." I stopped, sniffed. "What's that smell?"

"Cat's made a mess in the kitchen."

I pulled off my raincoat and threw it on a peg. "Well, why didn't you clean it up?"

"It's your cat. I told you, you should have had it put down years ago."

I pursed my lips, holding back a retort, and marched into the kitchen. A large puddle of diarrhea pooled by the sink. Marvin lay, curled on his cat bed, looking forlorn.

"Oh, Marv." I carefully crossed the kitchen and crouched down beside him. "It's not your fault."

I stroked his head. He purred, or at least he tried to. These days it sounded more like a dusty old rattle. Marvin was sixteen now. An old cat. Not a well cat. His kidneys were failing, his eyesight all but gone. Even his fur, once sleek and soft, was now patchy and matted.

Alan was right. Maybe it would be kinder to let him go. But I loved Marvin. The thought of having him put to sleep was more than I could bear. He might be a bit old and decrepit, but weren't we all?

I stood up. "I'll get this mess cleaned up, then," I said, in a voice loud enough for Alan to hear.

"If you could."

If I could. I always did. I couldn't remember the last time Alan had helped around the house, even though he was retired and had plenty of time on his hands. He'd rather slump in front of the TV or skulk off down to the pub.

It didn't use to be like this. Once, we did everything together. We were each other's world. We had to be. I was never able to have children. Perhaps that was the problem. Somewhere along the way, we realized it really was just us, forever. No extended family to call round, no grandchildren to brighten up those long hours of retirement. The love and laughter just seemed to drain away. Maybe all of us only have so much in the well. And ours had been dry for a very long time.

I scooped up the last of the mess with tissues, sealed them in a plastic shopping bag and popped them in the trash can.

"What's for dinner?" Alan called.

I shot a vicious glance at the living-room door. "Tuna."

THE NEXT MORNING, I returned to the Copy Shop. The same pretty young thing stood behind the counter.

"Hello," she said brightly. Because when you're young, your world *is* bright: yet to be darkened by heartache and regret.

"I've come to pick up my vase," I said.

"I'll just get it."

She disappeared into the back room and returned seconds later with a cardboard box. I pushed aside the tissue paper and pulled out my vase.

When Melinda was right, she was right. The vase was perfect. Pristine. Every color, every detail, every brush stroke exactly the same as the original. Except *better*. Before, the vase had looked like what it was: the work of a gifted amateur. This looked . . . well, this looked beautiful.

"It's . . . amazing."

"We're very pleased you think so."

I turned the vase around in my hands. It even felt different. Heavier. More substantial.

"Thank you."

"Well, remember, if you have anything else, anything at all, do bring it in."

"I certainly will. Now—" I took out my purse. "How much do I owe you?"

THE VASE DIDN'T look right on top of the TV cabinet anymore. I put it back on the mantelpiece, but the vibrant colors seemed to make the rest of the ornaments look faded and dreary.

I tried the windowsill, the bookshelf, the sideboard. Every day for the next week, I shifted its position, but nowhere seemed to quite suit my new, improved vase.

"Just leave the bloody thing be," Alan muttered.

"I want it to be right," I said.

He harrumphed and shrugged on his coat. "I'm off to the Dragon."

"Fine."

"Cat's made a mess in the kitchen again."

"Oh good."

After Alan had gone, I stood there for a while, staring at the vase. Not wanting to go into the kitchen. Not wanting to confront more evidence of Marvin's continual decline. He wasn't getting any better. Deep down, I knew that he wasn't going to.

With a heavy heart, I reached for the phone. The doorbell rang. *Saved by the bell.* I walked into the hall. Through the frosted glass, I could see a familiar haze of blonde hair. Melinda. I opened the door to let her in.

"Fran." She swept past me into the living room. "Just thought I'd pop over . . ." Her eyes alighted on the vase. "Oh, I see you took my advice."

"Yes."

She walked over and peered at it. "Oh, they've done a good job, haven't they?"

"Yes, it's excellent."

She wrinkled her nose. "What's that smell?"

I glanced toward the kitchen. "Marvin. He's not well. Alan thinks I should have him put down."

"Oh no, darling."

I felt tears welling. "I know he's old, but I can't bear the thought of losing him forever—"

"I understand. I went through the same thing with Lady Chatterley."

Lady Chatterley was Melinda's beautiful white Persian. But she wasn't an old cat. She was the picture of mouse-hunting, fence-scaling health.

Melinda caught my puzzled look. "The *original* Lady Chatterley, that is."

"Original? I don't understand?"

She smiled. "Let me tell you a little secret, darling . . ."

THE BLONDE ASSISTANT beamed. "Back again so soon?"

I felt my cheeks flush. This was stupid. Crazy. I didn't know why I had agreed to it. I put it down to the fact that I was emotional over Marvin and, well, Melinda can be very, very persuasive.

"My . . . erm . . . friend, Melinda, said you could help with my cat?"

I waited for Blondie to raise her eyebrows or laugh or call the men in white coats, but the smile never faltered.

"I'll just get the manager."

The same small, neat man emerged. He lifted Marvin out of his cat carrier. Usually, Marvin wasn't keen on being handled by strange people, but for once he acquiesced.

"Oh dear," the man said, examining him with a critical eye. "He *is* past his best, isn't he?"

"I suppose so," I said, sadly.

"Well, don't worry. We can definitely help."

"You can?"

"Leave him with us. Call back in two days."

I hesitated. "He will be . . . all right?"

"Of course."

"I mean, it will be the same old Marvin?"

He frowned. "Well, if that's what you really want."

I looked at Marvin, sagging in the man's arms like Bagpuss, the light in his eyes dulled by creamy white cataracts.

"No," I said. "No, I suppose not."

MARVIN MARK II—AS I now thought of him—was perfect. The picture of furry feline health. Glossy coat, bright eyes; even his old rich, deep-throated purr had returned.

Of course, there were a few downsides.

He went out more. I'd forgotten that. I had become used to him settling, snoring, on my lap in the evening. But now, most nights, he disappeared into the nearby fields, hunting.

I'd forgotten that too. Dealing with the headless birds and mice, and sometimes the not quite dead ones that scurried, bloodied and wounded, behind the fridge or the stove.

But still, it was good to have him back, healthy and fit again. Or so I told myself as I dropped another decapitated mouse into the trash can.

Alan barely noticed the change. I told him I had taken Marvin to the vet, who had put him on some new medication.

He tutted. "So, I've got to put up with him for a few more bloody years, then."

And then he belched and went back to his newspaper.

I think that was when I decided.

Although it's never really one thing, is it? It's all the small things. All those tiny little cracks, scuffs and chips you can never quite repair or glue back together. Not like they used to be. Not like the original.

It took some persuasion to get him to come with me. In the end, I used guilt. I told him it was a surprise for our anniversary. He grumbled, of course. But grudgingly, he went along with it.

The blonde girl at the shop did the rest: "If you'll just come with me, sir," she said, leading him by the arm into the back room.

His eyes lit up. "Absolutely."

I'd forgotten that Alan used to have a bit of an eye for the ladies. I looked at the small, bald manager.

"Oh, yes." He smiled. "We can definitely improve upon that."

ALAN IS JUST like his old self now. A new, improved old self. He's lost weight, got fit. Started dressing smartly. The other day, he even bought me flowers.

Of course, others have noticed too. Women especially. I always used to think I looked good for my age, but next to Alan Mark II, I seem a little tired. Dreary. Past my best, even.

Perhaps that's why, this morning, I found myself writing Alan a note:

"Just going away for a couple of days. Don't worry. When I get back, I'll be as good as new." I paused. "Better, in fact."

Dust

Introduction

I love creepy hotels.

Fusty lobbies; ancient, creaky lifts. All those mysterious locked doors. The endless maze of windowless corridors. I often take pictures of especially spooky hotel corridors. I blame *The Shining*.

In early 2022, my family and I flew abroad for the first time in three years, to Gran Canaria. The hotel we had booked was lovely but unusual, built in the style of a famous seventeenth-century Canarian church. The lobby had a massive domed ceiling, with tall pillars and chandeliers. Very Gothic. Outside, it was all whitewashed towers and huge arched windows. A mixture of Disney's Tower of Terror and The Eagles' "Hotel California."

Cool, I thought.

"You're lucky you weren't here last week," the receptionist told us as we checked in. "We had a huge sandstorm. Calima wind."

"What's that?" I asked.

"Cloud of dust. The wind blows in sand from the Sahara. Turns the sky red."

Interesting, I thought.

About halfway through our stay, as we were lounging on our sunbeds—no wind, perfect blue skies—my daughter asked, "When do we leave, Mummy?"

She's eight. An age where time is becoming more important to her. How much time she has to do fun stuff. How much time before she is forced to do boring stuff.

I smiled and said, "You can check out any time you like, but you can never leave."

She gave me her "eight going on fifteen" eye roll. "Mummy, you are so weird."

On the plane home, I was still thinking about the hotel. And time. And dust.

An idea for a story started to form.

So, welcome to the Villa de las Almas Perdidas.

Stay as long as you like. It's a lovely place.

Dust. It blew in from the Sahara and everything in the hotel seemed to be coated with it.

Fine and yellowish-brown, it crept through the slatted shutters and badly fitting windows, laying claim to all it touched. Olivia could feel the fine grains beneath her toes on the tiled floor and in the grittiness of her sheets, even though the maid had changed them only this morning.

A Calima wind, they called it. *Cloud of dust*. Occurring when high pressure hit the desert. The resulting sandstorm reduced visibility to near zero and turned the sky a scorched orange, transforming the volcanic landscape into something altogether more alien.

Even now, after the storm had passed, the sky seemed to hold a vague apricot tinge, especially at sunset. Rather than visiting a different country, it felt like visiting another world. Which was just what Olivia needed right now. To escape reality. To forget her life.

But that fucking dust, though.

She coughed as she brushed her hair in the mirror. Men always used to comment on her hair—long, glossy and brown. Now it was brittle and dry, streaked a dirty gray. Everything dried, sagged and drooped once you turned fifty, she thought. Your middle grew stouter, and your sight grew shorter.

Just like the Calima reduced visibility, so did aging. From sideways glances of appraisal and attraction, now men's eyes floated past her before settling on younger, fresher, plumper flesh. Olivia had faded in the storm of time, disappearing into the background. No longer bold or vibrant. Just a shadow in the periphery of their vision.

At least the dust had one benefit. It coated the mirror, the fine film softening her features, grown harder and harsher in recent years. In the dirty glass, she could pass for forty. Add in a few gins and maybe a worn thirty-five. Olivia smiled thinly. She might just be kidding herself, but self-flattery was all she had left.

She turned and crossed the room, walking outside to the balcony. She picked up her gin and tonic and took a deep gulp. It was warm and dust coated the rim of the glass. Olivia didn't care. She swigged the lot.

THE VILLA DE las Almas Perdidas was the oldest hotel on the island. Built fifty years ago and modeled on a famous seventeenth-century church, it was still beautiful but, like her, definitely showing signs of wear around the edges.

There was a grand central lobby, several additional wings and three pools, plus expansive gardens decorated with ornate urns and Roman statues. Ladies clutching their togas or half-naked cherubs pouring jugs of water into the basins of fountains. Odd, a little naff perhaps, but somehow the slight neglect and addition of the dust, bronzing them like rust, added an air of antiquity.

That was part of the reason Olivia had chosen this place. Its quirkiness. Its age. Its mostly two- and three-star reviews that proclaimed it past its heyday, frequented by those with one foot in the grave, who didn't mind its lack of atmosphere, entertainment or modern conveniences.

Olivia didn't. In fact, it was the perfect place to retreat. Away from other people. Away from feeling forgotten and alone. It was true that there was comfort in strangers. When no one knows who you are, they can't hurt or abandon you.

Like Gabriel did. A story as old as the Villa de las Almas Perdidas. Or perhaps the church it was modeled on. Olivia had loved Gabriel passionately, completely, had dreamed that they would have children and grow old together. Gabriel had loved her distractedly, transiently. He was older and he already had children from a previous relationship. He didn't want more. It turned out he didn't want marriage either. Or to be faithful. Olivia was not the love of his life.

She was merely a place holder, until something better and, inevitably, younger, came along.

Fuck. She had told herself she wouldn't think about Gabriel, with his casually long hair and hint of stubble, who was probably always too good for her, too charismatic, too handsome. Oh, Olivia had had her charms when she was younger. A good figure, that long dark hair and a pleasant face that she could make look attractive in the right light.

But she lacked that something that transforms pretty into sexy. She had tried. But with age comes weariness. Olivia was not "effortlessly" beautiful, and some days the effort was just too damn much. She had let herself go. Relaxed her grip, and Gabriel had slithered from her grasp.

But you made him pay.

She started. A voice, like a whisper on the breeze. Olivia looked around. She was standing by the main pool, although she didn't remember leaving her room and coming outside. The pool area was empty, except for an elderly couple lying on sun loungers by the main pool, crinkled brown bodies like shriveled conkers. Hard to tell if they were alive or dead, although something about them stirred a memory. Her own parents, sprawled on deckchairs at the beach. Nowhere "foreign." Skegness was as far as they went. Her parents had been tight with money. Even though they had plenty tucked away. The first thing Olivia did when she received her inheritance was to book a holiday abroad.

She shook her head. Why was she thinking about her parents, the past? It had been happening a lot lately. Since Gabriel, and the children. That was why she had come here. To forget. She turned and walked away from the elderly couple, down a tree-lined pathway toward the more secluded freshwater pool. Olivia preferred this area. Fewer people came to swim or sunbathe because the pool wasn't heated and the trees cast the terrace into shade.

Shade didn't bother Olivia. Full sun played havoc with her pale skin. Never one to tan, she just turned irritatingly red. And, of

course, sun was aging on the skin. Although wasn't fucking everything? Everything *good,* anyway. Sun, alcohol, fatty foods, life. Hide
away in a dark closet and you'd remain beautiful and wrinkle-free
forever.

Olivia sat down on one of the sun loungers. It creaked. The fabric was a little moldy around the edges. She laid her book, a dog-
eared Shirley Jackson, on the lounger beside her and placed her
drink on the small table. Then she paused. Something was different.

She was not alone.

Two children stood at the edge of the pool at the opposite end.
Around five or six, the girl was pale with fair hair in braids, and the
boy was darker, with tousled curls. Odd clothing, she thought. The
girl appeared to be wearing a plain white nightdress and the boy
wore what looked like a vest and pajama bottoms. Had they just got
up—at past four in the afternoon? But what did she know of the
strange habits of children? Still, something about the pair looked
vaguely familiar. Perhaps she had seen them before around the hotel.

As she watched, the boy dipped a toe in the pool and made an
exaggerated "Brrr" face before leaping back, giggling. Then the girl
did the same. Splash, giggle, splash, giggle. Olivia felt a twitch of annoyance. She knew they were only playing, but this was her place,
where she came to relax. Her own little oasis. There was a perfectly
good children's pool back up at the hotel. Why did they have to
come here and bother her?

As if feeling her watching them, the little girl suddenly looked
up. Her eyes, brilliant blue in her pale face, widened. She nudged her
brother, who followed her gaze.

Olivia tried to smile politely. "Hello," she said.

The children continued to stare at her with wide eyes.

"You should be careful by the pool."

Still no reaction. Were they deaf or just rude?

"Where are your parents?"

Olivia started to rise from her lounger.

The little boy screamed. A hideous, high-pitched thing, like an animal in pain. The girl glared at Olivia, wrapping an arm around her brother.

"Leave us alone," she shouted. "You're not our mummy."

"I know. I was just—"

"Stop hurting us. Why won't you just go *away*!"

The girl grabbed her brother's hand and the pair sprinted from the pool and disappeared into the greenery of the gardens.

Olivia stared after them, stunned. *What on earth?* Why had they reacted like that? All she had done was tell them to be careful by the pool. She hadn't been unkind. It was for their own good. If anything, she was the one who should be upset. They had disturbed her afternoon. They shouldn't be wandering around on their own. Someone should be watching them. *Taking care of them.*

She sat down again, a little shaken. But now she couldn't settle. The calm and tranquility had been shattered.

"Little brats," she muttered.

She swigged her gin and tonic. Then she picked up her book, marking the page with a folded corner, a habit that had always infuriated Gabriel. He disliked mess. Liked everything to be just so. Perfect. Even his children were always well turned out and cloyingly polite. Spoiled, if anything. He spent more on their clothes than he ever did on her.

She sighed, staring at the folded corner. A well-worn crease. She must have been stuck on this page for a while. She frowned and flicked through the rest of the book. A small shower of fine brown grains drifted to the ground. It was full of dust.

OLIVIA DIDN'T SEE the children again. She didn't see anyone in the hotel grounds, although past the stone wall that marked the resort's boundaries she could just make out the heads of tourists walking along the promenade. Olivia sometimes thought about taking a stroll along the seafront herself, but something always stopped her.

Instead, she limited herself to the confines of the Villa de las

Almas Perdidas. Leaving the pool, she wandered back through the gardens, skirting the main pool, which was completely empty now, just a few leaves floating on the surface.

Finally, she settled in the grand terrazzo—a large courtyard filled with wrought-iron tables and chairs. She sat in her usual spot, beneath the shade of an orange tree. Then she placed her book down and waited. Even though Olivia was the only customer, it was several minutes before she was aware of a presence at her table.

She glanced up. A waiter stood courteously nearby. He must have been the wrong side of sixty, dressed in the Almas Perdidas uniform—dark blue trousers, white shirt and blue waistcoat with gold trim. But his uniform looked worn, the waistcoat creased, rust-colored stains around the cuffs and collar of his shirt. Even his skin had a rusty kind of look, like dirt had become ingrained in the numerous lines and folds. His teeth, when he smiled, were as yellow as sand. Still, she thought, beggars can't be choosers.

"A large gin and tonic, please," she said.

He nodded. "Very good, señora."

"Gracias."

He lingered. Olivia smiled politely.

"You are enjoying your stay here, señora?" he asked.

Was she? Hard to say, really. But she said, "Yes, it's very peaceful."

He chuckled. An odd, dry sound. "Yes, all our guests think that, to start with."

All our guests? Well, that wouldn't amount to a lot. And what did he mean—to start with?

"After a while," he continued, "some feel they have been here forever—you know?"

Olivia was certainly starting to get that impression, and when would he get her *damned* drink? Her throat was as dry as the desert.

"Well, it's nice to have a break," she said.

"Yes." He chuckled again. "A break."

And then he wandered off, still chuckling to himself as if she had just told him the world's funniest joke. Christ. Bloody foreigners. Olivia massaged her temples and told herself to relax. She was on holiday, away from her problems. So why was she feeling so unsettled?

Perhaps it was those children, or maybe the solitude was starting to become a little claustrophobic. Or maybe it was just the heat and the dust. Even now, she could feel it scratching at the back of her eyeballs and catching in her throat. She really needed that fucking drink.

She blinked. A large gin and tonic sat on the table.

Olivia hadn't noticed the waiter return. She glanced around. The terrazzo was still empty. More than empty. There was something desolate about it. No sounds at all except the faint whisper of the breeze. There was quiet and there was . . . *abandoned.*

No, she thought. Not that word. This solitude was her choice. Not his. Gabriel no longer called the shots. She had shown him that. Him and that bimbo and his brats.

She picked up her drink and took a large gulp. She was drinking gin like water, but it was having the same effect. She wondered if they were pouring her short measures. Or perhaps her tolerance had increased. She had probably been drinking too much lately, but you had to have some vices, didn't you? At least it was low-calorie tonic.

She tipped the glass up again. Ice rattled at the bottom. Empty. Olivia stared at it disbelievingly. She couldn't have finished her drink already. She had only taken a sip—a large one, admittedly, but still. She placed the glass down on the table. Her hand trembled. Unease drifted across her skin. She used to worry she was losing her mind. Gabriel often made her feel like she was going mad. Called her unstable, hysterical, crazy.

The court had said she was completely sane.

She hadn't eaten today, Olivia suddenly remembered. She was probably a little light-headed. The buffet started at seven. She should go and get ready. She stood, chair scraping across the stone, and reached for her book, almost entirely coated now in yellow dust. She brushed it off, revealing the cover—an old Stephen King. Olivia frowned. Then quickly dismissed it. She picked the book up, stuffing it under her arm, and walked out of the terrazzo, sandals scuffing on the gritty stone.

It was almost sunset. The sky darkening from amber to magenta. Sometimes the dust cloud made it feel like a permanent sunset here. Eternal twilight.

Olivia walked along the pathway, past the gardens with their tall dragon trees, Canarian palms and pines. Old trees, probably planted when the hotel was built. Their leaves rustled like low conversation. And there was another sound too. A different sort of sound. A slow, rhythmic creaking. Like a swing. *A rope swing.* Gabriel's brats had one in the garden. The creaking sound used to drive Olivia nuts.

She hadn't noticed a swing earlier. But perhaps she had missed it. She seemed to be missing a lot at the moment. And it was none of her concern, anyway. Still, that insistent creaking grated on her. Perhaps it was the same children she had seen by the pool. Perhaps she should go and tell them that, once again, they were being an annoyance.

She turned. A winding pathway led down between the trees. Olivia followed it. The path opened out to a small space with seats and a fountain, now dry. It was an ornate piece, circular with a central conceit—two angelic-looking children pouring water from an urn into the basin. The boy had cherubic curls; the girl wore her long hair in plaits. Olivia felt her breath catch, heart thrumming in her throat. It was *them.* The children at the pool. They were the children *here,* sculpted in stone.

But that was impossible. She must be imagining things. Too much gin. They poured large measures. Except hadn't she just thought that she could barely taste the alcohol? Sunstroke, maybe. But the sun was stifled behind the haze of sand. What was *wrong* with her? And, still, she could hear that fucking creaking. Even louder now. What was it?

She walked faster past the fountain. The creaking was coming from her right. Olivia turned down another winding pathway. She didn't remember the gardens being this big, the trees so tall. Finally, she reached a new clearing. Grass, sprinkled with daisies, and ahead of her a large pine, boughs stretching out like muscular arms.

Tied to one were two sturdy lengths of rope. They swung back and forth in unison. At the ends, the boy and girl from the pool hung by their necks.

"No!"

Back and forth, back and forth. *Swing low, sweet chariot*. That song always reminded her of Gabriel's daughter—Charity. Max was his son. How could she have forgotten? Gabriel was always talking about them. Always doting on them, buying them things. Always putting them first. Two children for him, but no children for her.

Olivia took another step forward. *Creak, creak*.

The rope had cut into their necks. But Olivia hadn't strangled them. That was wrong. She had suffocated them with bags tied over their heads as they slept. Gabriel had been foolish not to take back her key. More foolish to go out, leaving the brats and bimbo alone. She had taken care of the bimbo with a kitchen knife.

As Olivia watched, Max raised his head. He screamed, just like he had when he woke, with Olivia kneeling on top of him. His cries had roused his sister, who had tried to fight her off.

"Stop hurting us. Why won't you just leave us alone?"

Charity was brave, but Olivia was bigger and stronger, and eventually both had succumbed. Olivia had laid them on top of their beds in their nightclothes for Gabriel to find upon his return.

But she hadn't come here to remember. She had come here to forget.

Gabriel had left her, and she had taken herself away on holiday. Nothing else. Nothing else had happened. How could it? If Olivia had done such a terrible thing, the police would have arrested her and she would be in jail, not here on the dusty isle of Gran Canaria.

They would never have let her leave the country. Never let her get away. How could she have escaped? How could she have carried on living, if she was such a monster?

Olivia turned and walked quickly back up the pathway. Dusty. Everywhere was so dusty. It was almost choking her. By the time she emerged back by the pool, she was gasping. She stared up at the hotel, white towers gleaming against the red sky. Villa de las Almas Perdidas. Such a pretty name. That was why she had chosen it. So why did it suddenly make her skin crawl with goosebumps?

She scurried across the patio, into the hotel's side entrance. It was cooler and darker in here. Olivia felt herself breathe a little more easily. Stress, that was all it was. The stress of Gabriel leaving her. She needed a drink. A strong gin and tonic to take up to her room before dinner. Or maybe it was the last thing she needed. Damned if you do. Damned if you don't. A sudden, hysterical giggle escaped her lips, which felt dry and chapped. Olivia licked them and spat. Dust.

Distantly, from the bar, she could hear the tinkling of a grand piano. She turned toward it. She was sure the piano bar had been on her left when she walked past earlier. But now, there was a wall on her left, hung with old pictures of the hotel and the staff. To her right, double doors led into the bar. She walked through.

The space was large but dark, despite the patio doors at one end. Chandeliers hung overhead. Velvet-covered chairs were arranged around small tables, and high leather stools perched along the bar. At one end, Olivia could see the grand piano but couldn't quite make out the pianist.

The patrons were few. The old couple she had seen by the pool sat, hunched over drinks, at a far table. A younger woman sipped wine in a shadowy corner. Olivia walked up to the bar.

"Hello?"

The barman turned.

"Good evening, señora."

The waiter from the terrace. He must have changed shifts.

"Can I help you?" He smiled, or at least he bared his butter-yellow teeth, dark eyes gleaming.

"I'd like a—"

"Gin and tonic."

He pushed a glass across the bar. Olivia looked down. A freshly made gin and tonic, brimming with ice and lemon. She hadn't seen him make it and the drink hadn't been on the bar a second ago, she was sure.

"Is something wrong, señora?"

"I don't know."

She rubbed at her head, and then her throat. It felt sore.

"I don't seem to be myself right now."

"Oh, you are very much yourself, señora."

"I'm sorry?"

His lips stretched wider. Not so much a grin as a leer.

He leaned over the bar. Olivia caught an odd musky smell, like rotten eggs.

"Do you not remember yet, señora?"

"Remember what?" she said, trying to sound irritated but sounding only feeble and scared.

"What you are? What you did?"

Olivia swallowed and reached for the glass, but the drink was gone. Instead, it was full to the brim with yellow dust. She looked up, heart thudding.

"What am I? What did I do?"

"See for yourself—"

Olivia spun around. The other guests stood behind her. She stifled a scream. The old couple she had seen on the sun loungers. No longer bronzed and wrinkled. Now, bloated with gas, skin mottled green and slimy with algae. As Olivia watched, the old man opened his mouth and a fish slithered out and dropped to the floor.

"You remember your parents, surely?" the waiter said. "You wanted their money, so you engineered a car crash, and they drowned?"

"No."

"And Jill?"

The young woman smiled and raised her glass. Blood oozed from defensive wounds on her arms. Her yellow nightshirt was ragged with holes and drenched in more blood.

"Gabriel's new girlfriend. You stabbed her twenty times. She was pregnant."

"I didn't know." Olivia clutched at her head and backed away.

"And you have already met the children, no?"

"*No*. I am on holiday. I am—"

"—a guest at the Villa de las Almas Perdidas." The waiter's smile was a snarl, eyes full of menace. "Do you not remember your Spanish?"

No. Because she had forgotten. Like she had forgotten everything else.

Villa de las Almas Perdidas.

In Spanish, *villa* meant village or town.

And *almas perdidas* meant—

A cold hollow opened in her stomach.

"Lost souls."

The waiter nodded. "Our longest resident, señora. Fifty years. And until you remember your sins, you will never leave." He held up her glass with a flourish. "Another drink?"

Olivia stared at him. "Fuck you!"

She turned and fled the bar, hurrying across the foyer and up the stairs to her room. She fished in the pocket of her shorts for the key, twisted it in the lock and shoved the door open.

The bitter, metallic smell hit her straightaway.

Blood. The room was covered in blood. It spattered the walls and soaked the crisp white bedding, staining it dark crimson. More bloody footprints trailed across the floor to the long mirror on the wall. Olivia followed them and faced herself in the dusty glass.

Her throat gaped in a scarlet smile. Both arms were sliced open from wrist to elbow. Blood dripped steadily onto the tiles.

She had come here to forget.

"And until you remember your sins, you will never leave."

But Olivia didn't want to remember. Would *not* remember. She had held out for fifty years. She would hold out for a hundred more if she had to. Gabriel had always said she was stubborn. He had no idea.

She walked over to the blood-soaked bed and lay down.

Outside, the wind rattled the shutters.

A Calima wind.

Occurring when high pressure hit the desert. The resulting sandstorm reduced visibility to near zero and turned the sky a scorched orange, transforming the volcanic landscape into something altogether more alien. Another world. Which was just what Olivia needed right now. To escape reality. To forget her life.

She closed her eyes.

Some souls should remain lost.

But that fucking dust, though.

Butterfly Island

Introduction

In my early twenties, I went on holiday to Turkey with two of my best friends.

I was skint and couldn't really afford it—in fact, I had to take out a £500 bank loan to pay for the trip. But I was young, irresponsible and it was two weeks away in the sun!

The resort we ended up in—Ölüdeniz—was still pretty uncommercialized in the early nineties. There was an amazing beach and a great crowd of young people and travelers who we soon became friends with.

We did a lot of cool stuff together and, toward the end of our stay, a bunch of us decided to club together to hire a boat to take us to a place called Butterfly Valley. Just across the sea from Ölüdeniz, Butterfly Valley was a beautiful and virtually untouched nature reserve. No permanent buildings, bars or restaurants. It had only recently opened up to visitors.

The plan was to stay overnight and the boat would pick us up the next day. There was no accommodation. Back then, there was really nothing there at all. Just a basic shack selling cold drinks and cigarettes. The tourist boats that now rock up hourly were nowhere to be seen. It was just us.

We took sleeping bags, food and *a lot* of booze. As the sun started to set, we built a huge bonfire, drank and smoked. Two of the group could eat fire and they put on an insane show. It was a brilliant, bonkers night. Sometime in the early hours, we curled up in our sleeping bags on the beach. As I drifted off, I remember thinking:

What would happen if the boat never came back for us? What if, while we danced and drank, something terrible had happened back on the mainland? What if we were marooned here on our own mini desert island?

The next day came . . . and eventually the boat returned. Of course. By that time, sunburnt, hungover and sleep-deprived, we were glad to get back to the mainland to shower and change clothes. Spending the night as a castaway is fun, but the novelty soon wears thin.

Many years later, I was sorting through boxes of old photos and I found some pictures of that holiday. It started me thinking about Butterfly Valley again. Around the same time, I was asked if I'd like to contribute a short story to a new British anthology. The two things came together, and "Butterfly Island" was the result.

It's one of my favorite short stories—and I might, one day, expand it into a novella.

For now, kick back, and I hope you enjoy the trip.

Almost every bad plan is hatched over a few beers in a bar. The end of the world won't finally arrive with a bang or a whimper. It will start with the words *Hey—y'know what would be a really great idea?* slurred over a bottle of Estrella.

I stare at Bill. I like Bill, as much as I like anyone. My affection is undoubtedly heightened by his ready supply of weed and loose attachment to his cash. That's why I don't punch him in the face. I say, "I need to go for a piss."

"No, wait." Bill leans forward. "Hear me out, man."

I don't want to hear Bill out. As I said, I like Bill, but he's a fucking moron. He's Australian, for a start, which has nothing to do with his intelligence but does make his stupidity harder to bear. I'd put it down to youth, but it's hard to tell Bill's age. His face is so weathered by years of sun and sleeping on beaches that he could be anywhere from twenty-five to fifty-five.

But then, to be fair, we're all a fairly motley crew at this beach bar. At first glance, you might almost mistake us for travelers backpacking our way around the world. That is, if the world still existed in any recognizable form. Look closer, and you might notice the ragged, mismatched clothing. The worn rucksacks. The guns and knives people carry quite openly these days.

What we really are is survivors. A ragtag bunch of nomads who happened to be in the right place at the right time. Or perhaps, more accurately, to not be in the wrong place at the wrong time. Killing our days with tequila and Thai noodles. Wondering when here will be the wrong place and where the hell there is left to go.

"This is the real deal," Bill says.

"Heard that before."

"You ever read *The Beach,* man?"

"Yeah. Long time ago. From memory, it didn't end so well."

"Yeah, but this is different. Look around. Look at what's happening. What have we got to lose? And what if what the dude says is true?"

"Big if. Huge. Fucking colossal."

"But if?"

He waggles his eyebrows at me. I still don't punch him. My restraint is admirable.

"I heard some mega-rich inventor bought the island years ago and turned it into a nature sanctuary," I say.

"*Butterflies,* man."

"What?"

"A butterfly sanctuary. Hence the name. Butterfly Island."

I stare at him in shock. Bill knows the word "hence." Maybe I misjudged him.

"Okay. Butterflies. My point is that I read he went to a lot of trouble to keep people like us away."

"But the dude's dead, and who gives a fuck about butterflies now, right?"

"True. But I do give a fuck about armed guards."

"Man, we're on the edge of the fucking apocalypse. Who's gonna waste their time guarding butterflies on an empty fucking island?"

He has a point.

"How will we get there?"

"I know a man."

Other famous last words. *I know a man.* There is always a man. I fully believe that our current apocalypse began because someone knew a man. Who had a really great idea over a bottle of Estrella.

I push my chair back. "I'll think about it."

I'm halfway to the toilets (a generous description of a lean-to with a hole in the floor) and not thinking about it, when two figures step out of the gloom.

I also know a man. Unfortunately, he is not the sort of man you have beers with. He is the sort of man who smashes a beer bottle on your head and uses the shards of broken glass to scoop out your eyeballs. Actually, that's wrong. He's the sort of man who pays people like these two goons to do the eyeball scooping.

"Well, look who it is." Goon 1 smiles at me.

"I'll get the cash," I say.

"I thought you had it."

"Soon. I promise."

"The sea is full of floaters who made promises."

"I mean it."

"Good."

He nods at Goon 2.

Goon 2 grabs my head and smashes my face into the wall. I taste plaster and feel a tooth crack. Pain shoots up my jaw. Goon 2 yanks my head back and smashes it into the wall again. This time I feel the tooth give and my vision blurs. Goon 2 lets me go and I slide down the wall to the dirty floor.

"No more chances."

A boot connects with my ribs. I scream and curl into a ball. "Please," I beg. "Please, no more."

"Fucking pathetic," I hear Goon 2 mutter.

I shove my hand into my boot and pull out my gun. I swivel and shoot Goon 2 in the kneecap. He howls and hits the floor next to me. I shoot him in the face. Goon 1 has his gun out, but I'm faster. I shoot him twice in the stomach and watch with satisfaction as blood splatters the wall behind him and he crashes heavily on top of Goon 2.

I push myself to my feet. I still need a piss. I walk into the toilet, relieve myself and splash some water on my face. Then I step over the dead goons and walk back into the bar.

No one has moved, or even looked up in curiosity. That's the way we roll nowadays. Bill is skinning up. He glances at me with mild interest. "What happened to your face?"

I spit the remains of my tooth into the overflowing ashtray. "So, when do we go to Butterfly Island?"

———

THE SUN PEERS over the horizon. Thirteen of us are spread between two ramshackle-looking boats, not including the drunken locals everyone is over-confidently referring to as "captains." A baker's dozen. Unlucky thirteen. I don't believe in fate or superstition. I do believe in drunken morons crashing boats into rocks.

The smaller boat to my right is filled with a group of five men and women in their twenties who already look trashed at just past 4 a.m. Or maybe they're still trashed from the previous night. I wonder where Bill found these people. If this is the best we can do, I think, we might as well concede defeat—and superior intelligence—to the cockroaches.

On our boat we have Bill (the man himself) and another Aussie, Olly, a wild-eyed guy with a pelmet of tattoos, a bandanna, and a hunting knife strapped around his waist, who I keep expecting to say *You don't know, man. You weren't there.* Next to him are a middle-aged couple in matching khaki shorts, black vests and sturdy walking boots, called Harold and Hilda. Probably. I don't actually know their names. They just look like a Harold and Hilda. Opposite them is an older dude with a shorn head and long gray beard who is calmly reading an old paperback of *The Stand.* Less fiction, more like a survival manual these days. Finally, only just embarking, are a muscular black woman with dreadlocks piled on top of her head and . . .

I turn to Bill. "What the fuck is this?"

"What?"

I point at the young girl climbing on board with the woman. "What's a kid doing here?"

"Well, her mum couldn't leave her behind."

"This is not a fucking trip to Legoland."

"Lego what?"

"Fuck's sake."

"You have a problem?"

The dreadlocked woman eyes me coldly.

"I just don't think this is a trip for a kid," I say.

"I'm not a kid," the kid says. "I'm twelve."

"I've got T-shirts older than you," I say.

The woman looks me up and down. "I can see that."

I address her. "Your daughter—"

"She's not my daughter. Her parents are dead. We travel together, or not at all."

"Man, we need her," Bill whispers, nodding at the woman.

"Why?"

"She's a doctor. If anyone gets sick—"

"You *did* check people out?"

"I don't mean that kind of sick, man. I mean normal sick."

He does have a point. I glare at the woman and girl and take out my cigarettes.

"I'm Alison," the woman says, smiling faux-politely.

"Good for you."

She crosses her legs. "Well, aren't you a treat."

I ignore her and light a cigarette.

There's a judder as the "captain" starts the engine. We're off. The crowd in the second boat whoop. I blow out smoke and wonder if having my eyeballs scooped out with shards of glass might actually be preferable. But it's too late now.

It's always too late now.

FORTY MINUTES LATER and the island draws into view. A jagged dark shape in the distance. It's mountainous, encircled by jungle and wide stretches of white sand. Years ago, back when I was in my late teens, it used to be a popular destination for backpackers. You could catch a skipper from the main island and stop over for a night or two, sleeping on the beach. They tried to keep it unspoiled. But, inevitably, it caved to commercialization. A beach bar sprang up. Then wooden huts were built for those who didn't like roughing it in sleeping bags on the sand.

At some point the crazy billionaire guy bought it and no one was allowed back on. But this was around the time a lot of shit was going on in the world, so my memory is vague, what with all the bombing, chemical weapons and new terrorist groups multiplying faster than the recently revived Ebola virus.

Good times.

I watch as the island grows bigger and more distinct, and the sea, which was a little choppy partway across, begins to calm, becoming more transparent. I can see several black shapes floating in the water, just beneath the surface. Not corals. Not sea creatures. One of the shapes briefly breaks the water to our right. Spherical with spiked protuberances. And then I realize. Fuck.

"Cut the engine!" I shout.

El Capitán turns. "*Khun phūd xari?*"

"Mines. Cut the fucking engine now and drop the anchor."

His eyes widen. But he quickly does what I say.

"Did you say mines?" Alison says.

"Look in the water," I say, pointing at the spiky objects all round us.

"Fuck, man," Bill mutters. "They're fucking everywhere."

I glance across at the other boat. Some distance away and a little ahead of us. One of the girls is trailing her hand in the water, centimeters away from one of the mines. I open my mouth to shout a warning.

Too late.

Kaboom! She explodes. Along with the boat and the rest of its passengers. One minute there. The next, gone in a flash of orange and a deafening blast wave. Flesh, limbs and shrapnel fly into the air and rain back down on us.

"Duck!" I yell, and throw myself down into the bottom of the hull, grabbing hold of the side as the aftershock hits. The boat rocks violently. Water crashes over the stern. I feel something smack into my head and realize it's someone's shoe, still attached to their foot. I fling it into the water.

Someone is screaming. The boat rises and falls, straining against the anchor. I remain splayed on the wet hull floor. The rocking calms. Water stops slopping over the sides. We're still afloat. Slowly, I sit up. The remains of the other boat and its occupants are spread out over the water, which is murky with blood and fuel; bits of bodies, wood, metal, rucksacks.

I glare at Bill, who is curled up next to me.

"Who's going to waste time guarding a fucking deserted island?"

He looks shamefaced. "I didn't know, man. I didn't know there would be fucking mines."

I want to punch him until his eyeballs pop out, but I can't afford to waste the time or energy.

"Is everyone okay?" Bearded Dude asks.

"We're fine," Alison says, helping the girl to sit up.

"They exploded. They just exploded," Hilda cries hysterically to her husband. "Why would they do that? Why?"

I'm not quite sure if she's questioning why someone would drop mines, or why people would explode. Either seems a moot point.

Our captain is gabbling in Thai.

"No," I say. "Don't touch the fucking engine."

"How are we going to get to the island?" Alison asks.

"We can't," Hilda says. "We have to go back."

"No," I say.

"No?"

"Look around. There are as many mines behind us as in front. We just got lucky."

"Well, we have to try," Harold says. "What else can we do?"

"We could swim, man." This from Olly.

"Swim?" Harold says. "Are you insane?"

Possibly, I think, but he might be smarter than his bandanna and tattoos suggest.

"We could do it," I say. "There's plenty of space between the mines for bodies. Just not boats."

"But what about all our stuff?" Hilda asks. "Clothes, food, water, phones."

"I doubt there's any electricity on the island, so your phone is going to be dead by dawn anyway."

Plus, who are we going to call? I think. If any of us had friends or family, we wouldn't be here.

"There's supposed to be a stream," Bearded Dude pipes up. "For fresh water. And maybe there's food left in the beach bar."

"If not, we can fish and hunt." Olly grins, and I reinstate my previous opinion of him as a survivalist wanker.

"You're all crazy." Harold shakes his head.

"Your call," Bearded Dude says calmly, taking off his flip-flops and sticking his gun into the waistband of his shorts. I follow suit. Bill and Olly chuck off their sneakers. Alison looks at the girl.

"You think you can swim it?"

"No problem."

Harold and Hilda exchange glances. "I can't swim," Hilda says. Jesus fuck.

"We're going back," Harold says. "He can take us." He turns to El Capitán and pulls out his wallet.

No, I think. Don't do this.

"We have money. See. Plenty money."

Harold smiles hopefully, waving notes. El Capitán smiles back, takes them and shoves them in his pocket.

"Khup kun krap."

Then he reaches down beneath the wheel and pulls out a semi-automatic gun.

"Get off my boat."

"What? But—"

"Get the fuck off, all of you. Now."

We don't wait to ask about the sudden improvement in his English. One by one, we all climb over the side and lower ourselves into the water.

"But I gave you money," Harold protests.

El Capitán jabs him in the chest with the gun. Harold falls back into the water with a splash.

Hilda yelps. "Please. Please. I can't swim. I'll drown. I can't go in there."

El Capitán nods. "Okay. No swimming."

He blasts her with a spray of bullets. Her body jerks and twitches, spitting red, and then crumples into the boat.

"Linda!" Harold screams. I was close with the name.

The engine splutters into life and the boat reverses in a small white wave.

"Linda!"

"She's dead," I say. "Swim."

I strike out and follow the others, not waiting to see if he heeds my advice. We all choose a sedate breaststroke, weaving carefully between the mines. Bearded Dude reaches the shore first and walks, dripping, up the beach. Alison and the girl are next. My feet have just touched the sandy seabed when I hear the boom.

I turn. A small mushroom of orange and gray rises up against the horizon.

"Shit." Bill spits out water. "You were right about the mines."

I stare at the smoke. "Yeah."

I don't say that the explosion is too far out at sea. El Capitán missed the mines.

Something else blew the boat up.

WE DRY OUR clothes on logs that line the edge of the beach. I shake water out of my gun and slip it back into the waistband of my shorts. Bearded Dude has taken a battered phone out of his pocket and is pressing buttons and frowning. I haven't had a phone for years. Like I said, no one to call. We've come ashore on a wide stretch of white sand. To our right, further down the beach, I can see the bar, now boarded up. The huts are further into the jungle.

"So," Alison says. "I suggest our first job should be to check out the bar and see if there are any usable supplies, bottled water, dried food and so on."

"Actually," Bearded Dude says, "our first job should be to introduce ourselves. I'm Ray."

"Alison," she says. "And this is Ellie."

"Bill, man," Bill offers.

"Olly," Olly says, sharpening his knife on the log.

Harold is sitting on the other end of it, huddled into himself. He hasn't taken his wet clothes off and is shivering, despite the heat of the mid-morning sun. Shock. Trauma. Or in other words, a fucking burden we do not need right now.

I realize people's attention has shifted to me. "The bar, did you say?" I start to walk across the beach.

"Dick," I hear Alison mutter.

Bill jogs to catch up with me. "Man, this is some trip."

"Yeah. I've watched a boatload of people get blown to smithereens and now I'm marooned on a fucking island, possibly facing death by starvation or dehydration. Some trip."

"Man, you really are a dick sometimes."

"I know."

I glance behind us. Alison is walking side by side with Ray and Ellie. I can't see Olly.

"Where's Olly?"

"Oh. I think he went to check out the huts."

And pretend he's Rambo.

We reach the bar. A few chairs rot outside. A faded and weather-beaten sign on the front offers a selection of beers and cocktails, crisps, noodles and chocolate.

"Guess this place didn't stay unspoiled for long," Alison says.

"Yeah." I smile thinly. "How d'you like it now?"

She turns and kicks the door in. "I'm reserving judgment."

I stare after her. Ray glances at me and chuckles. "I like her."

It's dim in the shack, sunlight filtering in through gaps in the roof and cracks in the walls. I blink, letting my eyes adjust. My nose is already on the case. Something smells off, rotten. Maybe food gone bad.

Tables and chairs have been piled up on one side of the small room. Directly in front of us is the counter. Glass-fronted refrigerators are lined up behind it, turned off but still half full of beer, water and soft drinks. So, we won't die of dehydration right away. And we can also get drunk.

"We should check out back for food," Ray says.

He disappears into the storeroom with Alison. Ellie walks over to the fridges and takes out a bottle of water. She checks the date, shrugs and uncaps it, taking a swig.

"Help yourself, why don't you?" I say.

She smiles at me, lifts the bottle again and takes several bigger gulps, almost draining it. She wipes her lips. "Thanks. I will."

I'm almost starting to like the kid. I turn and look around the rest of the room. The smell is still bothering me. I eye the stacked tables and chairs and walk over to them. Something on the wall catches my eye. A motley montage of blues and greens. Some kind of mural, or bits of paper pinned to the wall? I move closer and realize that it's neither. It's butterflies. Huge blue and green butterflies. Dozens of them. Dead. Nailed to the wall by their wings or through their large furry bodies.

"What the fuck is that, man?" Bill is at my shoulder, staring at the wall of crucified insects.

"Butterflies."

"I thought this was a sanctuary."

"Looks like someone found another way of saving them."

There's a couple of thuds from behind us as Alison and Ray walk out from the storeroom and dump two large boxes on the counter.

"Packs of crisps, dried noodles, sauces, chocolate. Plus, matches and firelighters. Enough to keep us going for a while," Alison announces.

I sniff again. "Does anyone else smell that?"

Ellie walks over and stands next to me. "Smells like when our cat crawled under the porch to die and we didn't find her for two weeks."

I stare at her again. This twelve-year-old is pretty hardcore. And she's right. Something is dead here, and not just the butterflies.

I reach for the chairs and start unstacking them and moving them to one side.

"What are you doing?" Alison asks.

"I'm expecting a busy day with customers."

"Are you ever not a dick?"

"Rarely."

I move more of the chairs and slide aside the tables. There's another door behind them. What used to be a toilet, I would guess. The smell is stronger here. I yank it open.

"Fuck!" Bill turns and retches.

"Shit," Ellie whispers.

Alison rushes over and pulls the girl back.

A body, or what remains of it, has been nailed to the door. Just like the butterflies nailed to the wall. It's been here awhile. The skin has mostly rotted away, just a few stringy tendrils of muscle stubbornly clinging to bone. Straggly clumps of dark hair sprout from a yellowed skull. The figure is dressed in a shirt and shorts, also rotted and ragged. I'd hazard a guess and say it's a man.

"What d'you think happened to him?" Ray asks.

"Well, he didn't nail himself to a door."

"So, there's someone else on the island?"

"And he, or she, is a killer."

He frowns. "We should check on the others."

HAROLD IS NOT on his log. I glance toward the sea, half hoping to see his lifeless body floating on the waves. But no. Damn.

"We need to go and check the huts."

The jungle is dense, the undergrowth beneath our bare feet littered with sharp bits of twig and thorns, and I'm only too aware of the potential for spiders or snakes. Above us, I spot the occasional flutter of bluey-green wings. Butterflies. I think again about the insects nailed to the wall. Weird shit.

The huts are set in a small clearing. Half a dozen of them. Arranged around a central firepit that must have once been used for barbecues.

Whatever has been cooking on it more recently certainly isn't sausages or burgers.

"Well, this just gets better and better," Alison says.

"Are those *skulls*?" Ellie asks.

They are. Five or six, along with an assortment of jumbled, blackened bones. We walk closer. I peer down into the pit. Then I pick up a stick and poke at the charred bones.

"Looks like our killer has been busy," Ray remarks.

I shake my head. "A lone killer couldn't possibly kill so many people at once."

"Depends on how big his gun is."

Alison crouches down and squints at the bones. "It looks like these bodies have been burned at different times."

"So, he kills everyone, then burns them one by one."

It still feels wrong to me. I'm pondering on it when Bill shouts, "Olly! Man, what happened?"

We all turn. Olly staggers down the steps from one of the huts. His right arm is bandaged with his torn-up vest but it's still bleeding profusely.

"Someone shot at me," he says. "Missed. No biggie."

No biggie. Ray and I snatch our weapons out of our waistbands and point them at the surrounding jungle suspiciously. None of us heard a gunshot. A silencer, maybe?

"You think they're still out there?" Ray asks.

Olly shakes his head. "I don't think so. Or they'd have finished me off, right?"

Rambo makes a good point.

"We should get out of here," I say. "Random shooters and burnt bodies aren't making me feel all homey."

"That's not all," Olly says.

I look at him.

He grins. "You should see what's out back."

THE CROSS IS staked firmly into the ground, in a small space behind the huts. The body lashed to it has been here some time, like the guy in the bar. All the flesh has gone. Stripped right back to the bone, which gleams in the dappled sunlight.

"This dude really pissed someone off," Bill says.

"It's not a dude," Alison says. "It's a woman. A young woman, I'd say, from the skeleton."

"You think she was killed and strapped up here?" Ray says.

There's a note of hope in his voice, and I get it, because the alternative is that she was strapped up here, maybe killed, maybe not. Maybe left to die or be tortured.

"Why would someone do that?" Ellie says. "Why would they hang her up like this? For what?"

For what? And suddenly something clicks. I can see it all with absolute clarity.

"A sacrifice," I say.

"A what?"

"They weren't all killed together. They were killed one by one. Chosen. Hung out here."

"Man!" Bill says. "Wild imagination."

"No," Alison says slowly. "I think he's right."

"But a sacrifice to whom or what?"

The fluttering in the trees has increased. I glance up. I can see more butterflies flying about now. My neck itches. A feeling of unease. The small patches of blue visible through the trees are starting to disappear. The jungle is darkening.

"I really think we should go."

"Me too," Alison says.

Ellie nods. "This place gives me the creeps."

We start to move away.

Olly remains, standing next to the skeleton of the young woman. "C'mon, it's only butterflies."

I glance back. A couple of butterflies have flown down and alighted on the skeleton. Two more perch on Olly.

"They like me."

It happens quickly. There's a rush like the wind and more blue and green bodies swoop gracefully down from the trees and land on Olly, predominantly on his right side. His injured arm. I see his face change, the smile morphing into a frown.

"Fuck, that's enough. Get off." He shakes his arm. The fluttering increases.

"Man, they really do like him," Bill mutters.

"Ow, shit. That *hurts*!" Olly cries.

More butterflies flock to him. I can barely see Olly now behind the mass of blue and green.

"Nooo. Aaagh. Get the fuck off. They're biting. They're fucking eating me. Help!"

"What the hell are they doing?" Ray asks.

I think about the staked body. The blood on Olly's arm. The frenzied beating of wings. It's quite simple.

"They're feeding," I say. "Now let's get the fuck out of here."

WE RUN, CRASHING our way through the jungle, paying little attention to direction. Olly's screams seem to follow us, long after his torment is out of earshot. We should have shot him, I think. But then, we only have so many bullets.

Eventually, sweat streaming down our backs, feet scraped raw, the greenery thins. We burst out into open air. Grass. Blue sky. Lots of blue sky. Ahead of us, the land runs out abruptly and drops off into a steep ravine.

We all stop, bending over, gasping, catching our breath.

"Guess we can't go any further," Alison pants.

"Nope."

"What the hell happened back there?"

"Flesh-eating butterflies. The usual."

"But how?"

"Who the fuck knows? Chemicals. Pollution. Experiment gone wrong. When a crazed billionaire buys an island and seals it off, it's not usually to make fluffy toys."

"You sound like you know a lot about it."

"Nah, just watched a lot of James Bond as a kid."

"You don't happen to have a parachute stuffed up your butt to get us out of this?" Ray asks.

We look back at the jungle and then toward the cliff.

"Caught between a drop and a fucked place," Bill says.

Alison walks over to the edge and peers down. "Maybe not. It's not so steep. I reckon we could—" She breaks off. "What the fuck."

"What?"

"There's something down there."

We all join her at the precipice. The drop makes me sway. And then I spot something, glinting at the bottom of the ravine. Something black and metallic with bent and twisted blades. The crumpled remains of a helicopter.

"Man," Bill hisses. "The dude was right."

"What dude?" Ray asks.

"The dude who said this island would make us rich."

"How is a crashed helicopter going to make us rich?" Ellie asks.

Bill grins. "Story goes that a helicopter carrying a new vaccine, one that could immunize against the virus, crashed on some uninhabited island. The dude was sure it was Butterfly Island."

"A vaccine?" Alison says. "That could save millions of lives?"

"Yeah." Bill nods. "And imagine how much someone will pay for it. I know a man—"

"What!" She stares at him. "You can't sell something like that. It needs to be delivered to an impartial health organization."

"Who asked you, Mother Teresa?"

"We're talking about the future of mankind."

"And I'm talking about *my* future."

"Could you all shut up!" Ellie glares at them. "First, we don't know if we can even reach the helicopter. Second, we don't know if the vaccine survived the crash, and third, we're stuck here on this island, remember?"

From the mouths of babes.

"And," I say, "we're stuck here with flesh-eating butterflies and at least one crazed killer running around sacrificing people. So perhaps we have more pressing concerns right now."

"Oh, I don't know."

We turn. Ray has taken a step back so that he stands behind our group. He is smiling and pointing his gun at us.

I shake my head. "Really?"

"What can I say? Good guys don't survive the apocalypse."

"Don't tell me—you heard about the helicopter too. You want to sell the vaccine for a load of cash, and you don't want to share?"

Ray shrugs. "Right and wrong. I heard about it, yeah. But my people don't want to sell the vaccine. They want to keep it for themselves."

"Why?"

"Imagine being immune from a virus killing millions. We'd be the most powerful people in the world. Invincible. Like gods."

Alison eyes Ray coldly. "So how come 'your' people sent you out here alone? Or are you one of the dispensable gods?"

He smiles at her. "Play nice. Maybe I'll let you be one of the chosen ones."

"I'd rather die."

"Fine."

He levels the gun at her.

"Wait." I hold my hands up. "Like Ellie said, the vaccine is no good to anyone if we can't get off this island. We need to work together or we're all going to die here."

Ray's dark eyes meet mine. He reaches into his pocket and takes out the battered phone.

"I got people waiting. I send this text; they know it's done. They come and get me."

"And get blown up by the mines."

"Already told them to drop anchor further out. Just got to swim to meet them. Home and dry."

"Got it all planned out."

"Damn right."

He grins a crooked yellow grin. I see his thumb press send. There's a roar from behind us. Animalistic. Desperate. Olly charges out of the thicket of trees, arms flailing, still half covered by butterflies. Most of his flesh has gone, eaten away to the muscle and tendon; one eye has popped out. His stomach cavity gapes. He shouldn't be standing. Yet he keeps going.

Ray shoots. Once, twice. Olly staggers but doesn't stop. I grab Alison and Ellie and pull them out of the way. Olly barrels into Ray, who clings to him like a desperate lover, but there's nothing he can do. Olly's momentum carries them off the cliff edge and down into the ravine. Ray's scream rises into the air along with the butterflies and then drifts away.

"Christ." Alison stares after them. "Fucking, *fucking* Christ!"

Ellie wraps an arm around her waist, and they hug tightly.

Bill looks at me. "Man," he says, and opens his arms.

"Don't even fucking think about it."

"So, what do we do now?" Alison asks, looking at me.

I consider. It doesn't take long.

"Well, we either chance the jungle or try our luck climbing down into the ravine. Either way, we'll probably die."

"Great."

"Plus, if what Ray said is true, there's another boat coming. And if Ray doesn't meet them—"

"You think they'll come ashore?"

"Maybe."

"And try to kill us."

"Probably."

"Oh, good."

"And we still have the problem of killer butterflies and a murderous psychopath roaming the island."

"And Linda's husband is missing," Alison adds.

I'd forgotten about Harold. And I have a feeling that I really shouldn't have.

"So?" Bill says. "We're fucked then?"

We fall into silence. I could really do with a cold Estrella.

I smile. "I've got a great idea . . ."

Acknowledgments

Normally, this is the bit where authors thank the people who helped them write their book and got it published. But this time around, I would like to thank the people who helped me to *not* publish a book.

Bear with me.

Sometimes, you know you've written a book that works. Others you're not sure—self-doubt is a prerequisite of being a writer—but a bit of distance and a bit of editing can usually iron out those kinks. And then there are the times you know something is wrong. You're not *feeling* the book and you don't know how to fix it.

When that happens, you can either try to rewrite the whole thing and end up with something (hopefully) vaguely publishable. Or you can call it quits. You can say: I don't want to put a book out that I don't love, I won't be proud of and, most important, that will disappoint my readers.

This is what happened with the book I wrote in 2020, the book I talked about during the introduction. I wrote it during a really tough year, finished it and hated it. It was simply the wrong book at the wrong time.

So, I would like to thank my wonderful agent, Maddy, and my brilliant editors, Max and Anne, for their kindness and understanding when I told them I wanted to ditch that book and write something completely different. Thank you for listening to me, backing me and *not* making me publish something that I wasn't happy with.

It's no small thing for publishers to have to change their plans. Book publication is worked out a long time in advance and involves a lot of different people—so I would also like to thank the teams at

MJ and Ballantine for their patience and hard work in accommodating me.

Thanks to them I was able to take the time I needed to write not just one but two books I love: this collection and my next novel, *The Drift*. I would also like to thank them for putting their all into this short story collection. Both editorially and with the absolutely wonderful cover design and artwork.

Obviously, publishing books is a business, but a good team is in this business *with* you. They believe in you, and they have your back. Not just when things are going well, but when you stuff up. Every writer has blips; every human being has bad times. Having people on your side makes a huge difference.

On that note, I must also thank my biggest ally—literally and vertically—my husband, Neil. As well as all my writer friends and non-writer friends. For making me laugh and listening to me moan.

And finally, thank you to *you*, lovely readers, for your patience in waiting for the next book. Your support is, ultimately, the most important of all.

Every book teaches you something new about writing.

But sometimes, not writing a book is just as useful.

Although I'll try not to make a habit of it!

ABOUT THE AUTHOR

C. J. TUDOR is the author of *The Burning Girls, The Other People, The Hiding Place,* and *The Chalk Man,* which won the International Thriller Writers Award for Best First Novel, the Barry Award, and the Strand Critics Award for Best Debut Novel. Over the years she has worked as a copywriter, television presenter, voice-over artist, and dog walker. She is now thrilled to be able to write full-time, and doesn't miss chasing wet dogs through muddy fields all that much. She lives in England with her partner and daughter.

Facebook.com/CJTudorOfficial
Twitter: @cjtudor
Instagram: @cjtudorauthor

ABOUT THE TYPE

This book was set in Sabon, a typeface designed by the well-known German typographer Jan Tschichold (1902–74). Sabon's design is based upon the original letter forms of sixteenth-century French type designer Claude Garamond and was created specifically to be used for three sources: foundry type for hand composition, Linotype, and Monotype. Tschichold named his typeface for the famous Frankfurt typefounder Jacques Sabon (c. 1520–80).